Mischief Corner Books Presents

INTERNMENT

Spirit Threads 1

Written By

Freddy MacKay

Illustrated By

Mila May

About the Book You Have Purchased:

Cover Artist: Mila May
Editor: Erika Orrick

Second Edition

ISBN-10: **0-9980903-2-8**
ISBN-13: **978-0-9980903-2-0**

Internment © 2017 Freddy MacKay
All Rights Reserved.
Published in the United States of America.

PUBLISHER
Mischief Corner Books, LLC

Dedication

We are, all of us, strange and wonderful mélanges of good
and bad. We dedicate this book to the bits of the angelic and
demonic inside of all of us in recognition of the necessity of
all of our component parts.

Trademarks Acknowledgement

The author acknowledges the trademarked status and trademark owners of the following wordmarks mentioned in this work of fiction:

Apple iPhone: Apple Inc.

Table of Contents

Part One
Monsters on the Mountain

Chapter One

Spring was alive and well on the mountain. Green buds covered the treetops, bushes bounced with the breeze, tulips and daffodils poked through the ground, and the smallest of forest creatures skittered about looking for their treasures from the previous summer and fall. Tadashi smiled as a familiar young squirrel scampered around his feet, chirping and squeaking at him furiously.

"I didn't take your nuts," Tadashi chastised, switching his broom to one hand. "You've forgotten where you've put them. Or they've decided to become wonderful new additions to the forest in the form of trees."

The squirrel stopped its angry barrage of noises and looked up.

"I'm telling the truth, Kou," Tadashi said. "I haven't hidden your nuts."

Kou chirped once.

"Look over there, by the arches." Tadashi pointed at the gate. "Why do you think a Black Oak is sprouting? I didn't plant it there."

The squirrel's nose twitched. He stared at the seedling then took off in the opposite direction for his oak by the temple.

"Aren't you even going to say you're sorry?" Tadashi called, shaking his head.

Kou climbed up his tree and went straight into his nest.

Tadashi chuckled and went back to his sweeping. "Little pest."

He didn't mind the forgetful little squirrel. The temple would seem big and empty without him. Company, in the form of the squirrel, was a welcome reprieve from his duties. Tadashi would have to remember to procure some of Kou's favorite treats. He had some hidden away. The spring was always a rough time of year for the small forest mammals like Kou, the poor squirrel could use a break.

Though he wasn't so small anymore. Kou had just turned a year at the end of April. It felt like just a moment ago that Tadashi had been up nursing Kou back to health after his mother abandoned the litter early. Kou had been the only one to survive. He'd been a fighter and would continue to thrive, though Kou had to be hungry. The winter had been an unusual one, the cold extreme even for the mountain, and food was hard to come by at the moment.

Definitely not an easy time for the animals, their stomachs empty, and they were looking for a mate. Tadashi stopped sweeping the grounds and searched for the squirrel. No wonder Kou was so upset. He must be preparing to lure a female. Were there any around? Tadashi scanned the trees and the forest floor beyond the gates. He couldn't see them, but he could smell them. Quite a few in fact. All of them were scurrying about looking for food.

Kou knew what he was doing, wanting his nuts. *Sneaky devil.* But then, Tadashi raised him. He only had himself to blame for the squirrel's cheeky behavior and slight, oh, awareness.

A squirrel raised by a kitsune. He must be getting lonely. Him, a messenger of the god Inari, taking in such a small pest. *What is the world coming to?*

Tadashi picked up his broom and headed back toward the small building next to the temple. At the same time, Kou popped back out of his nest, pinecone securely between his teeth. The little pest did have food. Kou ran by, dragging the pinecone with him.

"Be careful once you pass the gates," warned Tadashi. "It's not as easy to protect you once you leave the shrine."

Kou stopped and tilted his head, observing Tadashi.

"Here at the shrine, my powers protect you," Tadashi said. "Step off the sacred grounds, only my luck travels with you."

It wasn't the good kind though. Hadn't been for years, not since the Japanese engaged the Americans in the World War seven years ago. But Kou didn't need to know that. His happy aura was one of Tadashi's only lights. He didn't want to damper it.

"Go, have fun."

Kou chirped and ran off, scampering away with a sense of purpose.

Tadashi faced the temple and bowed, asking a favor from his god, Inari. "I know you and I haven't been on the best of terms, but please, protect Kou."

Tadashi straightened then resumed his course to the small hut by the temple, ignoring the larger house behind the shrine. He ducked into the doorway and took several long steps to the dresser by his bed. Tadashi rummaged around the top of it. He had kept a stash of Kou's favorite nuts for an occasion like this one… somewhere. A small, brightly colored cloth bag finally peeked out from under a pair of socks.

Yes!

He had used a little of his magic on the bag so it preserved and kept the nuts fresh. Tadashi grabbed the sack and stepped back. He gently placed it on the floor so he could grab it once he had shifted. Tadashi quickly pulled off his clothes, letting them drop to the floor.

Funny thing about real clothes, they wouldn't just disappear like the ones that formed when he used his magic. Getting tangled in real clothes was cumbersome and annoying. So was having to strip naked to shift.

Tadashi's view of the dresser top went from above it to eye level to not seeing it at all. He shook, adjusting to his new smaller size, and then picked up the cloth bag with his mouth. Tadashi trotted outside and over to Kou's tree. He leapt, deftly landing on the lowest branch.

Leaping from one branch to another, Tadashi quickly worked his way up the tree to Kou's nest. He dropped the bag into it for Kou to find then descended as fast as possible. Trees were a squirrel thing—foxes, not so much. Now if there was a den underneath, he could work with that. Tadashi made his final jump, the dirt kicking up around his paws when he landed.

Satisfied he had done his duty, Tadashi headed back toward his room when he stopped. The sun felt good. Birds chirped their favorite songs. The small animals chattered. *Maybe...* Maybe he could run around a bit, stretch his legs. It couldn't hurt to enjoy a fine spring day like this one. He didn't have to worry about intruders. The locals rarely came up the mountain.

Unsure of what to do with a 'Jap' or his shrine.

A subtle survey of the temple and its surrounding inhabitants put Tadashi's mind at ease. He wouldn't be gone long. His wards, however small, would be safe in his absence. They were happily shacking up with one another anyway. They wouldn't notice if he slipped away for a few hours.

With a turn, Tadashi headed toward the back of the property to an old and seldom used path. He was the only one who used it anymore, and the animals seemed to know to leave it alone. Bits of grass sprouted through the dirt, reminding Tadashi he'd have to weed soon. But that would be for another day. Today… today he'd run. Enjoy the sun and fresh wind blowing in from the ocean and let go for a little while.

Tadashi kicked, running along a path that led to nowhere but an isolated cliff, his tails swirling behind him as he traveled, the past and present haunting his footsteps as he raced to the one spot where he and Akatsuki once overlooked a sleepy California valley and its town.

A place he visited now by himself since Akatsuki died in the internment camps.

* * * * *

Trotting back to his room, satisfied with his run and able to work past the ever-present ache inside him, Tadashi stopped suddenly. There was a smell on the breeze—an unfamiliar scent. No. Scents. He whipped around and stuck his nose into the air, breathing deeply. It wasn't right. He growled. Something was wrong. Even the forest had gone quiet as if all the life bustling about earlier hadn't happened.

4

Tadashi sprinted toward the cause of his unease. The new growth and small buds peeping from the ground bent as he ran by, his speed kicking up a small wind where he passed. There should be some noise. The forest hadn't been this quiet in years. The last time the animals were this quiet was… Tadashi stumbled.

Had humans returned to the mountain?

Most left his area alone due to the stories that developed after the war. He had let the tales proliferate, encouraged them, giving the tales a helping hand or paw periodically.

No one wanted to visit a haunted shrine.

He lifted his snout and tested the air again. Eyes closed, Tadashi tried hard to remember what humans smelled like. It had been so long. Nothing. He lost the scent. Tadashi shifted, turning and inhaling the wisps of smell the wind brought him. Finally, he caught the unfamiliar odor again.

His heart raced, the forest a blur as Tadashi ran to meet his intruders. His sanctuary would not be poisoned by humans, even if he had to drag them away by force. A low rumble settled in his belly the closer he got to the scent. His memory might not remember the general odor of people, but it was close enough to the one person he remembered best.

When the smell hung in the air like a heavy perfume, Tadashi slowed. Other animal smells mixed with the humans. Tadashi sniffed the ground and sneezed. Dogs. The hair on his back stood straight as he growled. Of course this couldn't be easy, but he would not back down. If he could scare whomever was stupid enough to visit the temple, that would be easiest. Less of his dwindling energy would be consumed. Tadashi tilted his snout back again, trying to locate the offenders.

Circling through the trees, he searched desperately. No noise was being made. If humans were around, the bumbling idiots should be making some kind of sound. Trampling bushes underfoot, breaking low-hanging branches and squished flowers in their path instead of stepping around. They destroyed everything they touched. Took what they wanted and hurt those not like them. Like Tadashi or, more importantly, Akatsuki.

Tadashi needed to find the intruders before they hurt something valuable.

Finally, he found a piece of cloth hanging on a bush. The material was rather large and kind of looked like a shirt. Tadashi sniffed at it. *Yuck.* It smelled horrible. He sneezed. Humans were foul.

As he tore the offending material away from the bush, one thing did register with him.

The animals were chatting away again. Tadashi took it as a sign the intruders were gone. He shifted and took the piece of clothing in hand. He stretched it out, taking a good look at it. A t-shirt. His heartbeat went into overdrive, the emotions barraging Tadashi making it awfully hard to keep his form. His tails slid out, and the need to hunt battered away any reason he had.

Humans had gotten awfully close to the temple. Closer than any in so long. Tadashi would have to check the seals and barriers. He wanted no unwelcome guests.

Angry he couldn't find the humans, Tadashi spun around and began to pace through the trees. He struggled with allowing his baser instincts to come out and hunt versus going back to the shrine and regrouping. If he got too close to town, people would notice, especially right now. He wanted to know if someone new had come to the sleepy mountain village but his showing up could create problems. Tadashi only went to town for supplies, and even then, his trips down were when he could control his different forms.

No. He was too upset to make the journey down. He'd have to go back to the shrine, regroup, and make a plan. Tadashi also wanted to find Kou. Maybe the little squirrel could tell him something.

Chapter Two

"You saw nothing?" Tadashi asked again. He had to make sure. Kou didn't have the best attention span.

The little squirrel chirped, chattering angrily at Tadashi from on his knee as they sat on the steps of the temple. Kou dug his paw into Tadashi's thigh and nipped at his clothes.

"Ouch! Stop! Of course I believe you!" Tadashi wriggled his leg but Kou hung on. His squeaks became more urgent the harder Tadashi kicked out. He stopped in defeat, worried he'd hurt his squirrel. *I'm just not confident you would notice.* But he couldn't say that.

Tension knotted the muscles in Tadashi's back. They weren't going away any time soon either. Not until he found the source of the smell. His animals could be in danger.

"Ouch!" Teeth sunk into his hand.

Tadashi shook it, willing the pain away.

"Why'd you do that?"

Kou scrambled up his leg onto Tadashi's shoulder. The squirrel bit his ear.

"Kou!" Tadashi grabbed his ward and pulled him off. He stared at Kou, a stern edge to his voice. "What are you doing?"

"We're here to warn you."

Shivers streamed up Tadashi's back. He hadn't noticed intruders since he'd been so focused on his squirrel. With a barely controlled turn, Tadashi faced the owner of the cautionary statement. Hopefully his expression held the cool aloofness he didn't feel. A young man glared at him, resentment in his eyes, hands fisted at his side, his back ramrod straight. Everything in the man screamed he wanted Tadashi gone. Not like Tadashi didn't understand the sentiment. He didn't want the man on his land, and it was his.

"Why are you trespassing?" he asked as he stood. Tadashi tucked Kou into his robes, earning another nip. He refused to let his squirrel go despite the animal's annoyance.

The man sneered and took a step forward. Tadashi stood his ground, waiting, watching. Sweat streaked the dirt on the guy's face. His hair color was too hard to figure out considering the hat. He wore a ragged pair of overalls with a long-sleeve shirt. The gun held most of Tadashi's attention. If he retaliated, it'd only be used against him. Who knew if the sheriff or village would really care what happened to him. Figuring out a story when a 'relative popped' back up to claim 'inheritance' was a pain.

A hand wrapped around the man's arm and yanked him back. Tadashi blinked. Until then, Tadashi hadn't noticed the villager had friends with him.

Not a good sign in any way, shape, or form. A group could say a lot of things about him in town that would go against Tadashi's favor.

"Biff, he's not worth it," the friend hissed. "He's just some creepy Jap."

"He's—" Biff began.

"Right here," Tadashi interrupted, not willing to listen to games.

Biff rounded on him, only to be pulled back by multiple hands this time. One of the friends removed the shotgun from his hold.

Tadashi smiled, showing his teeth.

"Listen, Jap," snarled the man, "we're only here because the sheriff said we had to tell you."

"Tell me what?"

"We're up here hunting—"

"Not on my mountain!" Hair went up on his arms, a deep growl built in his chest, and every sense he had went on high alert. Words became echoes in his head. He stepped toward the group just as a gust of wind kicked up. "I own this land. You cannot hunt on it without permission!"

8

"The hell we can't," Biff answered, shrugging off his friends. "Something's going after our animals, we have the right to protect what's ours."

"On your land," Tadashi growled. "On *your* land. Not mine. So get off before I remove you."

"You don't own the mountain, Jap," his intruder spat.

"Oh, but I do," Tadashi answered, his voice low, rasping as he spoke and fought to keep control over his form. "I very much do own this mountain."

The ruddy color of the man's face brightened. "No fucking way in hell does someone like you own that much land!"

"Why did the sheriff send you?" Tadashi asked, stalking closer. "I haven't seen or heard from him in quite a while. He's never had anyone from town inform me that they're hunting on my lands before. He knows I wouldn't give permission. Why are you here?"

"You—wait—what?"

Oh, how pathetic, the poor man was confused. Tadashi inched closer. "Why did he really send you?"

This time all color drained from Biff's face. Okay, maybe the growl had been a bit much, but these men were here for a purpose. Tadashi intended to find out why. If he made them piss themselves in the process, the more fun for him. His grin came back and he narrowed his gaze, intent on the intruder.

"He… uh, he—" Biff cleared his throat, beads of sweat popped out on his forehead. "—he… he… we had to talk to you."

"Yes?" Tadashi motioned for his intruder to continue. Maybe this wouldn't be so difficult. The leader seemed weak. Tadashi inhaled and found fear rolling off the man in waves. He tilted his head, observing. Was he really the leader or the brawn?

"There's an animal," spoke another from behind Biff. A red head pushed in front. "It's taking our stock."

The real leader. "Not my problem."

The redhead gulped, his throat working furiously. "It is when it's coming up onto the mountain."

"I've had no problems." Not like he would. He was the most dangerous thing on the mountain.

"It's attacked one of ours," said the red head. "Shane died from the wounds."

"A human? It attacked a human?" Tadashi frowned. Nothing here would do such a thing. Not unless provoked. "What is it?"

"A wolf or bear," answered the young man. "Some kind of monster with a taste for humans."

Biff pulled on the guy's arm. "Red, be careful."

Oh, how fitting. Red puffed up a bit, apparently gaining some confidence for some unknown reason. That would never do.

"It needs to be put down," Red insisted. His hazel eyes glistened with an unusual eagerness. "Like the rabid beast it is."

"Not on my mountain."

Red lunged toward Tadashi, but a friend jumped between them, whispering, talking the man down, reminding Red they weren't in the South Pacific anymore. So… Red and his friends were vets. Vets who fought against Japan. That answered the why they hated him question, but it wasn't the reason they were there.

"Listen, Red, if you catch the animal on your lands, you can do what you want," Tadashi said with a bored sigh. "But I will not have you traipsing around my mountain, ruining everything you touch. Leave."

"That's ridiculous!" Red shouted. "This thing could kill you, maul you alive, and leave you for dead and no one would know, you stupid Jap."

"So that's why the sheriff sent you." Really, it did make sense. *Go see if the Jap is dead, boys.*

"Excuse me?" Indignation resonated in Red's voice.

"To see if I'd been chewed on or not," Tadashi answered. Now he was just pissed. "Trust me, there's nothing here stupid enough to do that."

The men stared at him with a variety of expressions from confused to angry to amused even. *Amusement*? Odd reaction.

"You think you're all tough?" Red was in his face, shouting. "You think you can tell us what to do? That no one can hurt you? Just 'cause we leave you alone don't mean shit. We let you stay here! You're here because we let you be—"

With his hand wrapped around Red's throat and dust billowing into the air, Tadashi leaned in close to Red as he pinned him to the ground. If his teeth looked a little longer than normal, whoops. Tadashi didn't care.

"I'm here because this is my home, my shrine," he growled, putting a little more behind it than usual. "Just because I'm a shrine priest doesn't mean I won't defend myself or what's mine against bastards like you. I listened once… it cost me everything." His voice faltered, sounds became nonexistent. Only when Red pushed at him did Tadashi come out of his haze and throttle the man again before letting him go. "I will not allow that to happen again."

Short, labored breaths fell from Red. "You're as nuts as Sheriff Fowler said."

Like he cared what the sheriff thought. Tadashi stood, patting down his robes, ignoring Red.

"We have to protect—"

A quick dip down, and Tadashi had Red's shirt in his hands, the man's feet dangling off the ground.

"You have to get off my mountain!" Tadashi tossed Red down, no longer caring about consequences. They had threatened him, subtly, but they had.

He would not leave his home. *Their home*.

"All of you need to stay off my mountain," Tadashi snarled. "And stay away from my shrine. You. Are. Not. Welcome!"

Red jumped up, surging toward Tadashi. It was his turn to be grabbed by his friends. The one who had been amused by Tadashi leaned forward and whispered into his ear.

"Not now. Not here. This is a place of worship."

Oh, one American had respect and reason. He knew they weren't all bad, but it was hard to see that sometimes, these days.

"Why do you think no one touched it during the war? It's holy," the guy hissed. "Besides, my mom would kill us if we did something here."

Mother complexes. Creepy but useful.

Tadashi sighed. He did need them to leave though. He could feel his human form fragmenting. Hopefully they would heed his warning. *Please, Inari, let them leave me in peace.*

"Leave." Tadashi turned his back on the men, speaking over his shoulder. "Please just leave. You have warned me about the animal. If he comes here, I will take care of him myself. You defend what's yours on your own land."

Dirt shifted, muffled voices all too clear to his ears argued, but Tadashi would not look at the men again. He couldn't. Not without them seeing too much.

"Please leave my mountain. Leave me in peace."

He just wanted to be left alone, even though the loneliness hurt. It was better than facing the villagers who turned Akatsuki over to the government and sent him off to his death in that god-forsaken internment camp.

"Go," Tadashi said, the loathing and warning clear in his voice.

The shuffles continued as Red muttered furiously to the muscle of the group and to their friends, but finally, they left. He waited until he could no longer hear their footsteps, which was a long while with his hearing. Then he sank to the ground, trembling. Alone once more, Tadashi buried the fury for the townspeople and focused on breathing.

It hurt sometimes. To breathe. He wished it was just an option on occasion—breathing. Now being one of those.

The effort it took to pick himself back up made Tadashi want to sit right back down. It had taken so much energy to confront those men. He wasn't used to expending so much of it.

Then pain sliced into his shoulder. "Oww!"

A pair of small teeth held onto his flesh. Blood seeped from the wound. The ferocity of the attack matched only one animal Tadashi knew.

"Ow! Kou! Stop! I said stop!" He tore at his clothes, desperate to get to the ferocious little squirrel. "Kou! Stop! Please! Why are you hurting me?"

Bites strong enough to break skin sunk into him. He wanted to slap at the pain, but he'd hurt his squirrel. Though…

"Ow!!" Okay, just a small smack wouldn't hurt. Much. Just enough to stun Kou. A growl deep from his chest rose up and he barked, "Stop or I'll make sure that bite is your last!"

The attack stopped.

Kou's rapid breathing, along with the stench of his fear and his fast heartbeat, registered in Tadashi's mind. He sniffed. Oh… *ohhh no*. A wet spot. Not on his robes. Oh, yuck. But then, he had scared Kou enough to urinate. He frightened his bright light.

Tadashi reached up and placed his squirrel on his palm. He lifted Kou so they were eye to eye. The dark beads were lit with distress. His little paws shook faster than his chest rose and fell. Tadashi closed his eyes, remorse weighing heavily upon him.

"I'm sorry I scared you."

Kou stilled in his hand.

"I am sorry, Kou." Tadashi hugged the critter close to his face. "So, so sorry."

A barely audible chirp came from his squirrel.

"I let my anger cloud my judgment. It wasn't you I was really angry at." Well, that wasn't completely true. "But why did you bite me?"

Tiny paws pushed against him and Tadashi drew Kou back so he could look at him.

Kou chirped and chortled at him, admonishing Tadashi for forgetting about him in the rumble with the young men. Oh dear, he had put Kou in his robes to keep him safe. Flattening Kou hadn't been part of the plan.

"Oh, ooohhh." Whoops. "I'm sorry I squished you. Everything all right?"

The squirrel sniffed. Could they do that? He then held up his tail. Oh, the squirrel had been spending too much time with Tadashi. His movements were becoming... *more,* and less animal. His eyes pleaded with Tadashi. Ah, it was too late to worry about the consequences now.

Tadashi lifted the tail as gently as possible, feeling more like himself now that his focus was firmly on his squirrel. "I see. Oh yes, the missing fur is a problem. Smarts, doesn't it? Don't worry, Kou, I'll fix it. I promise to fix everything."

* * * * *

Sleep evaded Tadashi, troubled by what he found out earlier in the day and because he had hurt his squirrel. He rolled to the side and reached out to his nightstand. He fumbled around for his matches then wondered why he bothered. He sat up and blew into his kerosene lamp.

A small blue light appeared, growing brighter as the flame fed of the fumes on the wick. One of these days he'd get a real lamp, one he could switch on. The problem was, he knew nothing of construction beyond what he learned long years ago in Japan. Electrical lines had been added before the war, but the boxes were left unconnected to anything. Electricity and he didn't get along. His one foray into putting electrical into the building had been, uh, a hair-raising experience.

It really was best they didn't cross paths.

Besides, the glow of the oil lamp was soothing.

A stretch and wiggle later, Tadashi swung his legs over the bed and sat at the edge. He wondered what time it was and checked. The clock said three. Tadashi groaned. It had to be lying. He took another look. Nope. Three. He was in for a long day. Going back to bed wasn't really an option. He'd be up in an hour and a half anyway.

He eased off the bed, standing gingerly. He must have slept weird because his back ached and his shoulders were tense. *Or I could be worried about the villagers who visited. Or Kou.*

Tadashi crouched down and checked the drawer hanging open from the nightstand. Kou slept peacefully in a nest of cloth and feathers, his favorite nut held firmly between his little paws. The bugger was getting spoiled.

Small pleasures, and Kou slept soundly. That made one of them. Tadashi stroked Kou once, patting him when he wriggled, willing the squirrel back to sleep. No need to wake him. Kou would worry.

Tadashi decided to check outside, knowing only seeing the grounds empty and in good condition would help him relax. The cool night air caused him to shiver, and really, it would be a bother to get dressed so Tadashi transformed. Keeping his human form was taxing at the moment anyway. He'd almost lost himself earlier. Thankfully, he hadn't thanks to Kou's intervention.

He slid a glance over to the squirrel. He stuck his muzzle in the nest and licked his ward. *Perceptive little bugger.*

A paw waved erratically and then pushed him away. Kou's high-pitched snores never missed a beat. Nothing fazed him, or so it seemed. Tadashi backed off and headed out of the hut, ready for rounds. Who knew what those pesky humans were up to?

Once outside, Tadashi gave himself a shake, just to make himself alert. The fur surrounding Tadashi kept him warm. Spring meant cold nights up on the mountain still so Tadashi was glad to have his fox form. Maybe it'd be better to sleep this way? The stove only emitted so much heat and once he fell asleep, it often went out. Tadashi hated being cold.

Waking up with the chills was the worst.

Maybe. Waking alone, without Akatsuki, hurt more.

With an ache in his chest and more determined than before, Tadashi took off into the night at a steady run. He had a lot of ground to cover. He'd be lucky to get back to the temple before the sun rose.

An unsettling mist lingered over the mountain, almost as if it knew there would be bad things coming to pass tonight. The air was electrified. The current crackled over him, sending his fur up and on edge. His muscles were tight as he ran, never fully loosening and allowing him to go top speed. His steps were short, but quick. The anticipation inside him pushed against his chest, ready to erupt any second.

Something. Something was going to happen. Maybe it was the subtle change of the wind or the way the night sky shone brighter. Or how the quiet echoed through the trees. All of those little things added up, telling Tadashi his world would change tonight. For better or worse.

The smell in the woods changed. From the crisp, clear, cool night air to a wave of heat, followed by a heavy cloud of smoke, burning Tadashi's lungs. He stumbled to a halt.

The glow. It hadn't been the moon shining brighter.

Rigid muscles held Tadashi rooted to the spot. He couldn't move if he tried. Tadashi's head swiveled unceremoniously as he searched for the source of the flames.

There! A small pocket down to the east. Tadashi's heart hammered as he finally found his footing and ran, swift as the wind. The grass nipped at this heels and the branches stung as he whipped past them, never slowing, his destination a small red glowing spot slowly becoming larger as he drew closer.

The heat fanned higher and higher as he got closer, but he wouldn't let that deter him. The fear of the fire spreading had him driving forward. If he could get there, he could contain it, make the rain fall. He just had to get close enough.

Ash coated his lungs; breathing became harder, the scorch on his lungs almost unbearable. His progress slowed as it became difficult to see. He blinked continuously to clear his eyes. The air was heavy upon him, tamping him down, trying to make him submit to the fiery wood. He wouldn't. Too many lives were at stake, including the town.

16

Town. No, he couldn't let anything happen to the sleepy little valley, despite everything that had happened.

When Tadashi got to the edge of the flames, close enough they caressed his fur like a lover's tongue, he shifted to his human form. He called out to the sky, drawing the wind down to him and splitting the clouds open. Raindrops began to fall. One by one, they splattered against his face. It wasn't enough though. He needed the sky to break open and pour down upon his mountain.

He encouraged the clouds to cry further, wanting the trees as wet as possible. Steam rose as the water came into contact with the flames, clouding the area with a fine mist. They danced with each other as Tadashi summoned more clouds, choking as he inhaled, coughing as he exhaled. His head buzzed, feeling airy and light. His eyes wouldn't focus and kept crossing, blurring the sights in front of him until it was a collage of yellow-orange and blue-black.

Cold, hard rain sliced into Tadashi's body as quick as the flames burned the skin. Hot and cold tore him up as the fire burned and the clouds cried over his forest. Luckily, the flames were getting lower and the rains were more like teardrops instead of the dense fog from earlier. It was then, when the fire finally began to recede when Tadashi smelt the gasoline. How could he not have noticed sooner?

Fury overrode reason. Muscles contorted and snapped. His skin crawled as fur sprouted and his bones broke, painfully forcing his change back into a fox. He should've seen it, should've known. If his feet touched the ground, Tadashi certainly didn't notice. He ran on instinct, something pushing inside him, telling him where he needed to go.

Out of breath, shaking, and in a state of absolute shock—though why Tadashi didn't know—he stood panting at the entrance of the shrine. The archway framed the grounds—and the trespassers on it. A low rumble started in Tadashi's chest, falling from his lips as he stalked toward the noisy and confused group of men, who seemed to be arguing with one another. They were so focused on themselves they hadn't even noticed him. He sat, catching his breath, deciding what to do next.

"He's not here!"

"Maybe the beast got him."

Tadashi was the only beast here at the present. Too bad they didn't take notice. They were about to be very dead trespassers.

"We need to leave, this ain't right," one protested. It wouldn't help him. Not now.

"Did you see the smoke? Something must of caught, we're going to be trapped on a burning mountain!" another yelled in a panicked voice.

"So it started early, we have plenty of time."

Ah, that was the cowardly bully from earlier in the day. Biff was it? Now Tadashi really couldn't let their belligerence go.

"No, you idiot! We're—"

"Just shut your trap," Biff ordered. "We need to find that Jap and teach him a lesson like the sheriff wants. It's time he got off this mountain. He's outstayed his welcome."

Fury. Anger. Pain. None of it could describe how Tadashi felt. This was his home, had been his home longer than those men had been alive.

"What about that animal? The one attacking stock? Maybe it got the Jap?"

Biff reached out and thwapped his friend. "That was Shane's dog, idiot. It got bit and went rabid. Thing's probably dead by now."

"Probably?"

"Yeah, now come on, we have us a Jap to hunt," the coward answered.

Oh no, I will be doing the hunting.

"What about the smoke?" Another man asked.

Biff lifted his arm and pointed. "Look it's mostly gone so stop bein—"

18

His voice trailed off. He was looking in Tadashi's direction. He stood, slowly walking forward, his head down. Tadashi growled low. The other men's heads snapped in his direction.

"Is that Shane's dog?" One of the men asked. He crouched down. "Here, Ace, come here, boy."

"Idiot." One of the others hit him. Biff had actually inched backward, away from the group. The friend chastised the man calling Tadashi. "Thing's rabid. You don't call it to you!"

"Right!" He shot up and backed away with the rest of the group. They lifted their rifles.

"Are you sure that's Ace?" A villager asked. "It doesn't look… right."

Tadashi pulled a memory from the man, his legs snapping and his fur rippling. He'd look like the damn dog all right, though he loathed to do so. He couldn't make the transformation perfect but close enough.

He barked, just for good measure. *Ew.* The sound gave him the willies. Foxes and dogs weren't meant to be.

"He sounds friendly," the stupid one said. He had to be stupid. Sad but true. "Maybe it ain't Ace."

He'd be the first to go, and well, there'd be one less stupid person for the world to worry about. Tadashi whined and limped forward. Stupid lowered his gun from his shoulder.

"He's hurt, come on, guys, let's check and see if he's okay."
Definitely stupid.

The contradiction between the man caring so much about a hurt dog and the willingness to 'teach Tadashi a lesson' was not lost him and only stoked his fury higher. Tadashi put his front paws out, dropped his front half, and dipped his head to the ground, cocking it to one side. He let out another whine, making it longer and higher. The man shuffled forward, his gun dropping farther.

"Don't, Jethro! It could attack you," said a cautious human.

"Aw, come on, you hear him whimpering," said Jethro. "I bet it's just lost and hungry."

Hungry, yes. Lost. They were the ones who were lost.

"Come here, boy. Come here, that's right." Jethro glanced over his shoulder. "It's not Ace. Not the right color."

Gig's up. Tadashi lunged.

"Sh—" Jethro fell back, and raised an arm, but not soon enough. One moment Tadashi's mouth was empty, the next he felt the soft crunch of stupid's windpipe as he bit down. Hands scrabbled at his snout. Tadashi shook. Jethro's garbled cries filled his ears followed by the sound of men arguing.

"Shoot it! Shoot it!" yelled Biff, fear lacing his cries.

"I'll hit Jethro!" shouted another.

"Maneuver around them!"

Was that Red?

"Quick, before the dog kills him!"

Nope. Someone else. Red seemed… intelligent, if an asshole. Too bad, too.

Tadashi adjusted his hold on stupid's neck. Jethro wasn't struggling, much. The hands so desperately swiping at him barely pushed against his snout. Tadashi ground down on the soft flesh, the small tears in the skin giving way to a new wave of blood hitting his tongue. Jethro whimpered. Tadashi snuffed, shook his head once more, then began to drag Jethro away from his temple. Didn't need the stupid human to sully his grounds any longer.

A shot rang out. A warm flare erupted in his side and in his shoulder. Guess they finally decided to shoot. Tadashi didn't care and kept moving. Humans, always too afraid to defend their own when they themselves could get hurt. Always stood to the side like a bunch of bystanders.

Tadashi dragged Jethro as fast as he could, making sure he was covered by the dying man. Didn't need to make himself a target for the villagers. Jethro wasn't exactly a light man and the effort it took to pull him was more exertion than Tadashi expected. He could feel a ripple across him and knew whatever form he had taken he was losing. He was becoming more like himself.

At first, he panicked. Humans shouldn't see his fox, but then he remembered it didn't matter. They weren't going to survive.

His shoulder burned and his stomach ached as more shots whizzed past him. They were wide, Jethro's friends wary of hitting him. Tadashi yanked and pulled, Jethro no longer fighting him. He listened closely, checking for a heartbeat. There was none.

Shots volleyed above and to the side of him. Shouts of angry men chasing him followed. They weren't fighting for Jethro anymore. They were looking for revenge.

How quickly they gave up on Jethro. So sad. So not surprising.

He spat out the foul-tasting flesh. Jethro thumped to the ground, no protest falling from his dead lips. He was dead after all. Tadashi ducked into a thicket of trees and waited. The men weren't far behind him.

"Oh, Jesus! Sweet Jesus!"

"Shit! Oh Hell."

"He, oh, I'm going throw up."

Guess they found Jethro.

"Is he dead?" asked Biff, a quiver in his voice.

No, his throat is dangling by a thread because decapitation is good for you.

"Somebody check," ordered Biff.

Stupid humans.

"I'm pretty sure Jethro's dead," said another man.

The air vibrated with a hunger. A need. Tadashi wanted flesh tearing from bone and so did the men. Muscles bunched and corded as they waved their arms, shouting at each other. They would be so fun to tear into.

"Shut up, Eugene!" snapped Biff.

"Biff, I'm just sayin—"

"Fine, he's dead, now let's go hunt."

Hunt they shall, but they will soon find they should also know how to run. In the dark, their human limitations would be harmful, to well, their livelihood. The anticipation sent a wonderful surge through Tadashi. He shook; ready to strike.

Someone cleared his throat, sounding nervous as he spoke. "Biff, are you sure that's such a good—"

"Shut! Up!" A gun cocked. Biff yelled, "Okay, Jethro's dead. That just means we have a dog to hunt and a fucking Jap!"

"Okay, Biff, okay," said Eugene. "Let's split into pairs and look around. The dog-thing couldn't have gotten far. We don't want that monster showing up in town anyway."

See? Now they're making it easy. First they wouldn't defend Jethro, but now they'll play the hero. How hypocritical. Humans would never make sense to Tadashi no matter how long he lived. Didn't Biff and his friends know they were the ones being hunted? How could they be so arrogant? Even with two bullets in him, Tadashi was still more of a threat to them than they were to him.

Guess they truly hadn't processed Jethro's throat being torn apart. *Ah, well, they will learn, and then they will die. Tonight. In the next hour or so.*

What good is a hunt without the chase?

Chapter Three

Twigs snapped. Leaves crunched. Panicked breathing filled the night air, giving the surrounding fog a sense of uncanny urgency. Frazzled veins pumped blood through exhausted prey. The hearts pumped loudly as they ran. How stimulating, how delicious was their fear.

"What is it?" One of the men yelled.

"I don't know!" shouted the other. "Just shoot it! Shoot it! Shoot! It!"

"I'm trying! Don't you think I'm trying?"

"Is it flying?"

"Can't be!" The first wheezed. He turned and let loose a shot, missing Tadashi by a mile.

His paws flew across the ground as he gained on the men, they were tiring and he was about done with this chase. He'd enjoy ferreting them out over the last fifteen minutes but he had business to attend to. Eight men had died by his fangs, two he'd tricked by transforming into a woman and using their perverse desires against them, two more were run off a cliff, and the last two had shot each other while trying to shot him. Life was good, and only four were left. He needed to take these men down before he could go for his prize. Biff was still out there. His instigator. His stench had crossed Tadashi's path multiple times but he wanted Biff scared, more scared than he'd ever been before.

"Shit!" The first yelled. "I'm outta shells, Dale!"

Finally. How many had they brought to kill him with?

"Here!" Dale shouted, tossing a small box toward his friend.

The friend missed and stopped. He dipped down to grab the shells.

A mistake.

"No, Alvin!"

Tadashi lunged, grabbing hold of the man's leg. His screams filled the woods. Alvin fell forward, pleading with his friend. His panic stoked Tadashi's hunger. He shook his head.

The man's leg snapped in his mouth. Alvin's screams became a high-pitched squeal as he scrambled. The metallic taste of his blood poured onto Tadashi's tongue. His sobs and cries fed Tadashi's mania.

He whipped the man into the air. He hit a tree with a loud thunk and fell. Alvin did not rise again. Tadashi went over to the body and listened. Dead.

Good. Three left.

The foul smell of piss caught Tadashi's attention. Dale stood twenty feet away in a small break, clear of trees, his gun forgotten in his hand. A dark stain covered his crotch.

"What are you?" he asked, more to himself than to Tadashi. He pressed against the tree, shaking so hard the tree danced with him.

He answered anyway. "I am a demon, messenger for the god Inari. I am the one that will bring your death."

Dale's jaw dropped. His breathing became more rapid to the point he might hyperventilate if he kept it up. Suddenly he turned, stumbling over roots, swearing.

Don't they know it's more fun when they run?

The man cursed and yelled, shouting for his friends.

"They will not come," Tadashi answered with a rasp.

Dale shouted louder.

They really made them stupid around these parts. Tadashi leapt, knocking Dale over with one blow. "They will not come for they are cowards."

A stench wafted into the thickening morning air as the man lost control of his bowels.

"And most of them are dead," Tadashi said. "Don't worry. You will be, too."

He bit down as the man screamed, tearing into the hunter. His claws sliced the skin open like a knife through butter. Blood sprayed forth, and Dale's screams echoed in Tadashi's ears, heightening his excitement in the hunt. Only when the whimpers became pathetic did he bite down on the man's neck, silencing him efficiently, Dale dead within moments. The flavorful coppery tang filled Tadashi's mouth once more and he savored it. When was the last time he enjoyed a hunt so thoroughly? He pushed off the ground and took in the scene below him, indifferent to the carnage. He felt nothing for the mangled mesh of bones and skin in a lump underneath him.

"Two." Tadashi lifted his head and walked away from the prone form. "There are just two now."

The woods weren't thick here. Sparse since they were at the base of the mountain, closer to the town.

The last time Tadashi scented Biff and his companion they were headed in this direction as well. They had probably abandoned their friends due to their cowardliness. Tadashi closed his eyes and focused his senses.

Biff's putrid smell caught Tadashi's attention after minutes of concentrating and sifting through the different odors. Without missing a beat, he turned toward the scent and ran. Biff wouldn't slip away. He would pay for his treachery. Tadashi had no issue of cleansing those evil men from the world forever.

Gravel spewed in all directions from the parking lot onto the road. Tire tracks scarred the surface of the street in the men's haste to get away. The truck would not help them. Tadashi was a messenger of Inari for a reason. He would hunt to the ends of the earth for the men who hurt his and him.

His paws stung as they hit the firm gray ground, the road beneath his paws hard and unforgiving. He ate up the distance between the mountain and the edge of town, to one of the outlying farms. Groves of orange and apple trees whirred by as he ran, focused and intent on his target.

Tadashi slid as he almost missed a dirt road the truck turned onto. Soon red taillights were beams in the distance, and with the speed of the wind, Tadashi found himself behind the vehicle. Dust from the road flew into his eyes. Tadashi moved off to the right, speeding up as he did so. The jump into the bed of the truck was easy.

The bed dropped significantly once his paws touched down, and the truck swerved. Oh, how the men screamed. They should. Tadashi's white fur was stained red. His nine tails billowed behind him. He was their nightmare come alive. The vehicle jerked right then left. Tadashi could see Biff working furiously to get control of his vehicle as he yelled at his friend.

"Dammit, get your gun, Gene! Shoot the damn beast!"

Gene scrambled to turn around, shotgun in hand.

That wouldn't do. Two bullets in his hide were more than enough. Besides, how smart was it to shoot inside the cab? Tadashi rocked his weight. The truck shook under him. A shot went off, blowing through the roof.

Not the smartest move.

"What you think you're doing, you dunderhead?" Biff shouted, pain lacing his garbled voice as it dropped off. The truck skidded, fishtailing to a stop.

Gene cradled his arm. Blood ran down his face as he whimpered. Biff was bent over the steering wheel, groaning and swearing incoherently. The two men had holes in various places from shrapnel.

All in all, this couldn't have gone better for Tadashi. Though it was a little disappointing on the chase end of things. The fun was in the hunt, the terror of the prey.

The only saving grace was the amount of pain Biff was in. He had to be hurting. A lot.

At least the bastard would suffer. The joy of knowing the last minutes of Biff's life were going to be miserable made Tadashi pause and bask in the moment. It was like a flood of all the pain and misery he held in the last few years burst forth from the sheer enjoyment of Biff's agony.

The passenger side door creaked. Tadashi tilted his head toward the noise. Gene was shimming out of the truck, looking over his shoulder. He gasped when his eyes met Tadashi's.

"No!" Gene fumbled forward, nearly falling on his face as he ran.

Tadashi leapt from the truck bed, easily overtaking the man in several great bounds.

"Please, no," Gene begged as he tried to escape. "Please."

Begging would do him no good. Tadashi plowed Gene over, throwing the pathetic excuse for a human to the ground.

"No-ahhh!" The man screamed as Tadashi tore into him.

Bones crunched, muscles shredded, blood flew into the air and soaked his fur. His teeth and claws ripped apart one of the men who had turned his back on him and his family years before when the war had started. The intoxicating scent of food and blood clung to Tadashi, feeding his frenzied state.

A thick bone snapped off in his mouth and Tadashi gnawed on it, chewing and sucking on the delicious treat. He licked at the bone until it was clean. He stood, intent on carrying it back with him to his den when Tadashi spotted the truck as he turned around.

That truck. It carried an enemy within, one that needed to die more painfully and slowly than anyone else. Biff. Tadashi shook his head. It felt clouded, his thoughts distorted. They were muddled. Something… something was different. About him.

Tadashi's ear pricked up when a laborious moan emanated from the vehicle. The prey within was wounded. Hurt. *Easier to kill*. Tadashi let the bone drop from his mouth, the prize forgotten with the promise of a new hunt.

Careful not to make any noise, Tadashi maneuvered to the large… he cocked his head… the words, they wouldn't form. What was that thing called? He searched his memory, coming up short. He knew. He really did know what it was called.

Why couldn't he remember?

"Ahh, ahh, hell," his prey groaned.

Tadashi pawed at the metal. The animal he wanted was on the other side. His mouth watered at the fresh scent of blood and sweat. His prey was so close.

The metal fell, causing Tadashi to jump back to get out of the way. It teetered before dropping forward. A poof of dust flew up into his face. Tadashi sneezed and then waited a moment.

Once the ground settled, Tadashi trotted over the metal. His prey was seated upright, but leaning over a round thing. He nudged it with his snout, getting another moan. Tadashi tugged on the weird fur covering it. His prey collapsed out of its hiding spot with a loud thump.

He nosed it, disappointed by its lack of fight. He wanted his prey to be hopeful, be able to hear its heart frantically beat as it ran, and smell its terror. Breakfast was much more enjoyable if it had put up a fight.

No. Tadashi sat down on his haunches. His morning meal didn't run from him. He was forgetting something important. What did he lose?

His prey groaned and lifted its head. He stared back at it, hoping it would get up and run. He wanted the chase. This particular prey had done something bad.

Bad? Why did he care if his food was bad or good?

"Oh my God!" His prey yelped as it scrambled backward. But it didn't get far. The… big thing… was in the way. "A demon! It's a fucking demon!"

"Yes," Tadashi answered. Wait? He could speak? Foxes didn't spe—he wasn't just a fox. Not any plain old fox anyway. He was a *kitsune*. He worked for Inari. He protected the shrine on the— Tadashi's legs buckled.

He had almost forgotten.

The man scrambled up, reaching inside the vehicle. "Where's that blasted gun?"

Oh no. Guns were bad. Tadashi lunged, grabbing hold of the man's leg with his teeth.

"Shit! No! Let go of me, you damn monster!"

Yes. He had become the monster. He became what they told stories about on the mountain. To protect what's his.

Tadashi tightened his hold on the man—Biff—and shook his head, pulling on the pant leg.

"No! Goddammit! Let go, you beast!" Biff swore. He barked a whole lot, but the man had no bite, an instigator that let everyone else do the dirty work.

Tadashi reared back and Biff fell to the ground, his swearing louder than before. He reached for his pants and unbuckled his belt. Tadashi sprang forward, covering the man. Biff sobbed, and Tadashi's stomach became wet.

"You are an evil man, Biff," Tadashi said with a gravelly voice, huffing when Biff stilled underneath him. "Bad men aren't allowed on my mountain. Not again."

Biff whimpered. "Dream. It's got to be a dream."

"Not a dream. I'm a nightmare." The muscles in Tadashi's back bunched and pulled. He shifted, uncomfortable, struggling for control. "One you helped create."

"No!"

Biff's denial was abruptly cut off as Tadashi bit down. It twisted in pure agony. Biff's screams filled the air, the area strangely quiet but for his cries. More blood coated Tadashi's white fur, which soaked it up. Tadashi only had to know it was as red as the morning sky.

He chomped, clawed, bit; every cry, every scream delighted Tadashi. Flesh split apart in his mouth, forming wide gashes in his prey. The muscles and pieces of arms hung with jagged edges. White bone—broken and stained pink—poked up from the form beneath him. His prey barely resembled the man he once was.

Tadashi loomed over the body, panting heavily. He trembled

with barely contained satisfaction and thrill. He had never felt more alive. His body thrummed and his fur stood on end. His hunt had gone well. His prey had died and he had lived. It ran. He caught it. It fought. He defeated the threat. His prey would never again rise. He could go back to his den and sleep. Content. Belly full.

He had been victorious... but over what? Confusion stole Tadashi's sense of accomplishment. Tadashi pawed at his prey, a low whine emanating from his throat. Why had he hunted? And why had it been... human? He felt lost and scared. His body renewed in its tremors, not because he was happy. No. He had forgotten something important.

Sheriff. Bad man. There was another bad man. A man who needed to be warned. How?

Tadashi looked down at the broken figure below him. Broken. Yes. Tadashi bit down with his large jaws snapping the prey's neck. He tugged and pulled until the head came off. He picked it up in his mouth and ran. Sheriff's den was near. He could be there quick as the wind if be wanted.

Why?

The question niggled at the back of his mind but he let it go. The wind danced with him and he wanted to play in return. He first had to drop off his prize though. He may have enjoyed the hunt but now that the taste sat in his mouth, it had become bitter and foul. He wanted to drop the head, go home, but he had show who was in charge.

Tadashi slowed when he saw the funny metal contraption that had a light on top of it. Sheriff. The den was large, irregularly shaped. It stuck out, sitting on top of the ground the way it did. Tadashi went up to the entrance. He pawed at it and butted it with the top of his head. His gut twisted, a growing sense of unease inside him.

The sun was just above the horizon. Maybe that was it. He needed to get back to his den, where it was safe. A white-yellow light casting its glow over the land. Not me though. Tadashi was awash in red.

Tainted.

Why would he be tainted? Tadashi shook himself. His gut churned, and a restlessness inside him came out as he began to pace.

The bad man should be up. The sun had risen. He should be up and moving like the other animals. Tadashi dropped the head and let out several large yips. He pawed the door again. If he had hands this would be so much easier.

Hands. What were hands? Why would he have such things?

Tadashi yipped again, ready to leave. Something told him he had to leave. The air smelt wrong. He smelt wrong. Tadashi began to back away. Scared and unsure. Why had he come here? What was so important?

He lifted his snout and breathed in. The forest. He could smell the forest. That's where he should be. But the scent was wrong.

"See you later, Leslie!" A man with fire-colored hair stepped into the doorway, adjusting his belt. "I'll be back lunchtime."

"Okay," called a male from within the… house. "I'll be here."

Tadashi jumped. Surprised by the movement. He was a fair amount away from the den so hopefully the human wouldn't see him.

The man stepped through the doorway and kicked the head Tadashi had left. It rolled away from him. The man mumbled and glanced around at the ground. His jaw dropped and he backed up a few steps, stammering away. "Sh-sh-l-l-Leslie. Leslie!"

"I'm comin'. I'm comin'. Quit your hollerin', boy." A man with sapling colors and a big black patch in his center met his companion outside. "What's your problem, Red?"

Red. The niggling at the back of Tadashi's memory returned.

Tadashi stared at the man, growling. He seemed familiar. The red, blazing hair. The eyes.

"Holy mother of God!" Leslie shouted as he stared down. He reached for his… belt and patted around. "Shit, where's my gun? The phone, we have to—"

Red pushed against his friend, eyes still glued to the head. "What is it?"

"Your friend." Tadashi jumped. Him. It was him… talking.

"What the Hell?" Red shouted.

The men scrambled back. Tadashi called on the wind. A breeze slammed their retreat closed. The men turned and banged on the door, swearing. Their distress provoked the hunter inside Tadashi. Words came. No thoughts, just words. He was here for a purpose. He had to bring the message, to fulfill his duty.

"I am the monster from the mountain. And you, humans, have run out of time."

The men stopped moving and rolled against the house, now facing Tadashi. Red actually leaned forward. Both of them shook their heads as if to clear them. Tadashi knew he was. His head felt light. His thoughts jumbled. He couldn't appear weak though. Not in front of them. Tadashi stood tall, his gaze even with theirs.

"Am I drunk? It's huge. Nothing's that big!" Red exclaimed, looking at Leslie. "Are you drunk?"

"No, Red," answered… *the Sheriff.* "I don't think we still are."

Tadashi spoke again, knowing he could, but not understanding why. "This is your warning."

"Warning?" Red parroted. His eyes were dilated. His heart was racing. He pointed at Tadashi again. "What the fuck are you?"

Red's and Leslie's fear excited Tadashi. He licked his lips. He had to hold back. Not pounce. Now wasn't the time. Tadashi let out a low whine. They were just standing there, dumbstruck. They weren't even trying to run.

The slow died. Those who did not run did not see another day. Any animal knew that.

"He some kind of mutant?" Leslie said—*the sheriff.*

Tadashi laughed. The sound cracked and dry. "Demon, though no more than you, Sheriff."

The protector had been the one who wanted to hurt me.

34

Tadashi let loose another growl, his fur on end. The men jumped again, pressing into the door. It'd be so easy. So quick to get rid of them, but who would listen if the sheriff was gone?

"Your kind is not welcome. Any attempt to return to my mountain, and you will—" Tadashi howled, the words taking effort to say. "You will meet the same fate as your friends."

"Friends?" Red gulped. "What friends?"

Tadashi trotted over to the head and nudged it with his muzzle. He turned the face toward the men. "Like this one."

"Shit," the sheriff swore.

"That's Biff," Red said, his pallor flashed a sickly green. "Jesus, that's Biff."

"He showed up with guns at the temple. He was there to hurt," Tadashi growled, showing his fangs, his anger surging up once more and fogging his mind. He stalked forward, relishing how every step he took toward the men made them shake more. "He was there because you told him to go!"

The sheriff whined and bared his neck. Red shuddered, his head twitched, and hands jerked. Tadashi leapt at the men. Their screams cut off when they slammed back against the door. Tadashi's large paws covered their chests.

His breath wafted against their faces with enough force their hair moved back and forth. The men trembled. Their eyes closed, lips clenched in teeth. Tadashi's body throbbed, feeding off their stark belief and misery. His skin stretched, pulling tight. His fur shimmed. He watched as his paws grew larger in front of him.

The power rushed through him. He leaned down and sniffed Red's neck. The man's breathing hitched.

"I could bite you right now, and you'd die," Tadashi said. He gave another lick. The skin was salty, tasted good. "I could have you for breakfast and no one would ever miss trash like you."

A high-pitched whine fell from Red's lips.

"This is your warning. Tell everyone you know," Tadashi said, his rough voice lowering. He scraped his teeth over Red. Elation warred with a sense of dismay. His heart squeezed in his chest. A wave of loneliness nearly knocked him over. Fear shot up his spine. There was nothing left of him, just a… "A monster waits for those who trespass on the mountain. Come if they want their deaths.

"You wanted a monster on the mountain? You have one, gentlemen."

With that, Tadashi backed off the frightened men. He watched as they slid down the side of the house, then he turned.

Tadashi sprinted away, using the wind to help pick up his speed. His mountain loomed before him, lit with red. Not from the sun, but from the fire raging upon it. Even when Tadashi met the flames, he didn't stop. He wanted as far away from the town as he could get.

His heart pulled and tugged inside him, ripping apart slowly. Horror filled him as the memories flooded back. He'd become what he hated most, and he enjoyed it.

He had one place left. One place he could go. He could only pray Kou was still there waiting for him, and hopefully, no one would ever come looking for the monster because they might find it.

That scared Tadashi more than anything.

Not even the newly formed rain pouring down on top of him could wash all the blood away now.

Part Two
Internment

Chapter Four

The winds caused Tadashi to shiver. Spring had descended upon him, but it was still cold as winter. In the fourteen years since the men had come to hurt and the fire destroyed much on the mountain, none of the springs had been this cold. Did that mean something? Tadashi hoped not. Tadashi debated shifting into his fox form but immediately grew nauseous at the thought. He avoided changing as much as possible these days.

It took too much from him when he did.

He had to retain control. To do that, he stayed in his human form as much as possible. There were times he got tired, though, and had to shift. Those times were a blur to him, choppy memories that weren't cohesive, mainly because his beast was in control then. He always felt hollow afterward.

Of course, staying in human form had a cost, too. *Like not being able to hide in my warm fur on a cold day.* Tadashi pulled his quilted jacket tight, holding himself. Not that it would make him any warmer, but the movement helped. He had cleaning to do at the temple, but with the wind nipping at him, Tadashi couldn't muster the energy to do so.

He slouched in his chair. Maybe he should get up and use another one of the blankets from the bed to cover his legs? Tadashi reached. Maybe he was close enough.

The soft fabric slipped between his fingers but he couldn't get hold of it. He scooted forward an inch and tried again, determined to get the blanket. Just a little more. A little more.

"Why don't you just stand up and get it?"

Tadashi fell forward, banging his head against the bed. "Ouch! Kou!"

He sat back, rubbed his forehead, and glared at his squirrel. Kou chirped, the closest sound he could get to laughing. Kou scurried up his leg and squatted on his knee. He held out a paw. Tadashi leaned into it.

"Are you hurt?" Kou asked.

"Would you stop laughing if I was?"

"No."

The squirrel ducked his head but not fast enough. Tadashi saw the mirth dancing in Kou's eyes. He sighed. "Thought not."

Tadashi rubbed his head again. It really did hurt. He wouldn't tell Kou though. The squirrel would worry, and he'd been fretting over Tadashi too much the last winter.

Two small paws pressed against his hand. Tadashi opened his eyes. Kou was leaning over the gap between Tadashi's face and his knee, anxiety rippling off his aura. He lifted his hand, allowing his squirrel on. Kou nuzzled up to him, pressing his little body against Tadashi. He exhaled slowly, relaxed by the squirrel's presence.

"Tadashi, maybe you should get in bed," Kou said quietly.

He really wanted to. "I have to clean the temple."

"You need a break. This shrine was meant to be taken care of by a family, not one person," Kou argued, squeaking when he finished. He often did so when he was upset. He never quite grew out of it, despite his altered state of existence.

"I know." They'd had this quarrel before. They'd have it again. It was no use disagreeing. It only made the row last longer.

"You could send word to your family," Kou said, pushing Tadashi with his tiny paws.

"I… uh—" Tadashi sighed. "They left for Minnesota a long time ago."

"Why?"

"Because if they had stayed here, they would've been sent to an internment camp." Tadashi didn't really want to have this conversation. It hurt every time.

"A camp?" Kou skittered closer.

"A place where people who were Japanese were sent to during the war," Tadashi answered, closing his eyes.

Kou must have sensed something because he asked, "Was it a bad place?"

"Yes," Tadashi barely managed to croak out. Images of Akatsuki being dragged away assaulted him.

"But the war is over," Kou said.

"It is."

"Maybe they want to come home."

But they hadn't. Tadashi had to grieve by himself.

"Do you know—?"

"They won't come."

"Why not?"

Tadashi ignored the question. He couldn't handle answering anymore. Kou seemed to sense his need to stop because his squirrel said no more. He took hold of Kou and carefully slithered into bed. One day wouldn't hurt. He'd been taking care of the temple for so long. He deserved a little time off.

"Tadashi?"

"Hm? What is it, Kou?" He placed Kou on his nest then maneuvered around, kicked off his house slippers, and adjusted the blankets. He leaned back against the headboard, bone weary. With a deep exhale, Tadashi closed his eyes and let his head drop. He felt so heavy, so cold, so very old and alone.

He felt Kou's tiny claws skitter across him and up his chest. Kou perched on his shoulder and snuggled against Tadashi's neck.

"Why won't they come?" Kou asked again following a spell of silence.

"Who would want to come back to the place they were thrown out of?" Tadashi said, tired and ready for sleep.

"You came back."

The words cut deeper than Kou knew. Tadashi didn't want to talk about why he came back or why he had stayed when he obviously had not wanted to. He scooted down, chuckling lightly as Kou used him as a ramp down to the bed. He rolled toward the wall.

"I'm tired, Kou. I think I'll listen to you and get some rest." He pulled the blanket over his frigid shoulders.

Kou scurried about him, making adjustments to the haphazard mess of his bed until he got halfway down. The squirrel stopped his fussing and let out a squeak. "Your tail is out, Tadashi."

"I know, Kou."

"Maybe you should—"

"No!" Tadashi snapped. He bolted up in the bed, twisting the wrong way and pinching his tail in the process. "Ow! Ow!"

He grabbed it, bent, and held his lone remaining tail to his chest.

"I'm sorry, Tadashi," Kou said. The apology was so quiet Tadashi had to think on whether or not he actually heard anything. How did his small voice manage to get smaller?

"Not your fault," Tadashi wheezed. He stroked his tail, soothing the ache. "I wasn't thinking. Did I squish you?"

"No, I moved in time," Kou answered, no longer sounding as upset.

Not knowing what else to do, Tadashi snuggled back down in his bed. His energy reserves were getting too low. He needed rest but he'd be forced to shift soon. Tadashi just hoped no one got hurt in the process, especially his Kou.

A furry body pressed against his face. When had he closed his eyes? Tadashi nuzzled Kou and gave him a kiss.

"Papa?"

Tadashi's throat caught, and he waited. Kou rarely referred to him as 'papa' anymore. He was almost fifteen now and had been asserting his independence though he was still a kit to Tadashi anyway.

"Papa?"

"Yes, Kou?"

"Can I take a nap with you? It's cold and I want to sleep a little longer."

"Want me to stoke the fire?" Had he let the fire die down too much?

"No, papa, I'm good." Two tiny paws pressed against his cheek and Kou gave him a kiss. "Sleep well."

"You, too, Kou."

His squirrel curled up on the pillow in the nook his head and neck created. The heat from Kou's body was welcome, as well as the company. The little squirrel, and his dependence on Tadashi because of what Tadashi did, was the only thing that kept him going some days.

He listened to Kou's breathing, finding the sound soothing in the relative quiet of the dreary morning. Pretty soon it evened out, and his squirrel was snoring softly. Tadashi chuckled, then soon followed Kou to the dream world. But unlike his squirrel, his fitful dreams were fraught with pain and nightmares.

* * * * *

The floor gleamed under Tadashi. It had taken hours to get it scrubbed but it was worth it. The temple looked presentable, even if it was only Tadashi who saw it. He stood, satisfied with himself, and happy to have several hours in which his mind was empty. The mindless task allowed him reprieve from his memories and guilt.

"Tadashi! Tadashi!"

He turned to answer Kou and saw his squirrel leaping off one of the high beams by the ceiling. "Kou!"

Tadashi dove, arms outstretched, praying he'd catch the crazy squirrel. Kou landed in his hands. Tadashi curled and rolled. Sharp pain shot through Tadashi's left shoulder, migrated to his head then back down his spine and finally settled in his knees once he stopped. Even his teeth hurt from clenching his jaw shut so hard.

Tadashi moaned.

Ever since the war, he just felt old. Now he qualified for ancient. Everything creaked, including parts of him that shouldn't.

"Why'd you catch me, Tadashi?" Kou whined. "I would've made it!"

"You so sure?" Tadashi struggled to his feet. He held up Kou in front of him. "I'm pretty sure you would've landed with a splat."

"Nuh-uh." Kou shook his head. "I've made bigger jumps in the trees. Sometimes it feels like I'm flying."

Utter terror rolled through Tadashi. Kou shouldn't be making those kinds of jumps. Not by himself. His powers shouldn't be anywhere close to being able to pull those kinds of stunts. Though, the troublesome squirrel was always ahead of the curve. Still.

An arduous squeak broke Tadashi from his fog.

Kou glared at him. His cheeks puffed and fur on end. Tadashi winced. He knew that look. Anger simmered just beneath the surface. Hopefully Kou wouldn't—

"Ouch!"

He bit him. The damn little brat bit him! Tadashi fanned his wounded hand, keeping hold of Kou with the other.

"You didn't have to do that!" Tadashi scolded Kou, frantic. "This behavior right here. This is why you're not allowed to go out on your own!"

"Tadashi!" Kou squeaked. His beady little eyes lit with outrage. "You're treating me like a little kit! I'm fifteen, not five."

"You bit me like you're five!"

"You deserved it!"

"Did not!"

Kou stuck out his tongue. "Did too!"

"You're just a little squirrel!"

"I'm bigger! I grow every year!"

"You don't know what it's like out there!" Tadashi argued.

"Because you won't let me!" Kou shot back. "If you'd just let me—"

"No, because you'll die!" Tadashi shouted. He shook—the idea of Kou leaving the grounds. He couldn't. He just couldn't.

"How—"

"Arg!" Tadashi let go of Kou.

"Hey!" Sharp teeth bit into his ankle.

Tadashi bent over, muscles twisted, bones creaked. "Run."

"Tadashi, you can't order me—"

"Run, Kou." He fell to the floor. He panted as he tried to hold back his shift. "Go to the room. Through your hole."

"Tadashi?" A tiny paw rested on top of his hand, which was quickly changing.

"Ruun!" The order came out with a low, rumbly growl. His chest vibrated as fur erupted on his arms. He throat felt as though it had hot coals running down it. "Stay saffee!"

Kou's frightened gaze met his. He was trembling, but had not yet moved, a determined intent in his stance. An attitude that would surely get him killed. Tadashi moved his head side to side.

"Run nowww!"

With a hesitant step in, Kou gave Tadashi a kiss then turned. He glanced over his shoulder, his distress clear in his eyes. Tadashi shook his head. Kou sniffed then ran as fast as he could, heading straight for their room. Problem was, the fox in Tadashi wanted to run after Kou. Fangs erupted from his gums.

"No! Argh!"

Tadashi curled on the ground, in pain and wishing it would all end. His mind warred with his body as he fought to stay sane. He had to let Kou get to safety. He had to hold on just a minute longer then he could let go.

"Ah! Ah!" Tadashi panted as fur pushed through his skin, stinging as it stabbed through the surface. "Run!"

He had no clue where Kou was, but he didn't want the squirrel turning around. Kou had to be safe. Tadashi screamed as his body contorted, his last thoughts of his squirrel. He couldn't live with himself if he hurt Kou again. Once had been enough. Unfortunately—or fortunately—it was also the event that allowed Tadashi to change back to his mostly human state.

A state he could no longer hold. One last painful pulse went through his body, Tadashi screaming as the change finally won.

Kou, be safe.

* * * * *

The mountain air smelled fresh, the pine scent sharp and satisfying to his nose. Tadashi snuffled the crisp air, filling his lungs as he ran. Odors from the other creatures revealed the forest was alive with activity, and thus, so was he.

The dirt under his paws was firm, but not hard. Maybe spring was finally coming. It had been a long, cold winter. The forest animals deserved a break. Much like Tadashi needed one, he couldn't remember why though.

Thirsty, Tadashi changed directions and headed for the mountain spring. Hunger gnawed at his gut as well, but he ignored it. Forgotten memories as to why he disliked the hunt pushed at him. The idea of eating made his stomach churn uneasily. Which was odd. Foxes were hunters, therefore enjoyed the thrill of the chase, but he was different. Tadashi couldn't remember why.

His hesitancy won out ultimately, but hopefully, a drink would help put him back to normal.

The long strides of his legs quickly ate up the ground between Tadashi and the river. He kept his eyes open for signs a life, and his ears pricked up. He'd been asleep for so long he didn't want to miss a thing while he was up.

There were buds poking through the ground, even a few brave flowers already blooming, and petite leaves covered the woody plants and trees. Spring would finally come. The animals had a fighting chance. Tadashi's pupils dilated, a distinct smell catching his attention.

Unless it's prey.

A rabbit darted out in front of him, its fear intoxicating. Hearing the rabbit's wild heartbeat drove Tadashi over the edge. He sprinted after it, mouth watering.

The rabbit ducked into some brush, but it wasn't enough to keep Tadashi at bay. He plowed through the tangle of wispy wood and kept on target. Long ears faked right, so Tadashi went left, blocking its escape. The rabbit jackknifed in the other direction, legs spinning on the loose ground. Tadashi yipped.

The fun had started.

He led the rabbit on a chase all over the woods, tongue out and enjoyment rolling through him. With the wind in his fur and the dirt in his paws, Tadashi couldn't remember the last time he had so much fun running after a snack. He kept pushing toward the stream so he had less work to do once the game was over.

Food and drink. That's all he needed. Life was simple and good.

Finally, when the rabbit's movements slowed too much, Tadashi took pity on it and ended their game, putting the rabbit out of its misery. One last burst of speed and Tadashi chomped down on its neck, breaking it swiftly, no need to draw its torture out.

He carried his prize to the stream, finding his favorite spot. Tadashi trotted over to a pine tree with a low-hanging branch shading the ground. It was close to a large collection of boulders, protecting Tadashi from surprises on two sides. The stream crossed in front of them and the tree. He plopped down and gave thanks for the food before tearing in.

Since it was a rabbit, it didn't take long for Tadashi to finish his meal. He licked his chops to clean himself, then got up to get a drink. The water felt cool against his muzzle, and his parched throat found some needed relief. Once he finished, he sat down and scratched behind his ear, ready for a nap. Under the tree would be nice. He'd feel protected, secure.

It was then, as he was turning around, an unusual odor caught his attention. He stuck his muzzle in the air. The aroma came from behind him.

Tadashi spun back around, regarding the other bank. Something was over there. He remained motionless, hoping he hadn't been spotted. His wary gaze traveled up and down the spring, his senses on high alert.

A whimper broke through the quiet. Tadashi's ears twitched. The sound came again.

Without an inkling of what he would find, or the danger he could find, Tadashi made for the noise. The sadness in the muffled sobs wove around Tadashi's heart and pulled on it. He splashed down into the water and swam across the stream. He didn't fight the current and allowed it to help him to the other side. He managed to pull himself up between two rocks much farther down stream, but he'd made it across.

His breathing was heavy from the exertion it took to cross the water, and his legs shook, but he remained upright. His ears swiveled back and forth as he searched for the source of the cries. He growled in frustration when he couldn't locate the noise.

The regular forest noises had died away and now a frightened hush filled the wood. Tadashi dropped to his belly and crawled. He had to find out what was hurt.

A soft sob escaped into the air.

Tadashi sprang, chasing the sound. He wove through trees and tripped over roots as he searched for the source of so much pain, because it *was* pain he'd heard.

Soon he found himself in a clump of trees. The sobs had turned to snivels, and they were coming from a hollow in one of the trees. Tadashi made careful steps toward the hiding spot, not wanting to spook what was inside. The snivels became louder until they were all Tadashi could hear. He wouldn't relent though. Something needed his help, and it was his job to fulfill.

Why? He didn't know. He just knew he had to.

Tadashi poked his head into the darkened hollow and looked around. Whatever the creature was, it smelled of forest but didn't. His jaw dropped. *What is that?*

"Doggie!"

A pink blur pounced on him.

"Doggie! Doggie! Wet, doggie!"

A paw went in his face. His jaw ached. A paw found his front leg and kicked it just right. He whined. Tadashi's legs shook with the added weight. Another paw found his ribs. Tadashi yipped as a sharp pain shot through him. The pink blur gurgled.

"Doggie, play with me!"

Tadashi circled, growling. He was no dog. The bundle fell off him.

"Bad doggie!" And then it started to cry. "You shouldn't be so mean."

Big, high-pitched howls filled the air. Tadashi stared.

How could something so small be so loud? Tadashi shook his head to get the ringing to stop. How did he shut it up? The wails increased tenfold every second they continued. Not knowing what else to do, Tadashi did what he would with any pup or kit.

He licked it.

All over.

Every inch he could.

The more he licked, the quieter the strange little creature got. Its little paws curled into his fur, its quiet desperation clinging to him. He switched from licking its bald spots to his long stringy fur. The golden locks were dirty and didn't seem thick enough to protect it from the cold. Tadashi snuggled closer to the pup, continuing to bathe the small, smelly creature.

Soon the snuffling sounds were replaced by happy little squeaks and gurgles. The pup wriggled and twisted, trying to escape its cleaning, but Tadashi kept gently pulling it back down into his lap.

A weird layer of skin covered its bald spots, and it didn't seem to harm the pup when he bit down on it.

The layer smelled. *Bad.*

Tadashi wondered if it needed to come off. Maybe the kit was shedding. A little early in the year but the creature was weird to begin with. He gave the loose skin a cautious tug. The pup gurgled louder, and then squirmed, front legs next to its head. The kit kicked and twisted until the loose skin fell off it.

Oh gods, the pup was bald. Everywhere but the useless fur on its head.

How would it stay warm? Maybe its fur just hadn't come in yet. Yeah, it was still small. He could hope.

The kit would freeze without—oh! More of its skin came off as the pup peeled it off its legs.

Tadashi shuddered. That was a little gross. Actually, it was repulsive. It really, really was.

The pup even kicked off a small white layer of skin, screeching happily. Tadashi winced. Loud.

Even with the extra layer of skin, the kit was dirty all over. Tadashi bent down to lick it, but the pup ran, warbling as it shot out of the tree.

Tadashi gave chase. Its sounds were different, but even he could tell they were happy ones. If the kit wanted to play, he was all for it.

The pup ran behind a tree, making that singsong sound again. Tadashi shook his head. Didn't it know how to hide? He trotted around the opposite side of the tree, huffing contentedly. The kit had its back to him, a paw held to its face. How could it walk on two legs? What a weird, little pink… thing. Its actions seemed familiar somehow, but the memories weren't there. Tadashi poked the pup with his nose.

It shrieked, warbled happily, and tottered away. He jogged after it. The pup had no balance skills and definitely didn't understand the idea of evade and hide.

Tadashi ran a couple circles around it, herding the pup away from the uneven spots. They relished the spring air, enjoying the sun and warmth that had descended on the mountain. Every time he got close, the kit would howl and spin around, heading off like a confused squirrel after a nut.

Squirrel.

Hm. Nope. The thought was gone.

Suddenly the strange kit toppled over and came up crying. See, running on four legs made so much more sense. Tadashi rushed over, nuzzling the hurt pup. It held onto him, howling into his fur. He wrapped around it, trying to keep it warm and began to clean it. The kit finally began to relax and let him, taking the comfort he offered.

When he got farther down, Tadashi stopped in his care. His kit was a her.

She smiled brightly at him. Tadashi felt the sudden need for a female. Where was her mother anyway? He had been so caught up in finding the little one he hadn't stopped to think about her mom.

No, she was too dirty. A mom wouldn't let her kit get so dingy.

Tadashi unwrapped himself from the pup. She garbled and pulled on his fur, levering herself up. He whined. That hurt. The female hugged him. She made sounds, but Tadashi could only understand two clearly.

"Sorry, doggie."

Okay, she could call him doggie. Tadashi rubbed his muzzle over her.

"Good doggie."

She still needed to get clean.

Tadashi glanced around. The river was above them. The current was too strong but he'd figure something out. Tadashi bumped her with his head.

"No, doggie." She wagged her paw at him, scolding. "Bad doggie."

51

He just wanted to get her clean. He had to make her understand him. Wait, why did he understand her? The female pulled on his fur. *Ow!*

"Ride. I want to ride."

He gaped at her. Did she honestly want to get on him?

"Up. I want uppie."

She pulled again. Tadashi thought about it. Fine. He could get her to the stream that way.

Tadashi lowered his head and stuck out his front legs. His kit climbed right on, no fear whatsoever. Pride bubbled up inside him. She may not have been his, but he found her. She belonged to him now.

"Gitty up."

She did not say that. His pup kicked his sides. *She did.*

Tadashi began slowly, not wanting her to fall. Once she appeared to have a good grip on him, Tadashi really took off, jumping and running through the forest. Her delighted squeals made him feel like he could go higher and faster than any fox around.

In no time, they were at the stream. She shimmied off him and leaned over the edge. A pleased yelp escaped her. She stuck her front paw in the water. Tadashi looked in and saw some small fish darting about. He huffed, tongue drooping out.

Tadashi stuck his paw in and splashed her.

The kit gurgled and scooped some water up, tossing it at him. Tadashi growled playfully. She howled and ran around and over him. He rolled, careful not to squish her. He nipped at her fur, and she only yipped. She squirmed away from him and ran to a tree, dirtier than before.

He hadn't meant for that to happen. If they continued to play, she'd never get clean. Tadashi glanced at the stream. If she were a normal pup, he'd bring her in and dunk her. She wasn't though, and Tadashi had a feeling she couldn't go in by herself.

His kit came out from behind the tree. "Doggie?"

Tadashi sat down, contemplating his problem. He had to wash her.

"Doggie?" The kit ran up to him and hugged him. "Is the doggie sick?"

He waggled his head back and forth and huffed, then an idea struck him. Tadashi managed to get her to let him go. He jumped in the small river, soaked himself, and then got back out. His kit watched him curiously the whole time.

She backed off when he got close though.

He ducked down and wagged his tail. She smiled. Tadashi barked. She inched closer. Tadashi crawled forward. She cried out with one of her singsong gurgles and leapt to him. His pup wiggled all over him, getting good and wet.

She was as clean as she would get.

Tadashi gave her a good lick to the face then stood, letting her slide off him. She never let go of him completely though, her front paw held tightly onto his fur. They walked together, back down to the den where he found her.

There were no visible clues that there had been any other strange animal like her around. He checked out the surrounding trees and brush to no avail either. He sat down with the kit snuggled up next to him.

Her stomach growled, and she shivered.

She needed food and shelter. A better shelter. Tadashi wanted to take her to his den but couldn't remember where it was. He could feed her there. Help her there.

His kit whimpered, and her stomach rumbled louder. Guilt set in. He should've known she hadn't eaten recently. No mom. Dirty. The signs were there, but in all their excitement, Tadashi forgot one of the most basic things she would need.

Tadashi stood. He needed to hunt something down for her. Something she could eat. He scrutinized his pink little… thing. If she was bald, that meant she was too young for meat, didn't it?

He was pretty sure it meant she still needed milk. Tadashi looked down.

He couldn't provide that.

Maybe if he chewed the food first.

His kit's stomach grew louder. "Hungry. I'm hungry, doggie."

Tadashi stood back up. His kit held onto him, her little paw buried deep within his fur. She wouldn't let go no matter how hard he tried to shake her off.

Well, he couldn't hunt with her attached. The next best thing was to take her to his den. Where was… home?

Tadashi stuck his nose in the air and breathed in. One familiar aroma caught his attention. He'd just have to follow that.

Chapter Five

Since the kit couldn't swim, Tadashi took her back down the mountain where the stream split and grew small and had rocks across it. It gotten him closer to the bottom than he liked, but it was the only way for them to get home, and they needed to do so quickly.

He didn't like how she shivered. Tadashi could feel every little tremble.

Her little body pressed against his as they walked. She had to be tired, but his stubborn little kit wouldn't let go of him, not even to climb on top and ride him. It was if she were afraid he'd disappear if she let go.

He wouldn't. Tadashi wished he could tell her he'd protect her and keep her safe. Tadashi couldn't, he may be a big fox, but he couldn't make the sounds she did. He consoled her the only way he knew how. He licked her face.

"Good doggie." The kit sounded tired.

Tadashi dipped down, putting his head against the ground. He let out a low whine. It was getting dark. They would move faster if she just got on. He could keep her safe, and she'd be warm. Warmer. Too bad she was too stubborn to listen.

"Berries! Look, doggie, berries!"

With a loud howl, his kit tore off into the woods. Panic ensued as Tadashi raced after her. What did she think she was doing?

Luckily, he didn't have to go far. Tadashi found her at a bush picking blackberries off it. So she wasn't a hunter but prey?

No!

She wasn't even close to being prey. His stomach revolted at the idea of her being something he would eat. Tadashi couldn't imagine harming a hair on her pretty little head.

55

Hair?

Tadashi ceased moving. The kit had hair. He stared at her and her smile as she stuffed her... mouth full of berries. Her fingers were a blur as she plucked the bush bare.

She wasn't a kit.

What was she? Tadashi knew somewhere inside him he had met a creature like her before. He knew what she was but he couldn't think of the word.

Tadashi paced as he watched her eat, disturbed he couldn't remember what she was.

It seemed important he recognized her. Now that he identified her with those words, a new urgency pushed at his memories, creating unease.

Her sky-colored eyes met his. The skin around her mouth was a deep purple and the color had stained her blunt teeth as well. She grinned, smashing some berries between her hands. The absolute joy on her face melted his heart, and his worries became secondary. His kit was happy; nothing else mattered.

Except she was dirty again.

How did something so small get dirty so fast? Tadashi licked her face, cleaning her and earning giggles. She buried her face in his chest, tugging on his fur with her hands.

A snap had Tadashi covering his kit with his body. A bang followed by a red-hot ache throb on his flank caused Tadashi to whimper.

"Doggie hurt."

Yes, but he was more worried about her. Tadashi nudged her as another boom echoed in the trees and more pain skittered up his side. This time his kit wailed, her expression showing pure fright. She clung to him.

"Doggie! Doggie hurt!"

Another loud bang went off, but this time Tadashi didn't feel anything searing into him.

"'Bad man stop! Hurt doggie!"

Man. The word jolted Tadashi's memories. He knew that word. He knew the humans.

He looked down. His kit was a human girl, a little girl—but still a kit—and they were being shot at by said men. Bad men. Tadashi growled and nudged the pup until she squatted down, shielding her from harm. His back leg was struck, a bullet tearing through him. Tadashi howled.

The kit howled with him. "Nooooo! No hurt doggie! Doggie good!"

The shooting stopped.

"Alva? Sweetheart?" called a deep voice.

She had a name. Like Tadashi. He had a name. That must mean something. The names. His mind was too clouded to figure out what.

"Alva? You okay, sweetheart?"

"Bad man!" Alva yelled, tears and snot streamed down her face. "Bad man! You hurt doggie!"

Tadashi turned around, bared his teeth, and growled. The bastard could've hit the pup. He took several steps forward, intent on finding the trespasser on his mountain. A whine behind him caused him to pause. He glanced over his shoulder and saw Alva standing behind him. Her face was blotchy and tears filled her eyes. A small hand curled into his side.

"No, doggie. Doggie get hurt." She pulled on him again, pointing away from the man. Tadashi followed, limping heavily.

Alva escorted him back through the bushes, in the direction they were headed before she ran off to get food.

"Alva, sweetheart, come to Berg."

"No!"

Her outright refusal made Tadashi huff. His kit had spark and knew better than to involve herself with men. Tadashi growled, anger surfacing. Men were always the problem.

Why?

"Alva!" Branches snapped, and footsteps thudded toward them. Berg was following them.

Tadashi tried moving quicker—stubbornly disregarding the pain shooting through him with every step—but Alva could only go so fast. Maybe she would get on his back again. He could run. It would hurt, but they'd be able to escape. Tadashi stopped, getting scolded in the process.

"No, doggie. We make doggie safe."

He bent down and nudged her. Alva's big blue eyes held worry. Tadashi didn't want her to worry about him. If he could get them to safety, she wouldn't have to.

"Alva!" The sounds behind them were getting louder, closer. "What are you doing? Get away from that... that..."

Her fist tightened its hold on Tadashi. He lay all the way down. Hesitantly, Alva finally climbed on top of Tadashi. Her little hands fisted his fur and she leaned into his back.

Smart girl.

"Alva? Holy shit! Alva!"

Tadashi sprinted through the trees. His body screamed in defiance but he ignored the bone-deep ache inside him. His breaths were short and labored. It felt like water was filling his lungs. Where had the bullets hit him? Still, he would run to the ends of the earth to protect the little kit.

A tree root got in Tadashi's way, tripping him. Tadashi stumbled, and Alva let out a frightened screech. He managed to stay upright but slid into the ground. The dirt and rocks ground against him, sending more twinges of agony through him. Tadashi tried to stand but couldn't. His legs shook and wouldn't stay under him.

Alva slid off him. She leaned into him and pushed. "Up. Doggie, get up. Doggie's okay."

He wanted to. Tadashi really did.

"Up. Get up!"

Finally, with a great amount of energy expended, Tadashi stood, his kit holding him up. He tried a tentative step forward. He wilted, falling toward the ground, but Alva pushed him back up. They repeatedly moved toward home in this fashion: Tadashi taking a few steps and falling, and Alva pushing him back up.

She murmured quietly to him, encouraging every step. Tadashi wondered how long it would be before they were discovered. He hoped they wouldn't be. Some hopes weren't meant to come true, though.

A shout interrupted their progress. "Alva?"

It was the man from before. Tadashi whipped around, growling. He nearly ended up head first on the forest floor.

A large man loomed over them. Pants, heavy sweater, long blond hair. A shotgun hung at the crook of his elbow.

"Alva!"

"No!" She pulled on Tadashi's fur.

Tadashi growled, his fur standing on end.

"Alva, sweethear—"

"No!"

The man knelt down. "Alva, that's not a dog."

Alva stuck her tongue out. "Berg bad. Berg hurt doggie. Berg mean man."

Tadashi agreed. He yipped, standing defiantly in front of Berg, between the man and the girl.

"Alva, that's not a dog. I think it's a fox. Maybe. It's a little big," the man said.

"Fine." Alva stomped her foot. "Berg's meannie. He shot nice fox."

At least they had that straight. Really, being called a dog. That would've gotten to him after a while. Tadashi was granted one small favor. He wanted to know one thing, though. Was Alva speaking better, or did he understand her better?

Both?

"Alva, you need to listen." The man scooted toward them.

Tadashi shielded the girl, growling at Berg.

The man held still.

"Alva, see, fox. Not dog."

"Doggie protects me."

Tadashi yipped and licked her face. She giggled and rubbed her face against him. Warmth spread through Tadashi like wildfire. He licked her back and rubbed his muzzle over her.

"Holy shit, I don't believe it," the man whispered. His voice sounded odd.

The man stood up.

Tadashi faced him again and growled.

Berg froze and swore again. His pure green gaze held Tadashi's. "I'm going to put the gun down."

Tadashi narrowed his gaze on the man, disbelief hammering hard at his chest, or maybe that was his heart.

"Did you just squint at me?" Berg asked. He shook his head and mumbled to himself. "I'm seeing things."

He stayed true to his word and put his shotgun on the dirt, then raised his hands. Tadashi sniffed the air. There seemed no bad intentions coming off the man. No lies hung in the air with their putrid odor.

"See, I put the gun down."

Good for him. Tadashi refused to move from his spot. Alva clung to him, not moving either.

"Alva, sweetheart, your family's real worried about you."

The words stung. Pain flared in Tadashi's heart. Alva had a family. But she was his. He whined. Berg gave Tadashi a long look.

"Alva, I just wanna make sure you're okay. Let your Mama know you're well."

"Mama?"

The word was no more than a gasp, but Tadashi heard it. The amount of hope that hung in it. He felt a shudder run through Alva.

"Yes, your Mama," Berg said. He stepped closer to them, hands still in the air.

A low-pitched whimper fell from Alva's lips. She buried her face in Tadashi's flank.

"We've been worried about you, Alva." The man's tone felt warm, soothing.

She hiccupped.

"We've been looking for you everywhere. Your Mama's been crying buckets."

Kits should be with their mothers. Tadashi didn't want to let Alva go though. It had felt good playing with her. He'd been happy. When was the last time he'd been happy? It'd been such a long time.

"I wished we'd come to the mountain sooner, sweetheart, I really do," Berg said. His voice was soft as the wind. He knelt a foot in front of Tadashi. "We've been trying real hard to find you. Your Uncle Red's been absolutely frantic. He misses his sweetheart."

Red.

Tadashi bared his teeth and rumbled. He did not like this Red. Why, he couldn't remember, but Red was a bad man.

Berg sat back on his hunches. "No one's going to hurt Alva, boy."

He wasn't so sure. Tadashi nudged Alva back.

"Have I hurt you?" The man grinned, like he dared Tadashi to prove otherwise.

The gun was on the ground and not in Berg's hands. That was something. Tadashi still didn't trust him though. The man had shot first, talked second.

Not knowing what to do, Tadashi turned his back on the man. He needed a moment to think. And while he thought, Tadashi cleaned Alva. Her hands and face were purple from her earlier feast. No matter how much he licked her fingers they wouldn't go back to the normal color.

"Jesus, you're really thorough when bathing pups, huh? Or don't you want to get in trouble with her Mama?"

Tadashi ignored the man. He knew. He did. She'd have to go back to her mother. She should be presentable at least. As he placed one final swipe across her cheek, Tadashi noticed her shiver. His gaze went to the horizon. The sun was setting.

She must be cold, being naked and all.

Ah, yes, that was his fault. He had forgotten humans wore… clothes. Tadashi curled around Alva. She settled into him and rubbed her head against him, giggling. She hit one of the wounds from the gunshots. Tadashi shuddered. It hurt. He situated Alva, tucking her in so she couldn't move.

"I can help."

Tadashi raised his head, meeting the man's deep green gaze.

"Both of you."

Berg was still on the ground, but he sat with his feet crossed.

"I'm a vet," Berg said. Like that meant anything to Tadashi. "I treat animals."

That did.

"If you give me Alva back, I could fix you back up."

Tadashi growled at the man. Berg was the one who shot him in the first place.

"Least I could do," Berg said. He scooted forward.

Too close. Tadashi yipped at him.

"She's cold," Berg stated, he nodded in their direction. "She's shivering, right? Alva needs her clothes. Needs her Mama."

"Mama," Alva mumbled in a sleepy voice.

Tadashi whined. He didn't know why it was so hard to let her go. She was a human, but she wasn't like the brute in front of him.

"Listen, fox, Alva can't stay with you," Berg explained slowly. "More men are going to show up, looking for her and people could get hurt. There's a monster up here. A heartless monster that attacks all comers."

That couldn't be true. Tadashi was safe.

"The only safe place is the shrine." Berg pointed. "Tadashi—the priest of the temple—and his family are the only ones who are allowed."

But he was Tadashi. That made no sense.

"Please, fox. I need to get Alva to safety."

Confused and unsure, Tadashi faced his kit. She smiled at him. Her little hand waved then dug into his side. Alva's tiny fingers curled around a lock of his fur. Tadashi gave her another lick. Maybe his last one. An ache filled him, but Tadashi understood the urgency coming from Berg.

He genuinely seemed worried there was danger. Berg sighed, and then reached for the buttons on his shirt. He undid the first few, exposing a white undershirt. "Let me give her my flannel. It's getting cold."

He had his shirt up off over his head in seconds and then tossed it to her. Alva pulled on the fabric until she had it bundled up next to her. She cooed happily.

"Soft. Berg warm."

"That's right, Alva, warm. Put it over your head, sweetheart. That's a girl."

Alva managed to get the shirt on with some effort and rather clumsily, but she did it. Tadashi huffed, proud the small little kit could dress herself. She had been cold. It was better to be warm.

"Please," Berg said softly. "Please let me take her home to her Mama. We've all been so worried since the picnic. She's been gone for a while now and we need to make sure she's okay. I promise nothing bad will happen to her."

Fine. Tadashi would let her go to her mom. He rose, slow and stiff. Alva slid away from him, standing up, wobbling on her feet.

Berg held out his arms. "Come 'ere, Alva."

She glanced at Tadashi. He gave her a nudge with a snout.

"Hey! Berg! We heard shots! Berg!"

"Shit!" Berg twisted up, staring off into the distance. He jumped down toward the racket, sliding over the dirt.

The voices shouting sounded familiar. Tadashi's ears pricked up, listening to the shouts as they drew nearer.

Berg turned around. "Alva, hurry, sweetheart."

He waved her over. Alva wobbled toward Berg. Tadashi leaned against to give her support. Tadashi nudged her, encouraging her to move faster, sensing and smelling the man's urgency. The same feeling skittered through him. His heart pounded faster, his fur stood on end, and he had to fight the impulse to stretch out and run.

"Berg!"

The man in question locked eyes with Tadashi. "You need to run."

He wanted to. The blood pumping through his body told him to leave. Except Alva was still holding onto him, her tired little body leaning against him.

"Berg!"

"Shit!" The man scrambled back to Alva and Tadashi.

"Berg! Wait. I see him!"

"Run!"

Alva still needed him, the ground was bumpy and the light was fading fast. He wouldn't let her fall.

"Berg, what are—holy hell, Red! Look!"

"Shoot it! Shoot the fucking beast!"

"No!" Berg screamed, spinning around. He threw his arms up.

The men didn't listen. Shots rang out through the wood.

Tadashi pushed Alva down and covered her with his body. He trembled with anger and fear. Please don't let her be hurt.

"Alva!" Berg yelled as he sprinted down the mountain. "You'll hit Alva!"

Red-hot bullets burned Tadashi, ripping deep inside him. Alva whined under him. Tadashi panted, relief painting itself through his body. She was okay.

"Alva's up there! Stop!"

They did. The echoes of shots piercing the air died away.

Perplexed murmurs followed the noise.

Berg skidded to a halt. "Alva's safe! Just don't shoot!"

"How can you say she's safe!" A familiar voice yelled. "That monster is on top of her!"

"Because you were shooting at her!" Berg retorted, livid. His hands were up in the air, waving about as he shouted at the men.

Alva chose that moment to let out of heart-wrenching wail. "Doggie!"

I thought we covered this. Tadashi bent over and nuzzled her, trying to get Alva to relax.

"He's eating her!"

"The dog is comforting her. Look—" Berg pointed at Tadashi and the girl. "Alva's calming down."

Another man spoke up. "Are you sure it's a dog?"

"Yes," Berg answered with vehemence. "I made the same mistake at first. Maybe he's some kind of wolf-dog hybrid. But I do know he's been protecting Alva. Hell, he's probably the only reason she's still alive right now."

Why would the human lie? He knew Tadashi was a fox. But… if he was going to go that far for Tadashi. It took a great deal of effort to push back on his feet. In fact, his legs wouldn't stop dancing under him. Tadashi held his head high, as dignified as he could, and barked.

Gods, what an awful sound.

He barked again and threw in a tail wag for good measure.

Berg strode up to him like he did it all the time. "Hey, buddy, you did good."

Tadashi whined and pawed at the mountainous man.

"That's it. Good boy." Those deep green eyes held too much anxiety. "Will you give Alva to me?"

Tadashi didn't miss the subtle movement made by Berg so he stood directly in front of the girl and him. Berg stretched out his arms and cooed at Alva. She turned her face and smiled back at him.

"Alva, sweetheart? You okay?" Red called. The strain in his voice seemed real, but Tadashi didn't like the man. How could Alva be related to him?

"Red!"

"Yes, sweetheart." Red stepped toward Berg. His shotgun hung from his arm.

Tadashi let out a low growl and got tapped on the nose for it. He swung his head at the idiotic man, eyes wide.

"Bad dog," Berg admonished, but there was a spark of amusement in his eyes. "Red won't hurt Alva."

"I don't like this Berg," Red said. He shifted, his hand moving to the barrel of the gun. "It's an animal."

"You've got a goddamn shotgun in your hands," Berg ground out. His deep tone was rough and terse. Shivers went through Tadashi. "Back off, and he'll give Alva to me."

Tadashi barked in agreement.

Berg gestured to him in a manner that said *see?*

Red spat on the ground, a sneer disfiguring his face. Hate dripped from every word he spoke, but his voice had a slight tremor. The humans couldn't detect it, but Tadashi could. "That thing is a beast. It will kill anything that gets—"

"Has he hurt me or Alva?" Berg interrupted. "No. It's protected Alva, from us. Besides, does that look like some mutated wolf with multiple tails? No. Some husky probably got lucky and had a litter. Let it go, and let me get your sweetheart. Your sister is frantic and what's important is that Alva's safe."

"Hey, Red," another man called. "Look at it. The dog, or whatever it is, is barely standing. It'll probably die soon anyway. Let's get Alva and go. It's almost dark and I do not want to be here when the sun is down."

"Yeah," Red agreed reluctantly. "I suppose." He sent a sidelong glance to Berg. His eyes clearly filled with dread, and the scent poured from the foul-smelling man. "Will the dog let you take her?"

"He was about to until you idiots started shooting," Berg answered. Even Tadashi could hear the censure in the man's tone. He smiled, letting his tongue hang out. Tadashi was all for making Red uncomfortable. He'd let the fact Berg shot at him as well go for that alone. The man had probably saved him.

"Pick her up then," Red ordered, his lips were still warped into a frown. He ground his jaw together as Berg backed away from him.

"Okay, okay, I'll get her." Berg turned and moved closer to Tadashi. "Mind letting me have our girl, boy? I promise she'll be safe."

The men laughed, why Tadashi didn't know, but he dipped his head.

"Why you always talk to animals like they know what you're saying, Berg?" One asked.

Another called out, "See if he'd like a good bath, too."

"Would he like a bone, Berg?" Another teased.

Berg ignored the razzing. He picked Alva up, the young girl snuggling into him. Berg didn't immediately stand up, pretending to juggle the girl, but he spoke quietly to Tadashi.

"I'll stay in front of you as long as I can, but run first chance you get. Red shoots anything he sees as a threat."

Tadashi nodded again.

"I'll be back to help. You know the temple?"

Again, yes.

"Go there. I'll find you."

Sounded fair to Tadashi.

Berg stood, clutching Alva, mumbling, "Weirdest damn day of my life."

Yes. It was. The whole skin-peeling experience made a whole lot more sense now.

Berg headed toward Red, short, purposeful steps.

"Why's my girl got your shirt on, Berg?"

He laughed, head falling back. His blond locks brushed his shoulders. "It was hot earlier, Red. Alva was doing what kids do best in that kind of weather."

"Oh?"

"Yeah, she was running free as a jay bird." Berg chuckled again and patted Alva. "Weren't you, girl?"

"Free as a jay bird!" she parroted, throwing her hands up in the air.

The men laughed, the tension dissipating, but Tadashi kept his ears cocked for the slightest sound. Their ease could turn into hatred real fast. He kept his gaze on Red, watching the man for any signs of aggression. Out of the corner of his eye, Tadashi caught Alva waving over Berg's shoulder.

He turned to her and smiled, a fox smile anyway. Her face was so open, so honest, so caring. He wished she'd never grow up.

Twin cries—one loud and deep, another a high pitched squeal—erupting from Berg and Alva had Tadashi whipping his head back in time to see Red leveling the barrel of his gun at him. Tadashi spun around, but not before a loud bang went off and a cataclysm of agony ripped through his body.

Chapter Six

As the fox fell to the ground, Berg stood there in shock, holding Alva's head against his shoulder. The way his heart lurched as the animal went down threatened to bring Berg under. The fox had been a protector, not some savage beast. There'd been no reason, none, to shoot it. Berg knew Red had wanted to go after the animal, but he didn't think he would actually shoot the fox on front of his niece. The man doted on her too much to be so insensitive.

Apparently I'm wrong.

"Jesus, Red," Harwood gasped, exhaling slowly and speaking for the guys. "You are one heartless bastard."

The other men in the search party chuckled nervously, agreeing with their friend.

Red spit on the ground, then chomped down on his chew again before answering, "One less rabid dog to worry about. Let's go, boys."

Everyone cleared a path as he stalked back toward the group. Berg followed but kept at a distance, angry with Red for outright dismissing Alva's feelings.

"It wasn't rabid!" Berg answered in a short, clipped tone. Alva shuddered against him, followed by tiny, wet drops soaking his shirt. "And what about Alva?"

Red twisted around and frowned. "What about her?"

"Did you stop to think what seeing an animal shot would do to her?" It took so much effort not to yell and pummel the man. Alva had been through enough already in the last day.

A few of the men murmured their agreement but they quieted down right quick when Red glared at them.

"Hand her over," Red ordered. He gave his shotgun to Harwood and then held out his arms.

Berg didn't want to hand Alva over. Not one bit, and considering how balled up his shirt was in her hands, she didn't want to go to her uncle either. Red hopped back up the rocks to Berg.

"I said hand her over."

Berg dipped his head, he'd lose the argument, but maybe he could make things easier. He talked slowly and quietly to his sister's goddaughter. "Your uncle's missed you, sweetheart. You gave him a scare. Why don't you make sure he's okay?"

She shook her head.

Red fumed. Deep lines furrowed on his forehead and around his eyes. "Alva, sweetie, Uncle Red wants to hold you."

"No," Alva whined, sniffling. "Red bad."

For the first time since Alva had gone missing from her birthday party, Red looked truly forlorn, his tough guy façade crumbling in front of his niece.

"Alva, sweetheart, I had to shoot the dog."

"Nah-huh."

Berg shifted his bundle. A small part of him rejoiced at Red's distress. "You really going to argue with a two-year-old?"

Red pressed his lips together, the vein in his neck ticking wildly. He took a couple deep breaths before speaking again. "Honey, that dog was hurt real bad. The nicest thing we could do was put him down. It had to be done, sweetheart."

She whimpered, burying her face farther into Berg. He understood. He'd made the mistake of hurting the fox, and he'd been good. If only he'd been a little faster, they wouldn't be in the situation and Alva wouldn't be so sad, and maybe the fox would have had a chance of surviving. Now though… he'd be dead before he got to the temple. Probably, and that really bothered Berg.

He pressed his cheek against Alva, fighting to keep his voice steady. "Let your uncle love on you, sweetheart. He's been looking for you all night and all day."

Alva began to cry. *So much for helping.*

"Just let me carry her, Red," Berg implored, holding Alva tighter. "She's had a rough go of it."

"Fine," Red snapped. His hands fisted at his side and he glared at Berg. "Let's get back before Jean Ann has a heart attack."

Berg shifted Alva in his arms, patting the small girl to reassure her. "Sounds good."

Red twirled around and headed back toward the search party. Everyone started the move with him. Berg followed, quiet like everyone else who had watched as they argued. As Berg passed some of the guys, the men called out to Alva and patted her back, everyone happy to see her safe and sound. Alva, however, refused to answer anyone.

Hell, Berg didn't want to talk either. The fox getting shot... the fox! Berg spun around, frantically searching for the fox. He wasn't by the tree where he collapsed. The fox couldn't have just disappeared. He'd been right there.

A flash of white in the distance caught Berg's eye. He squinted, focusing in on the movement. There! Through the trees, the fox was limping away. In the direction of the temple. Thank God.

Then again, how was the fox even alive?

Berg wanted to go and check on the curious animal, the urge hard to fight, but with Alva in his arms, he couldn't. He'd have to sneak away later, once he got Alva back to Jean Ann and away from Red. Speaking of Red. A chill caught Berg, and he trembled in response. Berg spun back around, meeting Red's unfocused gaze.

There was nothing in Red's eyes. No anger. No fear. No happiness. It was just... empty. That was more disturbing than anything else Berg could've found there.

Nervousness skittered through Berg. Something in the way Red stared after the fox made Berg uneasy. The vacant expression on his face and how his eyes were fixated in the distance... Berg feared Red knew the fox was still alive. He feared for what Red's warped mind would want to do. The man had lost his marbles when Berg had been younger, and only Sheriff Fowler could keep Red in check.

The sheriff wasn't around. He'd stayed back in town, searching the lake.

Not wanting to draw more attention to the situation, Berg shuffled forward, carrying the tiny Alva, probably taking as much comfort in her arms as she took from his.

"Hey, Berg," Red said, putting a hand on his arm.

"Yeah, Red?"

"Where's your gun?" Red inquired. The harsh edge to his voice made goose bumps jump up all over Berg's skin.

Some of the men glanced over their shoulders as they walked, closely watching the exchange. God, it would be all over town tomorrow.

He gritted his teeth and answered. "I put it down to get Alva."

"You mean you weren't armed?" Harwood's shocked question stopped everyone. They all watched him, waiting for a response.

He shrugged, uncomfortable with the attention. What could he say? Animals usually like me 'cause I'm a vet? No, this crowd would just razz him some more.

Red slapped him on the back, making Berg jolt. "Should we go back and get it?"

Berg surveyed the blue sky. It was darkening into purple-black, rays of red and gold bursting from the setting sun, and stars were twinkling overhead. He shook his head. "It's gonna be dark soon."

"But, still, don't you—" Red began.

"I think we need to get Alva home, don't you, Uncle Red?" Berg said, unwilling to hear more.

Red's expression softened. He reached out and caressed Alva's check. "Yeah, time for my girl to go home. She's all tuckered out."

Soft snores filled the vast hush in the group. *How did I miss Alva falling asleep?*

"Come on, boys, let's go," Red said, walking past Berg and picking the pace back up. "Shame about the gun, Berg, it was a beaut."

"Yeah, well, it's fine." Berg didn't have a huge attachment to it. He was a vet after all. He was for saving animals' lives. "Besides, I can always come back and find it."

Now he had an excuse to look for the fox.

"Maybe you'll need some help."

"I'll be fine," Berg answered, not sure it was the truth or not. It had been years since the last attack.

"Sure you will," Harwood said. He clapped Red on the back. "Now let's get sweetheart home to Jean Ann."

Red jerked his head once, and everyone followed, the trip passing in silence. Those whose hands were free had their guns cocked and ready to shoot, while he and Red escorted Alva. Walking back to town was the second-worst experience in Berg's life. Almost losing Alva was the first.

The uncomfortable trip paid off though. Jean Ann's cries of relief would warm any cold heart. The cheers from the townspeople who had gathered at the house helped too.

"My baby girl! Oh God, my girl!"

Jean Ann rushed over to Berg, nearly causing him to drop her as he handed her over.

Alva woke with a whimper. "Doggie."

Jean Ann cradled Alva to her. She looked up at Berg, tears streaming down her face, confusion in her blue eyes. "Did she say doggie?"

"Yeah, a dog found her and was taking care of her."

"A stray dog?" Fear belied Jean Ann's question.

"Yes, probably," Berg answered.

"Berg's the one who found her though. All by himself, too," Red interrupted. He'd brought Jean Ann's husband over. Edwin looked like death warmed over. An extra decade hung on him like a worn shirt.

Two pairs of distraught expressions met Berg's, but their agony was swiftly replaced with rapture.

"Thank you," Edwin murmured, his voice hoarse and unsteady. His eyes were red rimmed. "I can't ever thank you enough."

"Oh, no, I didn't—" Berg began to protest, only to be cut off by Red's loud voice.

"Three cheers for Berg! Thank you for finding my niece, safe and sound."

The crowd chanted, drowning out Berg's protests. Red's interference puzzled Berg, and he wondered what the man was up to. Finding out would take a careful hand. Berg stared at Red's empty eyes until a hand touched him. Jean Ann stood close and went on her tiptoes, placing a soft kiss on his cheek.

"Thank you, Berg," Jean Ann choked out, then the tears really began to flow.

Edwin hugged his girls to his chest, burying his head in Alva's hair. Alva squeaked, waking up completely. Her yelp of happiness made Berg chuckle with contentment. The three of them cried together.

With a step back, Berg tried to give the family some privacy in their moment, but there were too many people around to do so; people wanting to congratulate him immediately surrounded Berg.

"Well done," Jean Ann's father said, his smile nearly as wide as his face.

"Good job, Berg, where'd you find her?" queried her mom.

"Uh, well, I—" Berg bumped into someone and turned to apologize. Red was pushed up against him, that strange vacant look in his eyes again. Why is he standing so close? Red's gaze moved to his parents.

"On the mountain," Red supplied before Berg could say anything.

There were several audible gasps in the room. The women began to titter as the men crowded around wanting to know what happened. Berg got drawn in one direction while Red went in another. Dammit, they needed to talk. Berg moved through his friends and neighbors, his irritation growing.

The noise became deafening as the gossip started. Red was soaking up the attention while Berg just wanted everyone to calm down. Hell, Edwin was squeezing Jean Ann and Alva so tight Berg thought his friend might break them.

"Luckily Berg got there in time."

What?

He turned and twisted, trying to locate Red. He was sure the voice had been Red. Who knows? The other men from the search party were bathing in the attention as well. Everyone surprised and excited by the prospect they had made it up the mountain and back with no incident.

"The mutt was big and white, even had blood dripping from it."

Well fuck. He scoured the room some more, about to give up, until he saw red hair. Finally. Red stood laughing in middle of a gaggle of women.

"The beast's razor-sharp teeth were huge," Red said, holding his hands apart. "Luckily our guns were on us."

Liar. The fangs weren't that fucking big.

One of the women, Bonnie, leaned into Red. "Were you scared?"

The beast hadn't been sighted in at least six years. Chances were the mutated dog, or whatever it was, died a long time ago. Berg drove in Red's direction with purpose, every step excruciating because of how wound up he was. Not to mention Red was being an idiot. The fox couldn't be the beast Red informed everyone about. Dogs didn't normally live over fifteen, no matter the breed. Now Red was stirring everybody up again. It needed to stop.

Berg pushed into the throng of people, anger riding him harder than he had expected. He raised his voice. "There wasn't anything to be scared of."

Bonnie turned around, her skepticism toward his claim clear as day with one shapely raised eyebrow. "But Red here says you met with the Beast."

"A mutt, some kind of husky-wolf hybrid," Berg agreed partially, his words strained as he said them. "But I doubt it was the Beast."

"It was a pretty big dog then," Red spat, his face giving his name a run for its money. Scarlet was not a good look on the man. "And we don't need any mangy mutts running around."

"He could've been one of the resort developer's dogs or someone on their construction crew," Berg retorted, his voice heavy and cross. Why did Red have to cause so much trouble? Berg could feel his right eye twitching, its steady beat letting him know a headache was coming on. Damn. "Have you thought of that? Maybe you killed someone's pet? After it saved Alva."

Wow. It got really quiet. Fast.

Berg didn't think he'd ever been in a room this quiet before. Not with this many people. The good people of Orange Grove were too talkative for their own good.

"Did you say the dog saved Alva?" Jean Ann's father—Mr. Engström—asked.

"Yes, sir, I did," Berg affirmed. "The thing was trying to protect her from me when I found her by some blackberry bushes. He even let her climb on his back."

The room turned to Red, whose demeanor had gone rigid, and unfortunately, his expression said he was outright pissed.

"You let her ride him?" Edwin asked, his voice rising as he pushed through the crowd. Oh see, now, he sounded pissed. Berg looked for Jean Ann. Nowhere in sight. Damn. She must have decided to put Alva to bed or something. "What do you mean this, this dog, whatever, let Alva ride him?"

Berg sighed. This was going to be an uphill battle, wasn't it? By the expressions everyone wore, yes, yes it would.

"Berg?" Mr. Engström said quietly, holding up a hand to stop Edwin. "Would you care to explain?"

"The dog was spooked because I shot at it. He was cleaning her, but I couldn't tell that." He pointed at Red. "My brain went to the Beast stories and I reacted, shooting it. Anyway, Alva was scared, too, and she climbed on him and they took off. I had to trail them.

"When I got close, he stood in front of her and shielded her." God, if he could take it all back he would. The fox had tried so hard to protect her and he… *he's probably dead because of it.* "So, you see, I don't think there was anything to worry about. Even shot, that dog protected her with its life. I tried to tell Red, but…"

If only he could do it over again, reacted faster. He was supposed to fix animals, not kill them.

"I'm sorry," Berg said after a moment. His throat hurt, was all twisted up. He gulped a few times to moisten it. How had it gotten so dry? "I just… I dunno. I think shooting it was a mistake, is all. Red probably did put it out of its misery, but I'm having a hard time reconciling it all."

Mr. Engström patted Berg. "You never did like hunting, boy. Only ever did it when you had to. It's why you make such a good vet. We understand."

The room murmured, but Berg knew the other guys would talk. They always gave him a hard time over his 'squeamishness'. This episode wouldn't help things.

"What matters is you found Alva, made my girls happy," Mr. Engström continued. "Isn't that right, everybody?"

The dreariness lifted some from the room as people agreed. People dispersed into groups now that the spectacle was over. Others began to say their farewells. A quick glance outside showed a black sky. Much like Red's mood. Red stood not far away, staring daggers, his jaw ticking something terrible.

God, what kind of harassment was he going to have to put up with this time? Mr. Engström followed Berg's line of sight. He sighed and rubbed the back of his neck.

"You'll have to excuse Red," Red's dad offered. "After… after that incident on the mountain. His friends being killed the way they were, he's… he's never been quite the same."

"I know." Everyone did, but still. Being around Red felt like an accident waiting to happen.

"Why'd you think about going up on the mountain?"

Huh? Oh. "Um, well, the park butts up to it, and it was the only place we hadn't looked."

Mr. Engström frowned, his eyes unfocused until he looked back up to Berg. "I'm just glad you boys are safe."

"Thank you, sir." Berg glanced around, exhausted. He wanted to say his goodbyes. "Where are Jean Ann and Alva?"

Edwin spoke up. "Alva was dirty and tired. She went to bathe her and put her down."

Berg nodded, glancing at the grandfather clock in the living room. It was well past eleven o'clock. Had they really been here that long? God he was tired, and he had to see to Mr. Grahn's sick heifer tomorrow, then go over to the Hanssons', and somehow, he had to find that fox.

"Berg?"

He looked up, blinking rapidly a few times. Did he drop off? His gaze met the clear blue eyes of Mrs. Engström.

"Thank you."

Berg dropped his head. "You're welcome."

"You look like you're about to drop, dear."

Berg scanned the room. The others from the search party looked about as wrung out as him. "I think we all are."

"You boys worked hard, looking for my granddaughter."

"I haven't been a boy for some time, Mrs. Engström."

She chuckled, her dimples showing. "If you're wondering where your wife is, your sister brought her home hours ago. The waiting around isn't good for a woman in her condition."

Hell, he hadn't even thought about Freyja since he found Alva. Shit, what a horse's ass he was.

Mrs. Engström patted his arm. "Why don't you get home? Freyja's been worried sick. You might want to head off the rumors before she hears 'em all tomorrow."

There was a twinkle in her blue eyes. Berg winced.

"Thank you, I think I will." Berg kissed her cheek and made for the door. Freyja was going to blow a gasket. Especially when she heard he led everyone up the mountain.

Dammit. He was going to be sleeping on the couch for the next week.

* * * * *

Sweat poured down Berg's face, his shirt was soaked. His leather vet bag thumped against his side with every step. How in Hell could it be so hot when it was so cool the day before? He had found his gun and stashed it so he could retrieve it on his way back, found the blood trail, and was on his way toward the temple. His legs were shaking from the exertion it took to climb so fast up the mountain. His morning started early after having a late night. That wasn't helping his condition.

The couch was small.

Berg woke not long after finally falling asleep. Rays of sunlight rudely penetrated the curtains through the window. At least he had a jump on the day. He was able to get his important stops out of the way so he could come back up the mountain.

Hopefully, Freyja won't know. He laughed. Yeah. He could wish all he wanted but someone would tip her off.

Better to ask for forgiveness. He'd had to do that a lot lately.

Berg checked his watch. How was it only ten o'clock in the morning? This day would never end. The past forty-eight hours were a blur anyway, might as well count as one long ass day.

The terrain got steeper and rockier, so it took all of Berg's concentration to hike up the haphazard path of blood he followed. How the Mizunos went up and down the mountain with supplies for their temple was beyond comprehension. The family had to be part bear or something. Well, it explained why the temple keepers were all so skinny. A gleam drew Berg out of his meandering. His grimace deepened into a frown.

81

The fox obviously couldn't walk a straight line. Not that Berg expected the animal to, there were trees and bushes, but the amount of stumbling disturbed him. He knew the animal had been wounded badly. He had just hoped, just a little, to fix his blunder.

He kept a certain amount of optimism though. Berg was sure the temple had to be nearby, so if the fox made it this far, he could still be alive. Maybe the Mizunos found it and helped the fox. The shrine had kitsune statues as its gatekeepers since it was a temple devoted to Inari. If they saw a wounded fox, they'd certainly do something. Their beliefs wouldn't let them not take action.

Hopefully.

After rounding a particularly large rock, Berg stopped, and then relief put an extra kick in his step. The rooftops of the temple were visible. Maybe they would help him look for the fox. It was hard to believe the animal made it this far even with the blood trail dotting the ground. He kept his eyes on the prize and hurried forward.

"Thank God for m—Hell!" Berg tumbled face first into the ground. His hands hit the ground first. A painful tremor worked through his body. His elbows twinged with a sharp needling. But something soft broke his fall and kept his knees from knocking into the ground. One half of him wouldn't hurt.

Berg twisted around to see what saved his knees from being obliterated against the hard ground.

"Shit!"

The fox lay motionless under him. Panic overtook Berg's relief. His hands moved, all thought stopped as he checked for a pulse. His heart pounded, the sound echoed in his ears, and for a moment, he didn't breathe.

God, he couldn't feel anything, and damn, the fox was cold. Shit. Berg pressed his lips together. His teeth hurt from the pressure of his jaw as he ground his teeth. He dropped his head on the animal, buried it in his fur, and squeezed his eyes shut.

It was ridiculous. Really. To cry over a damn fox that would eat your chickens as soon as your back was turned. But there had been something different about him.

Intelligence shone in his eyes. He had protected Alva. He responded to Berg. An animal, no matter what kind, shouldn't be shot down in cold blood.

Berg turned his head, trying to catch his breath but it stuttered. Damn. It was all his fault… if he hadn't insisted on checking the mountain. But then they might not have found Alva. If he had gotten to her faster, made the fox understand the danger he'd been in, something.

But he hadn't and now the fox was… what was that?

God. A heartbeat. The fox had a heartbeat! Nothing could've made Berg happier. He knelt, got his arms under the ragged animal, and slowly got to his feet, cradling the fox close to his chest.

It wasn't easy. The damn fox was huge. But, god, he was a gorgeous specimen.

Carefully walking toward the temple, the trip took longer than he thought it would, and by the time he made it to the gates, Berg's arms were shaking. He called out, announcing himself so as not to take the Mizunos by surprise. No one answered. In fact, the place seemed unusually quiet. Not like Berg would know per se. But some noise, even regular forest noises should be audible, but nothing. Absolutely nothing.

Honestly, it was a little creepy. His arm hair stood on end, Berg spooked. Definitely spooked. He wanted to turn around, but he needed to see to the fox.

"Mizuno-san?" Berg called again. "Mrs. Mizuno? Anybody?"

Hell.

Berg stepped into the courtyard and tried again. Nope, nothing. He scoured the grounds for any sign of life. It was completely devoid of any.

God, this did not feel right.

Berg totally had a case of the heebie-jeebies.

Not one to admit defeat, though, Berg headed to the temple. Once in the main room of the building, Berg stood, stunned. No one was in there but it was gorgeous, well kept, though a bit dusty.

Someone must be here… right?

A quick search through all the rooms showed the same care and attention to detail. They also revealed no one had been there in a few days. A fine layer of dust coated every surface. The pit of Berg's stomach began to knot up. Between the silence and the dust, Berg feared for the Mizuno family.

Maybe they had just gone on vacation. Ha! Probably not, considering their distrust of the town, but it would make Berg feel better about the situation if they weren't here rather than thinking the worst.

Once back in the main worship chamber, Berg stared at the Inari shrine: beautiful, eloquent, and in sore need of a dusting. Holding his fox against his chest, Berg knelt down in front of the old-world god, and a sense of familiarity rung with Berg. His dad and mom never shut up about the Nordic gods. All the deeds, good and bad, they had done went through Berg's head. Inari, in a sense, wasn't any different than them: a god before Christianity. Worshipped by simpler people at a simpler time.

Maybe it couldn't hurt to ask for a little bit of help. Berg wasn't picky where it came from at this point.

"Inari, um, this is Berg Engman. You don't know me—at all." What does one say to an ancient god? "But I just want to say… I hope the Mizunos are all right, and if you could look out for your fox's welfare, I'd be much obliged."

There. That couldn't hurt anything. With one last little prayer, Berg lifted the fox and went to check the one place he hadn't yet, the hut on the side of the temple.

"Mizuno-san?"

Berg gave the door a good kick. It shuddered under the assault, creaking and groaning. No one yelled back or said to wait a minute. Hm. Chances were the hut was just a shed or storeroom, but his gut said it was something more. Berg couldn't let it go. Instincts were meant to be listened to, not ignored.

He kicked the door again. The timber shivered, making all the same noises as before. "Mizuno-san? Mrs. Mizuno? Tadashi?"

Again, no answer. Berg sighed and shifted the fox in his arms. They hurt so bad, but he wouldn't put the animal down. As long as he could feel the sluggish heartbeat under his palm, he knew the fox was still with him.

Ready to pull out his hair in frustration, Berg kicked the door. A loud crack, and it swung open. Damn. He'd broken the door. It'd been a flimsy door, but still, Berg winced. He hoped the Mizunos didn't carry a grudge.

Well, the door was open. Nothing like the present. Berg ducked into the small space and then was shocked by what he found.

A small bed pressed against one wall with nightstand and dresser next to it. A chair sat by a wood stove and a painted box lay close to it. Damn again. Who would live in such a place? What was with all the other rooms in the temple then and the attached building behind it? Wasn't that the house?

The mussed-up sheets told a whole other story. Someone did sleep here. Berg walked closer to the bed. He closed his eyes, shifting the fox again. The animal was so dang heavy. Maybe he could put it down for a minute. He really needed to look at its wounds.

If anyone were to show up, this seemed like the most reasonable place to be. Opening his eyes, Berg debated where to put the fox. He eyed the comforter. It was gorgeous. With a sigh, Berg maneuvered it down then set the fox on top of the worn bedding.

It was clean, just… old.

"Finally," Berg said with relief. He stretched his arms. Goddamn they were tired. He then slung the strap of his bag over his head, ready to set it down and get to work when he was interrupted but a brutal cry.

"Murderer!"

Chapter Seven

Berg spun around, looking for the small—*squeaky?*—voice. He found nothing but a damn squirrel in the box by the stove. God those dirty rodents were a nuisance. Berg took a breath. Not the time. Better to ignore it. He glanced out the door. No one there either. He could've sworn he heard a child's voice.

It had shaken him, too. He felt like a murderer.

Berg looked down at the fox, its white fur stained red. It was a travesty, and he had started it. Now, he would fix it. He bent down by its side, reaching for his bag.

"Murderer!"

There was a soft thump against his back. "What the Hell?"

"Killer!"

Tiny claws ripped through his shirt as something crawled up his back.

Berg twisted, trying to grab hold of the creature, as well as look for whoever was shouting at him. No one was in the room. Teeth sunk into his shoulder.

"Fuck!" It bit him again. Berg grabbed for it but the lithe little body ducked down into his shirt. It nipped and skittered about as he tried desperately to work the clothes off, but every time it took a chunk out of him, his hands automatically went to the spot it hurt.

Berg looked at the box. The squirrel was gone. God, he was being attacked by a squirrel. He'd never live it down. Death by squirrel.

"You bastard!"

What did he do to deserve this? "Get the fuck off me, you damn squirrel!"

"Murderer!"

"I am not!" Berg yelled in response, needing to defend himself.

The squirrel bit him again. This time, his hands were fast enough and he trapped the squirrel against him. Berg wrapped what fabric he could around the squirrel and began to excise the shirt off him.

"Please don't be rabid!' said Berg in a pained voice. He hurt in places he really shouldn't.

"You killed Tadashi!" The mysterious voice shouted again.

What? Tadashi wasn't even here. Berg searched for the voice as he finally worked the shirt over his head. He tossed it.

The squirrel dropped from it as the fabric fell to the floor. It glared at Berg, chirping wildly. Berg backed toward the bed, keeping a wary eye on it.

"Would you leave me the fuck alone and let me help this fox before he dies?" God, he was going nuts if he thought a squirrel would listen to him.

The squirrel stopped chirping. It stood alert, rapidly breathing just like Berg.

"Holy hell," Berg gasped. No. No, it was just done attacking him. Squirrels were stupid vermin. He really hoped it didn't have anything catching. Like rabies. "You didn't have to bite me!"

The squirrel backed off. Great. Foxes and squirrels listened to him. Why couldn't it be a useful animal, like horses and cows? Then he'd know what was wrong with Mr. Grahn's heifer. Berg had heard of horse whisperers, but oh no, he was a squirrel whisperer.

Berg shook his head and turned to the fox. Might as well do something good.

"Tadashi's alive?" A small voice asked.

"As far as I know!" Berg spun around, surveying every nook and cranny. He was getting real tired of this game. "Whoever's there, please come out. I promise I won't hurt you." He pointed to the squirrel. "Him I can't speak for."

The squirrel skittered up to him. Its little beady eyes were damp with unshed tears. *God. I must be tired. I'm seeing things.* Berg rubbed his eyes.

"He's really okay?"

Berg opened his eyes again, leaned forward, and ignored the steady gaze of the creepy squirrel. He softened his voice, hoping to coax the child—he assumed child by the voice—out. "As far as I know. You'll have to ask him when he gets here. Right now, I need to help this fox. It's hurt real bad."

A squeak drew his attention down. The damn vermin actually looked upset. Great. Now he felt worse than before.

Berg shook the thing off. It kept crawling back on his boot though. He did not have time for this. Berg noticed a broom leaning against the wall, leaned, and grabbed it. Using the bristle end, Berg poked the squirrel.

"Get off, I have work to do."

"Hey! Don't hit me!"

Did that come from the squirrel? It looked like its mouth opened. Creepy. "Come on, off!"

The squirrel danced around the broom, determination on its face. It sat back on its hind legs and pointed at him. "Bad human!"

"Argh!" God, it talked. It really fucking talked. The broom came down on instinct, landing right on top of the demon squirrel. It squeaked. That seemed normal.

"Stop trying to squish me!"

That did not! Its tail flicked wildly under the bristles.

"Get this broom off me!"

"Stop talking!" he demanded, his chest heaving. His head felt kind of light. That couldn't be good.

A talking squirrel? No way, not ever.

"Help Tadashi!" The squirrel retorted.

"I'm trying to help the fox!" Really truly. He was arguing with a possessed squirrel. How fucking nuts was he? He let out a gruff laugh.

"Then let go of the broom and help him!" Its tiny head popped out from under the broom. An arm wriggled free and it pointed at him again. "Stop being a bastard and save—"

Berg thumped the squirrel again and jumped back. "Fuck!"

The demon squirrel, possessed squirrel, whatever it was, held its head in its paws. "Why would you do that?"

Berg lifted the broom, pointing it at the rodent. "Stop talking!"

It opened its mouth then stopped. The squirrel snapped its teeth together—Berg shuddered, because damn those hurt—and, was it squinting at him? The damn squirrel reminded Berg of the fox.

"The fox!" Berg whirled around and dropped the broom. He knelt down next to the bed, his hand searching for his bag. Then he felt it, but it pushed against his palm.

Without looking, Berg knew how it had gotten there, but he checked anyway. The squirrel had pushed it into his grasp. It kept getting creepier. Berg didn't have time for this. He opened the bag and pulled out his supplies, laying them on the bed next to the fox. He ignored when the squirrel jumped up on the bed and started arranging his needle, scalpels, tweezers and bottles, and everything else.

Just no.

Berg found his clippers and trimmed the blood-soaked matted fur down to the skin. He prodded and examined the wounds. The harsh breaths falling from the fox worried him. *At least the animal is breathing.* Berg reached for the bottle with painkillers. It met his hand.

He flinched. "Thanks."

"You're welcome," the squirrel answered. "These things? They will help the fox?"

"Yes." Berg suppressed a shudder. Too weird.

"Is it going to hurt him?"

"No." He drew some of the liquid into the needle before prodding the fox's flank. "At least I hope not. I'm going to give him some shots so it doesn't hurt so much when I cut—Ow!"

The damn squirrel's teeth were in his hand. He shook it, trying to dislodge the little demon. The stinker had a death grip.

"I have to get the bullets out somehow!" he yelled.

The squirrel let go. It looked… confused.

"Do you have to bite me?" Berg asked.

The squirrel shrugged. It really shrugged. How… human. "You said you wouldn't hurt him!"

"I have to cut the wounds to dig out the bullets. The needle puts in medicine so he doesn't feel so much," Berg explained, his temple throbbed. A headache was coming. He didn't need this… weirdness. "Are you going to attack me every time I do something you don't like? Or can I do my job?"

"What is your job?" The squirrel puffed up. If a squirrel could look skeptical, this one did.

"I'm a veterinarian. I take care of sick animals." Insane. This whole experience, dream, whatever, was insane.

"Fine." The squirrel sniffed and crossed his front legs. Berg tried not to stand up and bolt from the room. He had made a promise to the fox, to himself. "But if you hurt him more, I'll be the one you answer to."

Really? The squirrel is threatening me? No one would ever believe Berg in a hundred years. *Death by squirrel may happen after all.*

"Go on, fix him." The squirrel gestured to the fox.

"You could say please, you know? Weren't you taught manners?" Berg snapped.

The squirrel's tail drooped. "Please fix him."

Crap. The guilt. It tore through him. Berg closed his eyes. *Ignore the squirrel. Just ignore it.* Slowly, he reopened them. The fox lay before him, struggling to breath. *Focus on the task at hand.*

He plunged the needle into the fox's flank. The skin jerked but the fox made no sound. Not a good sign. He waited. When he thought the medicine kicked in, Berg picked up the scalpel so he could open the wound. He paused and then turned to the squeamish squirrel.

"You might not want to watch."

The damn rodent sniffed. "I can handle it. I'm fifteen now."

"There's going to be more blood," Berg clarified.

"I... I'll be fine." The squirrel gulped a couple times. His gaze flicked to the fox then back. "I can help."

"You sure?" Because Berg wasn't.

The squirrel lifted his head, chin out. "Yeah."

Berg shook his head. "Fine."

Never in his life would he have imagined this. God, what a weird-ass day. Possessed squirrels and all.

* * * * *

Berg wiped his hands on his pants. God, he'd never been so tired in his life. Hours had passed. It took forever to find all the bullets, carefully extract them with as little damage to the muscle and blood vessels as possible. All he needed to do was stitch up the wounds and the fox would be set. Berg put out his hand.

"Needle."

"What for?" The squirrel asked.

"I need to sew up the holes," Berg explained.

"Like clothes?"

"Uh, yes?"

The squirrel chirped. It sounded... disapproving.

"What?" Berg couldn't help but be a little miffed. What room did a talking squirrel have to judge him?

"Holes can be ripped again. They're weaker than before."

"Well, the scar tissue—"

The squirrel held up its paw. "Quiet!"

"Uh?" Did the squirrel just shush him?

"I can do better," the squirrel said, flicking its tail.

"What, by licking it?" Berg responded sarcastically.

"No." The squirrel climbed up on the fox. Did it just smirk at him? It put its paws over a wound. "Like this."

"Like—shit!"

A white glow formed, and if his day hadn't been freaky enough, the skin started to knit together.

"Hey!"

The squirrel glanced up with a look of concentration on his furry little face. "I'm busy!"

"If you could do that before, why the hell did I operate on him?" Berg stood, completely agitated. "We could've—"

"I can only do this," the squirrel answered. His ears even flattened against his head.

How could something so small make Berg feel so bad?

"I-I'm not that strong yet," he squeaked. "I can only do small things like this. Papa says I'm still young, and while I can do more than him at my age, I don't have the control necessary for my powers."

Was he talking about magic? But magic didn't exist. Berg's gaze moved back to the white glow. Okay, hadn't existed.

"Papa says it's energy of the universe."

And now the squirrel is psychic.

"He's been teaching me how to control it, reluctantly." The squirrel scampered up to another wound. "But Papa says wisdom is better than ignorance."

"Where's your dad?" Berg asked. He might as well go for it at this point. The day couldn't get weirder.

The squirrel squeaked. Oh, Berg had a bad feeling about this. The squirrel's eyes got watery, and then to Berg's dismay, he looked down. "He's my papa."

Oh, it could. It definitely could. A talking squirrel with an abnormally large fox father. Made perfect sense. Hold on. If the squirrel could talk and use universal energy, which he learned from his father the fox… fuck, Berg's head really hurt.

"So, my Papa's going to be okay?" The squirrel's black eyes pleaded with him to say yes.

"It's a wait and see game, squirrel." Berg sighed. "It's up to the fox now."

The squirrel sneezed. "It's Kou."

"What's Kou?"

"I am." The animal pointed to himself.

Fine, the possessed rodent had a name. "Okay."

"And this is my papa, Tadashi."

Now wait a minute. "Tadashi is the son of the temple priest."

"He's also my dad," the small nuisance insisted.

"That's a fox. A big fox, but he's a fox."

Kou ran up to the fox's head and tapped it with his front paw. "He's also Tadashi."

Berg may be a little off, but an animal couldn't turn into a human… even if there were talking squirrels.

Kou pressed his paws against the fox. The white glow came back. There had to be a logical explanation for that, too.

"Why're you doing that? There's no scar there."

"To make him shift. The change will help jumpstart the healing energies inside him," the squirrel answered.

Next time I won't ask.

"Put your hands on his side," the little tyrant ordered.

"Why?"

"Just do it!"

Berg exhaled. What would it hurt? Maybe Inari had answered his prayers. But the talking squirrel was in poor taste. Really. The humor the gods had sometimes. He didn't understand it. Berg moved his hands to the fox's side. Warmth surged through him, and then, a glow came from his hands.

Of course it did.

Freaking out wouldn't do him any good, so Berg watched the fox instead. His chest rose and deflated easier than before. Berg smiled. Thank you, Inari. Thank you for listening. *Even if you gave me a freaky talking, magically possessed squirrel.*

"How are you doing that?" Berg asked in awe.

"I'm just getting a boost from your energy," Kou answered.

"What's it going to do?" The skin wasn't knitting together and turning into a puffy pink scar like before. The fox's body was… rippling?

The squirrel met Berg's eyes, looking at him like he was stupid. "Like I said, I'm forcing the shift."

"Listen, Kou, animals don't just—" Fuck, was that skin? Where was his fur going? Why? Oh shit, Berg began to withdraw.

"Don't move!"

Crap. Berg pressed harder against the fox-human-thing. Hell, it was really turning into a man. A flat stomach replaced the furry one. Long, hairless legs grew. Black hair flowed from the fox's head. The only thing that remained was the tail.

Berg reached out and stroked it. Yup. Felt real enough. A naked man with a fox's tail.

The tail was softer than he expected. And it really did grow from the man's butt. Oh, geez, that tick behind his eyes was going wild. His head throbbed painfully, and yet, it felt light.

"Stop stroking Papa like he's some pet!" Kou demanded.

Yeah, the day was officially too weird for Berg.

Chapter Eight

The incessant chirping needed to stop. Tadashi's head hurt. No. His whole body ached, and he just wanted a little bit of rest. He'd been cleaning the—oh, gods! Kou! Tadashi transformed in the temple and Kou had to make a run for it.

If he hurt Kou again, he wouldn't be able to live with himself. Tadashi jerked up, scanning wildly about. Where he was hit Tadashi about the same time he realized the man—*Berg?*—was lying on the floor, half-naked.

I remember! Excitement and confusion warred inside Tadashi as his time as his fox came back to him in spurts. No, he didn't remember it all, but a fair amount. It was a start. He'd analyze why once he figured out how he got back to his hut. But first, Kou was on the man's face, pawing at him.

"Kou? What are you doing?"

His squirrel looked up at him, still poking the veterinarian. "I think something's wrong with him."

Obviously. "Okay. Let's start with why Berg is shirtless and bleeding. Are those bite marks?"

If a squirrel could blush, Kou was doing it. "Maybe."

"Did you put those there?" Tired, Tadashi scooted back on the bed and leaned against the headboard. He didn't like having trouble on his doorstep, but he owed the vet.

The squirrel shuffled and stepped onto Berg's left eye. He sniffed.

"*Kou*," Tadashi said in warning.

"Maybe."

"Would you get off the poor man's face?" Tadashi rubbed his forehead.

Kou 'struggled' to get of Berg's face and then ran across him, nearly 'missing' some important parts on the poor man. His squirrel jumped to the bed and sprinted up to Tadashi. Kou flew at him, little paws out.

Tadashi hugged his squirrel to him, pressing his cheek against Kou's warm fur. "I'm sorry. How long was I gone this time? More than a couple days?"

"A week." Kou shuddered, pressing his nose against Tadashi. "You were gone a week."

"I'm sorry." Tadashi squeezed tighter. "I really am, Kou."

"Who hurt you?" Kou asked, pushing away from him.

"Ah, well, that's complicated," Tadashi answered, glancing at Berg.

Kou clicked, then pointed. "Did he hurt you?"

"What do you have against Berg?" Tadashi set the squirrel down on his lap and began to pet him. "He saved me, didn't he?"

"Why are you avoiding the question?"

"You helped him fix me, didn't you?"

Kou turned over for a belly scratch. "Maybe."

Tadashi pointed to the scattered doctoring supplies on the bed. "Fine, I did."

"Who brought me here?" Tadashi asked, hoping to fill in gaps. "Last I remember, I passed out before I reached the temple archway."

Kou squeaked and went still. Tears gathered in his eyes.

"What?"

"You were that close?" Kou sniffled, then wiped his nose with his paw. "Berg brought you in."

"He did?"

"Yes, this morning." A tear fell out of one of Kou's eye. "You had so much blood on you."

Being shot does that. Tadashi petted his squirrel. "I'm fine now, right?"

Kou nodded, his tears drying.

"Thanks to the man passed out on the floor?" Tadashi inquired, nodding down at Berg.

"Yes," Kou answered with hesitance.

"And why is he passed out on the floor with bite marks?"

"The bite marks were there first!" Kou answered defiantly.

Tadashi crossed his arms. The movement hurt, tugging on him in weird spots. He bit his lower lip and grunted. Kou flicked his eyes to Tadashi then rolled over. He curled up on the edge of the bed.

"When he brought you in, I thought he had hurt you. So I, um—" Kou motioned to Berg.

"I see."

"Then he helped."

Tadashi was too tired for this. "Okay. That still doesn't explain him on the floor."

"I think you shifting in front of him overloaded his puny brain. But he liked your tail, I think."

"My tail?"

"He stroked it."

Shock dwarfed any other emotion. Tadashi wouldn't expect someone who… oh no. Several things clicked at once. "Berg saw me shift?"

"Uh-huh." The squirrel jumped down onto the gentle giant.

"Is… is that all?" Tadashi knew it wasn't.

"He didn't like me talking," Kou replied, perturbed. His tail flicked about furiously betraying his calm tone. "He squished me with the broom."

"He talked with you?" Did his voice go up an octave? No, that shouldn't be the priority. "And squished you?"

"Only a little, and besides, how else do you think I could help him if I didn't talk to him?" Kou turned around, looking at Tadashi like he'd lost a few IQ points, paws on his sides. "He doesn't understand squirrel."

"No, no, he does not."

Just then, Berg groaned. Kou squeaked and ran over to his box. Tadashi froze with the exception of his fingers. They pulled at the sheet on the bed. His need to cover himself overrode reason. He should be coming up with a way to explain everything. Remember how to pull the memories from the kind man.

There's no way. None.

"My head," Berg moaned. His large palm pressed against his forehead. He used his other arm to push up off the floor. "All that had to be—"

His emerald green gaze locked onto Tadashi. Those eyes. Tadashi remembered a young boy with those eyes. Inquisitive. Troublesome. Kind.

Could this be the same boy?

Berg searched Tadashi's face, and then his gaze moved down. His honest eyes told Tadashi everything the man thought and saw. Berg's examination didn't miss a thing. Not the way Tadashi's chest rose and fell quicker. The way his hands fumbled about even caused a smile to cross Berg's lips. His eyes became troubled when they fell on Tadashi's groin. They flicked away only to settle on Tadashi's tail. Those green gems could've burned a hole in the sky considering how hard Berg stared.

He sighed, hunching forward. "It wasn't a dream."

Tadashi should lie, but… "No."

There was no point in denial.

"I'm sorry." Apologizing seemed the right thing to do.

"So you're a kitsune?"

How? Unadulterated—and unreasonable—hope rose inside Tadashi. "You know what I am?"

"My parents told me all about this shrine, even brought me as a kid," Berg explained. "Before the war, people came to your parents' festivals and parties all the time."

"They did." Those were good times. Time before hate.

"They shared the temple stories just as much as the ones from our homeland." Berg scooted, leaning against the bed. "I was pretty young during those parties. I came, but that was a long time ago, the memories are fuzzy. I loved this place, though. The architecture fascinated me, but then, to a little kid, they were these weird, unusual buildings. Anything shiny was attractive. You were… always making mischief."

Tadashi laughed. Berg was the same young boy he remembered, but all grown up. No wonder his fox had given in.

"But you also were…" Berg watched Tadashi with keen interest. "I guess you being a kitsune explains why you look the same."

"Oh, I, well, yes." Why was he so flustered?

"You should try to look older, the townspeople will start to talk."

"I, um, yes?" Why had he lost the ability to speak? It was ridiculous.

"They thought you were in your twenties back when I was kid, so that'd put you in your late thirties, early forties now." Berg knelt. His hand went to Tadashi's face. His fingers were so warm. "Though, Japanese folk like you are known for their youthful appearance, but a few wrinkles here"—Berg touched Tadashi's temple, then traced down around his mouth—"and here, should dissuade people."

Tadashi's chest felt tight. The room, it was stuffy.

"I don't think they would make you any less beautiful now as you were then. Just more… mature."

Did Berg know how he sounded? By the unfocused countenance on the man's face, Tadashi thought not. "Handsome would be a term better suited to me, I think."

Berg jerked back, withdrawing his hand. Tadashi almost followed the warmth, but a stitch in his side when he moved forward stopped him. "Sorry. I… was lost in memories."

"Must be fond memories."

Berg dipped his head and covered the back of his neck with his hand. His laugh was nervous and forced. The tanned fingers stood out against the bright red neck and ears.

Interesting.

Berg's head rose, but his eyes didn't met Tadashi's. "Are you feeling better?"

"I should ask you. I wasn't the one passed out on the floor."

Berg could get redder. How... cute.

"Are you all right, Berg?"

"Yes. It was a lot to take in, I think my brain needed a moment." Berg rubbed his neck and gave another tense chuckle. "I'm still thinking I'm going to wake up on the couch and find out I dreamed all this."

With his declaration, Berg's shoulders slumped. Like a weight dropped down on top of him. The younger man drew his legs up and clasped his hands around his knees. He lay his head on top of them and closed his eyes. Tadashi wished he could ease the man's burdens, but he had a feeling the memories were embedded too deeply. If he tried to pull them out, he could take a part of Berg with them.

Besides, I don't know if I can do that anymore.

"Where is your family, Tadashi?"

Being called so casually, Tadashi usually bristled, but he had allowed the boy to do so, therefore, he could allow the man. It was the inquiry about his family that really got to him. "They left a long time ago."

"But I've seen them."

"No, they moved east," Tadashi answered sadly.

"You had a grandpa, dad, mom, and a sister," Berg insisted. His head had come up off his knees. His eyes... they were full of conviction. "A brother, too and... a friend."

"I can change forms, Berg."

"Yeah, but the time in town this winter, that wasn't you. Couldn't be. It was everyone but you."

"This winter?" Tadashi bent forward, then immediately regretted it. "Ow!"

A large hand pressed against his chest, nearly spanning it, and pushed against Tadashi gently. Berg's other arm wrapped behind him and eased him back. His heat rolled off his body in waves and Tadashi soaked it up.

"Watch it! You were badly hurt. You should be dead." Berg's voice had wavered on that last sentence. "I'm sorry."

"Not your fault," Tadashi assured him.

"It kinda is."

Tadashi smiled up at the man. "But you fixed it."

"I tried." Berg backed away from Tadashi and looked around until his gaze settled on the ground by the wood stove. "Kou helped."

Kou? Oh gods, Tadashi had forgotten about his squirrel. His attention snapped to the box. He grimaced. The death glare he was receiving said Kou knew, too.

"What's up with the, uh, squirrel anyway?" Berg whispered, turning back to Tadashi.

He tore his gaze away from Kou. "It's a story for another time."

"So talking squirrels aren't a Japanese thing?"

"Not at all."

"I see."

Awkward. They all shifted restlessly in their spots. Tadashi slid down in the bed, exhausted. Berg placed the back of his hand against Tadashi's forehead and then stood. He gathered the comforter and drew it over Tadashi.

"I know it's hot, but you may want it later on. You can toss it off if you get uncomfortable."

Wow, Berg was close. A thump in his chest made Tadashi gasp.

"You all right?"

All Tadashi could do was nod.

Berg checked his wrist then sighed. He pressed his lips together before he spoke again, his low voice soft and reassuring. "I have to go. I've been gone from town for a while and someone is sure to notice, but I'll come back again as soon as I can."

Gods, Tadashi hadn't even stopped to think about any of that.

"You rest up." Berg patted Tadashi's leg. "I hope Kou will be able to play nursemaid for me for the night."

As if summoned by his name, Kou jumped up on the bed. "I can take care of him myself! Not just for tonight."

Berg narrowed his gaze on the squirrel, then pointed to the stove. "So you're telling me you can cook for him?"

"Uh, sort of, I—"

"Or fill his pitcher with water?" Berg continued. Kou shrank back, crawling up to Tadashi. "Or help him to the bath—where's your bathroom?"

"I have a wash basin here and an outhouse out of the way," Tadashi answered.

"You don't have indoor plumbing?"

Tadashi shook his head.

"Oh. What about baths or showers?"

"Like I said, I have a water basin."

"Isn't there a bathhouse on the property?"

Tadashi looked agape at the man. "How did—"

"I used to come here when I was little, remember?"

"Right. Well, there's only one of me."

"Oh. Sorry." Berg paused. "Well, why don't when I come back we make sure you get a real bath. I want to know your wounds have been cleaned properly."

"Okay."

"You want me to bring some wood in? I know it's hot, but it could cool tonight."

"That would be nice." This conversation was... odd. Yes, odd was a good word for it.

Berg began picking up his scattered supplies, packing them away. "Hopefully I'll be back by tomorrow. You get some rest."

He let his head fall against the pillow. He felt a furry body curl next to his neck. "I will."

He was tired. A nap couldn't hurt. His eyelids weren't cooperating either. The room's focus kept warping.

A warm hand brushed against his forehead, lingered. "I promise you'll be safe, Tadashi."

Tadashi sighed, confused, but more content than he'd been in years. Something had changed. He hurt, but the never-ending hunger inside him was gone, or at minimum, quenched for now.

Once he sorted himself out, he'd have to figure that out.

* * * * *

Maybe if he drunk a little more, then the day could be written off as a dream. Talking squirrels, foxes coming back from the dead and changing into men with tails, it was all a little more than Berg could handle. He kept thinking he'd wake up and the whole search for Alva and the subsequent discovery of mountain demons would be a bad dream.

The day just kept going. Kind of like Berg, one foot going in front of the other. It hadn't been a dream. Tadashi had been the fox who saved Alva, and Berg couldn't tell anyone. He wouldn't.

"Berg, honey?" Freyja called out. Her swollen stomach entered the living room before she did. "There you are."

Berg nodded. "Need something, dear?"

She exhaled and put a hand on her back. "Just hot and tired and couldn't sleep."

He put down his beer and motioned to the couch. "Come 'ere."

Freyja waddled over and slowly descended to the cushions. She grunted, a smile crossing her face.

"Happy?"

"My feet are killing me." Freyja fidgeted, obviously in a fair amount of discomfort.

"Give me your feet."

Freyja turned at once, putting her petite legs across his lap. Berg took one of the small feet in his hands. They engulfed it. He pressed a thumb into her arch and began rubbing. Freyja groaned, her eyes fluttered closed, and she leaned back against the arm of the couch.

"God, this feels so good," she moaned.

Berg chuckled. "Does this mean I can come back to bed?"

"Don't push your luck." But the corner of her mouth twitched.

"I promise not to bite," he teased.

"Unlike the… rabbit that got a hold of you today?"

"You noticed those, huh?"

"Hard to miss welts covering my husband," Freyja replied.

Berg sighed. There was just no winning lately.

"I see you got your shotgun back."

No winning at all.

"So you went up on the mountain?"

Berg switched feet.

"That's not going to help you," she warned.

"I did. It was uneventful."

Freyja opened her eyes and stared at him. "Did you run into the dog?"

Berg flinched and knew she saw it. "Yes."

"And?"

"The Mizunos will be taking care of it." He wasn't exactly lying. Berg felt the guilt though, another rock in his gut to weigh him down.

Freyja pushed up. "The Mizunos? Really?"

Berg nodded.

"Wow. I knew they still lived up on the temple, but they rarely talk to anybody," Freyja said, awe in her voice.

She had enjoyed the old festivals just as much as he had when they were little. Berg smiled at his wife. Their love of architecture and of old stories had brought them together.

"They were nice to me," Berg answered.

"That's good." Freyja yawned. "Did you run into Tadashi?"

Berg nodded. The uncomfortable ache from earlier shooting through him.

"You used to follow him around like a lost puppy during festivals." Freyja laughed, shaking her head.

"Did not!"

"You thought he was a girl at first, too," she teased then snorted. "I remember when you found out he was a boy. You said 'I don't care, he's beautiful'."

Berg groaned. He remembered those feelings, and he did not need the reminder. Especially after the day he had.

"Honey."

"Hm?" Berg stopped and looked up.

Freyja was smiling, her hand on her belly. "The baby's kicking."

"Really?" Excitement coursed through Berg as he reached for her. Little motions pressed up from Freyja's stomach. It was so weird. Berg still couldn't believe his kid was inside her. Yes, he knew the mechanics, but he was in awe of the life growing within his wife's belly.

A laugh pulled Berg from his wonder. Freyja grinned sleepily. "This baby is part of the reason I can't sleep, you know."

"Sorry. I can't wait to meet him."

"Still insisting it's a boy?" Her blue eyes sparked with amusement.

"Sure am."

Freyja closed her eyes and stretched. "If you keep rubbing my feet, I may just fall asleep."

Berg picked her feet back up. He pushed the heel of his palm into the arch of her foot. "Hey, Freyja."

"Mm—what?"

"Why do you think the Mizunos are so scared of the town?" It really bothered him, but he didn't expect her to answer.

When he was younger, Berg didn't understand why the family fled. As he grew older, he learned about the internment camps. It frightened him that the government had so much power to control people. That had been years ago though. Surely things had gotten better since then?

Freyja pulled her feet off Berg, drawing his attention. "Honey."

"Hm?"

"Would you like to invite them to dinner? Let them know people would welcome them back."

Berg stared. He'd never expected Freyja to make that offer.

"Well?"

"Let me talk to them," Berg said in careful consideration. "I have to check on the dog, and I'd like to know why they're frightened before putting any pressure on them."

"That's my husband." Freyja smiled at him.

"I try."

"I know." Freyja swung her legs around and pushed up off the couch. "One of the many reasons I love you."

A familiar ache, one Berg thought he'd pushed away, bloomed inside his chest. "Me too."

She held out her hand. "Come on, let's go to bed."

"Yeah, okay."

He tripped getting up, making Freyja laugh. He gave her a lopsided grin in return. Freyja held out her hand and he took it, glad to be able to sleep on the bed. With Freyja? He should be, but… no, there was just guilt there.

Damn, he was all out of sorts, and Berg feared he would be for a while.

Chapter Nine

Berg set his bag down by the stool. He waved to Ruth, hoping to get a cup of coffee. She smiled at him and sashayed over. Catcalls from some of the men in the diner went up. Ruth winked at them.

"What can I get for you, Berg?"

"Coffee? Please?" He slumped over.

One dark eyebrow went up as her mouth pursed together. She tapped her lips with a manicured nail. "Late night?"

"Mr. Grahn's heifer took a turn for the worse last night." Berg stretched, yawning loudly. "Got a call about three in the morning. Then Mrs. Johansson's dog went into labor. Kate's horse got bit by something. Charlie's—"

Ruth held up her hand. "I'm sorry I asked. One strong Cup 'o Joe on its way up."

"Thanks, Ruth."

She nodded and yelled back behind the bar, making Berg jump. She slid a hand to her hip. "You really are tired. You do know it's only eight in the morning?"

Berg cringed. "Can you make that two cups?"

Loud, hearty laughter filled diner.

Ruth tapped a nail against the counter. "And maybe some food?"

"A sandwich?" Berg asked. He was hungry.

"Turkey? Ham? Chicken? Beef?"

Berg gagged with the last offer.

"No beef."

He shook his head. "No."

"Heifer that bad?"

"Yeah."

"Chicken it is," Ruth replied, spinning around. "And a couple aspirin."

"Thanks." Maybe he should put his head down. Just for a few minutes.

The counter was cool against his face, the heat and running around getting to Berg again but before long, the sweet smell of coffee got a rise out of him. It was quickly followed by Sheriff Fowler's voice.

"So you've decided to join the land of the living?"

"Huh?" Berg shot up, blinking. Was that drool? He felt his chin. It was. Damn, what was he, two?

Fowler patted him on the back. "Your snores could wake the dead, Berg."

"Sorry, Sheriff."

Snores? Fowler sat down next to him and pushed a cup of coffee in his direction. "Best drink it while you can."

Berg cradled the java in his hands and groaned appreciatively when the flavor hit his taste buds. The pounding in his head even scaled back some. Funny how knowing he was drinking coffee helped make him feel better. He took another long appreciative drag from the mug and moaned.

The diner erupted in laughter.

Berg swung around, confused by all the noise. He had half the town's population staring back at him. Well, it felt like almost everyone was there. When did it get so busy? His head spun from trying to figure out how people magically appeared from thin air.

Sheriff Fowler chuckled next to him and thumped Berg on the back. "You look a little worse for wear there, Berg."

He pointed at the crowd, not turning his head. "When?"

"Check your watch," Fowler answered, his tone filled with mirth. The other people in the diner smiled or started laughing again. Berg tore his gaze away from his friends and neighbors and looked down.

The watch had to be lying. No way was it already eleven thirty. Just no. Berg still had people he was supposed to see and needed to check on Tadashi. Going up and down the mountain would take time. Time he didn't have. Shit. He had to check and make sure Tadashi was okay.

Someone tapped Berg's shoulder. He jerked and spun around on the stool, meeting Ruth's laughing eyes with his own. "Here, take some aspirin. Might help get your head back in the game."

He barely caught the pills as his eyes decided to cross. Damn. He was tired. His head pounded more than it did this morning. Sheriff's and Red's snickering caught Berg's attention, and he bent forward, watching the men. Had Red been there the whole time? Berg's lip curled, his anger festering. He just couldn't shake the man lately.

Red was up to no good. Berg felt it. He couldn't prove it, but he felt it. Just like he knew what kind of men the Sheriff and Red were. Men like him. Did they know they were the same as much as they were different?

What Berg didn't understand was why Fowler and Red spent so much time together. They put themselves at risk when they spent lunches and evenings together all the time. Or did they not think people would question their relationship, other than one of the sheriff looking out for a troubled friend?

"Berg?"

A large hand waved in front of him.

"You there?"

Berg blinked, refocusing. "What?"

The corner of Fowler's mouth twitched and he shook his head. "You haven't heard a damn word Red and me have said, have you?"

"Absolutely not," Berg concurred. He popped the aspirin in his mouth and took a swig of coffee. "As you said, I needed more coffee."

"And something to eat," Ruth insisted, bringing out a couple plates. "You probably haven't eaten anything since what? Yesterday morning?"

"Probably," Berg admitted. "Thanks, Ruth. I appreciate it."

"I'm just trying to stay out of Freyja's war path, honey," Ruth joked as she set the plates down. She had a turkey sandwich made up, some soup and apple pie. Berg began stuffing his face.

"You think you can eat and listen?" asked Fowler, leaning toward Berg.

He grunted as he scooped another spoonful of heavenly soup into his mouth. He really didn't have time to waste. Freyja would have his balls if he came home late again.

"Well," the sheriff began. "The thing is… Red and I've been talking with some of the guys from the search party."

Berg stopped eating. His body tensed, and he put down the spoon and gave Fowler his full attention. "Yeah, about what?"

"We think we should go to the mountain."

"Why?" Bad idea. So bad.

Red poked his head over Fowler's shoulder and spoke. "To look for that wolf-dog hybrid. Or dog. Whatever it is."

"Dog," Berg lied. "Again. Why?" The hairs on the back of Berg's arms rose. His spine tingled but in a bad kind of way.

Red gave Berg a crooked smile. "To hunt it, of course."

A rumble of protest erupted from Berg, making both men jump back on their stools. Red teetered on the edge of his, eyes wide.

Fowler scowled at Red. "Shut it, Red." Then he turned back to Berg. "If it's one of the resort owner's dogs, then we should find it and make amends."

"And if it's a wolf-dog hybrid, it needs to be dead," Red added.

Fowler elbowed Red, making him cringe. "Shut it, Red."

Like that would ever happen.

Berg frowned. In all the years he knew Red, the man never wanted to go near the mountain unless absolutely necessary. What changed?

"You seem really gung-ho about this, Red," Berg said.

Red looked taken aback but quickly recovered for the most part. "Nothing happened to us on the mountain, or Alva, seems to me there's nothing to be afraid of."

Hm. Berg didn't agree. Fear remained in Red's eyes. Red wanted to hunt down Tadashi. He saw it coming, but not this way.

"So, what do you think?" Fowler asked, regaining Berg's attention.

"I think it's a bad idea, and chances are the dog's already dead," Berg swore, maybe a little too forcefully.

Fowler gave him an assessing glance. "You think so?"

"The dog had been shot multiple times," Berg explained. "And had excessive bleeding. If we go up, we'll find a dead dog. If you're afraid that it's one of the resort owners, why don't you go on over to their site and ask? Before we go high-tailing after a dead dog."

Fowler's resolve wavered. Berg could see it by the slump in the man's stance. Red, unfortunately, had gone, well, red. Berg was surprised Red hadn't shouted at him, yet. Then he saw Fowler's hand and how it rested on Red's chest. *Those men, they're asking for trouble. Someday, someone will see the small gestures between them and see more.*

"Sheriff," Berg said, needing to keep the men away. "Let me talk to the Mizunos while you go up to the resort. I can check to see if I find anything, or if they have, and it'll save a lot of trouble for all of us."

Incomprehension fell on Fowler's face. "The Mizunos?"

"The shrine priest and his family," Berg provided.

"Ah." Comprehension filled the man's expression. "Yes, them. I suppose."

Red growled something incomprehensible to Berg, but the sheriff must've understood. He grunted and made a soothing motioning with his hand.

"We don't see much of them," Fowler said. "You sure they can help? They haven't been… friendly."

Berg flicked his eyes to the diner. People were pretending not to watch the conversation with rapt interest. Kind of like how Ruth kept hovering over the pie rack pretending to check them. Nosy busybodies.

"If I don't find anything, then we can revisit going up on the mountain," Berg added. "I talked to them yesterday"—boy, the diner sure got quiet—"and they hadn't seen a dog around, but would look for one."

"They would?" The sheriff asked in disbelief.

"Yup." Liar, Liar, Pants on fire.

"Why would they help us?" Red spat. "They're just—"

Fowler whipped his hand over Red's mouth.

Huh. Interesting. Berg scrutinized the pair. "Why wouldn't they?"

Red shrugged off the sheriff and spun to the counter, putting his elbows down and staring at his plate.

Fowler gave Berg a tight smile. "Like I said, we don't see much of them."

"Sheriff?" Berg waited until he had Fowler's undivided attention. The sheriff's demeanor changed. He shifted in his seat, blocking Red from view. "Something happened… something that shook them."

"What?" he asked irritably when Berg didn't elaborate.

"Why do you think they're so afraid?"

* * * * *

Tadashi pushed at the rude object trying to wake him. He didn't want to wake up. He was warm, happy, and at rest. He could spare a few minutes before temple duties needed to be attended to.

"Tadashi."

"Five more minutes, Kou, just five."

A deep chuckle caught Tadashi's attention. "I'm sure I've never been compared to someone so small before."

Wait. That wasn't Kou.

"Who?" Tadashi shot up in bed then groaned. Moving like that hurt. He glanced up and found Berg watching him with concern.

"Berg?"

The large man nodded and then helped situate Tadashi on the bed. The heat from Berg's hands soaked into him. Tadashi wanted to bask in the warmth. How could he trust a virtual stranger so easily? Was it because the man had been as open and friendly as the boy he remembered? It would be better to be cautious, wouldn't it? Even during his weekly supply drop-off, the contact with the town was minimal. Just because Berg was friendly now didn't mean he'd stay that way. But… Tadashi could only smell concern and worry from the man.

Tadashi grabbed Berg's hand as he withdrew. "You came back?"

"Mm-hm. I promised I would. How are you feeling?" Berg asked, squirming in place. His green eyes darted around the room. Berg's anxiousness belied the kindness he had been showing.

Tadashi felt bad for the poor man and patted the bed. "Why don't you take a seat?"

"Sure." Berg eased down, watching Tadashi intently. "You still haven't answered my question. How are you feeling?"

His skin prickled, self conscious of the eyes upon him. "Fine."

Kou chirped. "You are not fine."

Crap, I forgot about Kou again.

Berg pointed to the squirrel. "I agree with him. You were shot. Many times."

Tadashi sighed. One worrywart was more than enough to deal with, now he had two? Oh, and he had one more pressing issue. In fact, it was urgent.

"Could you, um, excuse me for a moment?" he asked, crossing his legs and arms.

"Would you like to get dressed? I can—"

"No!"

Berg frowned. "No?"

"I, um, have business to attend to," Tadashi answered, squirming because now that he knew he needed to go, he really had to go.

Berg's face lit with understanding and put out a hand. "Ahh, well, let's get you to the outhouse."

"No—I—whoa!"

Suddenly Tadashi was in the air, blanket hanging loosely from him as strong arms held him close against Berg's chest. It felt familiar. Wait, no, now wasn't the time to let someone coddle him. Tadashi protested, kicking about. It didn't do him any good. Berg held on and shushed him. Tadashi gave in and directed Berg to the outhouse, did his business knowing Berg was on the other side of the door, and then endured Berg carrying him back to his room.

Being fussed about once they were back in the room proved to be too much.

"I can do it!" Tadashi snapped. "Really, and if you don't mind, I can put my own clothes on! I'm not an invalid."

"Sorry." Berg ducked his head, his neck turning that red color. "I-I-I d-don't know what exactly I should be doing for you."

"You don't need to do anything!"

"You could barely sit up," Berg answered defensively.

"I've been shot!"

Berg held out his arms, palms up. "Which is why I'm trying to help?"

"At least let me get some cloths on!"

"Oh, that bothers you?" Berg shrugged. "I kinda thought it didn't so I didn't want to bring it up and be rude or anything."

Oh gods, the poor man. "Have you been embarrassed this whole time?"

"Yes." Berg's voice was low and tentative.

Tadashi laughed. A deep down, honest-to-goodness laugh. Oh, it hurt his sides but he didn't care. It just felt good to chuckle at Berg's expense.

"It's not that funny," Berg said quietly, rubbing the back of his neck with one hand. He wouldn't look at Tadashi.

"Yes it is." Mainly because they'd both been too embarrassed to say anything. They were grown men acting like kids figuring out the difference between boys and girls the first time.

Berg rolled his eyes but didn't protest any further. "When was the last time you've eaten?"

The human liked to change subjects a lot. Tadashi was about to say he wasn't sure when his stomach answered for him by rumbling loudly. Kou chose to interject in their conversation, too.

"He wouldn't wake up, so when he was a fox, probably," Kou said.

Tadashi's stomach protested its lack of food again.

Berg frowned, his eyes losing focus. "Not at all?"

"Nope," Kou answered. "I even gave him a nibble and he didn't move."

"You bit me in my sleep?" Why wasn't he surprised? Kou bit everything. Still, he'd been defenseless in his slumber.

The squirrel shrugged, and Berg shook his head. "Does he bite everything?"

"Probably," Tadashi conceded, a smile cracking on his face when Kou puffed up. "It's a squirrel thing, I think."

"Hey! Fine," Kou squeaked. With a chirp, Kou skittered out of the room, tail flicking about wildly. "I'm going to go find some nuts."

Berg laughed, and Tadashi with him. Oh, wow. It looked good on Berg. Tadashi gulped and pointed to the chest of drawers. "If you wouldn't mind?"

"You'll be able to eat some food after you get dressed?"

"Yes."

Berg riffled through the drawers, pulling out a shirt and pajama bottoms. "This good?"

"Yes."

"Here." Berg pushed the clothes in Tadashi's face. He automatically took them and chuckled as Berg turned around and faced the window.

How… sweet? Tadashi dressed as quickly as he was capable. "Done."

Berg returned to the bed, checking Tadashi over. His mouth twitched, and his fingers wiggled about, but he didn't waver in his examination.

"Do you know what you are doing?"

"If you were a dog or fox, yes."

Tadashi snorted. "Then you don't really—"

"I can still tell if you're hurting or not, you only need eyes to do that," Berg snapped, and then he coughed, his anxiousness showing. "Sorry, but you obviously don't take care of yourself. And asking your little squirrel, that's too much for a little one like him. It shouldn't be his responsibility."

"So now it's yours?" Tadashi asked, frowning. He didn't like where the conversation was going, nor did he welcome pity. "Do I really look deplorable?"

"Yes and no." Berg sighed, rubbing the back of his neck. "But you are malnourished."

"No I'm not," Tadashi argued, his frown deepening.

"I can see your ribs."

Why did that matter? Tadashi became ruffled at Berg's disapproving tone. "I don't see how that's your business."

Berg opened his mouth but paused, narrowing his eyes on Tadashi. "Was Alva your business?"

The little girl. "Is she all right?"

If Tadashi could wipe off the knowing smile on Berg's lips, he would.

"Is she?"

A heavy sigh fell from Tadashi as his frustration mounted. Berg really needed to learn how to answer questions. Instead, he sat there, smug-like. The girl had to be okay. Berg wouldn't be acting like such as ass if she weren't, but Tadashi needed to hear the words. Otherwise he'd never be able to relax. Tadashi was about to throttle the man when Berg finally spoke.

"Alva's just fine. According to town gossip, she's talking up a storm about a white dog." Berg chuckled before nodding toward Tadashi. "You wouldn't know anything about that, would you?"

"You're impossible."

"Nah, just improbable," Berg teased. "So do you need to turn into a fox to eat or do you eat people food?"

"I eat regular food!" Tadashi huffed and crossed his arms.

Talk about putting a guy on the spot. Berg didn't hold back any punches. But then… Berg's straightforwardness and his honesty, were what Tadashi found endearing in the man. He also could manipulate the hell out of a conversation. Tadashi wondered if the man knew how to lie. He hadn't smelled any from Berg yet, which had to be the reason Tadashi felt so relaxed around the man.

Of course, his calming aura didn't hurt. Berg might have been a huge guy, but his tender care… it lulled Tadashi into the vet's pace too easily.

"Why are you so nice?"

A sad gaze settled on Tadashi. "Why are you surprised by kindness?"

No answer was forthcoming. Tadashi didn't… didn't what? "Why shouldn't I be? It was the town that turned the other way when we were taken away, and the town tried to run me off the mountain. The sheriff sent his dogs, and as far as I'm concerned, they got what was coming to them.

"This temple has been my home longer than any town has been here," Tadashi continued, swallowing past the lump in his throat, ignoring the ache there, too. "Why should I have to leave? Of course, why would I stay?"

Gods, what a mess. Tadashi hung his head, letting his hair fall in front of his face. The last thing Berg needed to see was Tadashi crying. His humiliation really would be complete. Why couldn't Berg leave well enough alone?

Anger. Tadashi focused on it and wrapped around its energy. He glared at Berg. The big man actually flinched and moved back.

"You need to leave," Tadashi groused. "Now."

But he didn't. Berg didn't move a muscle. He stayed on the bed, holding Tadashi's gaze with his. The deep green eyes were like pools of water. Reflective and clear. Gentle.

"I'm sorry," Berg whispered after a spell. "I really, truly am."

Tadashi closed his eyes, unable to watch Berg's sad fidgeting. He didn't want to do this, have this conversation, or talk to someone who couldn't understand. Berg would never understand the persecution Tadashi dealt with. Berg's kindness hurt. An ache spread across his entire body. How did he deal with a man like Berg? He couldn't. Tadashi hadn't had to interact this way with humans since he came back to the shrine.

"What happened to Akatsuki? Where's your family? Someone should be here to look after you."

Tadashi's eyes flew open. He shook, fighting hard not to shift. "Out!"

Fur sprouted on his arms. A tooth nipped his lip. Tadashi growled. Berg hadn't even moved an inch. He paled, but the firm set of his jaw said he wouldn't go anywhere. Berg barely flinched when Tadashi took a swipe at him.

"You're not wanted!" Tadashi yelled, his voice broken as his soul. He ignored the pain in Berg's eyes at his rejection. "You don't know what it's like to be hunted down like some freak! To have what you care most about taken away from you. Killed! Don't come in here making presumptions!" Tadashi roared. "Get out of my room!"

"No."

What?

Berg's gaze shifted away from Tadashi, looking down. How could the man challenge him, tear up his scabs, then ignore him? Tadashi snarled, glaring at Berg, but the man seemed unperturbed. A sad smile even crossed his lips. Why would Berg be sad?

He jolted when something tough stroked his arm.

Tadashi's chest rumbled, perturbed, as he looked for the offending object. But it wasn't an object. Berg's firm fingers were trailing up and down his skin. Goose bumps popped up wherever the digits caressed him.

It was a caress. There was no mistaking it was touch offering comfort, but there was more to it. Confused with the development, Tadashi failed to find the words to ask Berg if he'd lost his mind. No one, no matter how big or how stupid, would let a predator growl at him or her and be unaffected.

A dozen questions crossed Tadashi's mind, but none of them were slow enough for him to process, let alone ask. Instead, he watched as Berg continued to stroke him. By the gods, Tadashi wriggled even closer. No. He had an itch and had to move. He didn't want to be close to anyone. To lose them hurt.

The steady motion on Tadashi's arm lulled him though. His eyelids drooped and he fought the battle against sleep. He'd just gotten up. He had work to do. The shrine wouldn't clean itself.

"Do you want me to?" Berg offered quietly.

"Want you to what?" Really. The man was an enigma. An annoying one. One that could just bowl Tadashi over with a simple touch.

"Do you want me to clean the shrine?"

Had he said that aloud?

"If you could tell me where the supplies are—"

"Why do you insist on helping?" interrupted Tadashi, exhausted and no longer able to fight back. "Why won't you just leave me alone?"

That really was the center of the problem. He was angry he felt too weak to do anything or get Berg out of his room.

"I don't want you here."

"Somebody needs to be here besides your little squirrel," Berg answered, the rough palm of his hand rubbing delicious circles on Tadashi's forearm. "He's too young, too small, and a little too… *different* for the job."

With a snort, Tadashi smiled and agreed. "He's a handful, but I love him."

The motions on his arms stilled for a fraction of a second before starting again. Berg's rumble came out with a "Must be nice."

"Really, you need to go," Tadashi insisted. Sort of. Maybe. Actually, he was saying it to keep up appearances. Tadashi didn't like how Berg affected him and made it so he didn't care what the man did or did not do or listen to. "You… you confuse me."

"Sounds fair to me."

Riddles were not kind, especially subtle, half-spoken ones from Berg.

No retreat came from Berg. The bed didn't rise nor the soothing caresses stop. Berg's presence consumed the small space. Tadashi's eyes had closed, giving up the fight, allowing Berg to show him affection.

"I know what it's like."

"Hm?"

A rough cough from Berg had Tadashi attempting to open his eyes, but he didn't have the energy.

Berg cleared his throat, his breathing hitched. His fingers temporarily halted their pursuit of unknown attentions. "I know what it's like. Maybe not everything you've been through, but the being a freak, people wanting to hunt you or take what you love away from you. Those feelings I do understand. Maybe not in the same way, but…"

When Berg trailed off and didn't continue, Tadashi managed to get his eyes open. The defeat hanging off Berg made Tadashi inhale sharply. The slump of Berg's shoulders, the way his eyes became unfocused. His voice had softened, turned into a crackly rumble, and how his tender touches turned into a pressing need for a connection caught Tadashi off guard. Berg came off as confident and unflappable, but now… now he was a picture of a slow burning hurt that consumed a man until his very soul screamed out.

Tadashi would know. He'd been there, was still there, seventeen years after he learned of Akatsuki's death. He reached out to Berg, curling his hand around Berg's large one. Tadashi squeezed. Berg's gaze rose, meeting Tadashi's, crumbling all anger he had been holding onto.

"I'm sorry."

"Me too."

"You don't even know what for," Tadashi answered, his voice cracking.

"Does it matter?"

No. It didn't. To hear someone say sorry and mean it lifted a crushing weight off Tadashi. He squeezed Berg's hand a little harder.

Chapter Ten

The loud clattering had Tadashi bolting upright in bed. He looked around frantically. He quickly spotted his continued source of enjoyment and aggravation.

"What are you doing?"

Berg glanced up temporarily, then put his shoulder back to the old wood stove. "If you're gonna stay in this room, you need better heating."

"So you're removing it?"

With a huff, Berg stood and pointed toward the door. "I have a replacement."

So he did. Tadashi frowned. "That doesn't mean you get to take my old one!"

"So you want Kou freezing to death?" Berg shrugged. "Fine. I'll just—"

Bastard. "No! It's, uh, fine. I don't want Kou to suffer."

Berg grinned triumphantly. "Just give me a few minutes and this will be out of here in a jiffy."

"I'll help," Tadashi proposed, swinging his legs out of bed.

"Are you up for that?" Berg leaned against the stove and pushed his baseball cap up.

"I have been in bed for two weeks, I think I'm all right," Tadashi responded with exasperation. Between Berg and Kou, he barely managed to go pee without help since he was shot, and both of them insisted on him staying bed. Considering their turbulent start with each other, Tadashi had been surprised by the united front they showed. *Against me.* "Please, I'm going to waste away to nothing lying in this bed any longer."

Berg glanced to the stovetop. "What do you think, Kou?"

Oh, gods, he was never getting out of bed.

Kou rubbed his chin, a habit he'd started since Berg showed up… every day… without fail. "Well, we don't want him to keel over."

"Nope, not so much," Berg agreed. "And he does need to get exercise to keep up his strength."

"He'll get fat if we let him stay in bed too much," Kou added, his black eyes sparkling.

"Oh, now, that would be bad," Berg concurred . "Laziness is not a good trait for foxes. They'll never survive the wilds of—"

"Enough!" Tadashi shouted, jumping from the bed. "I'm right here. How can you talk that way in front of me?"

Berg beamed. "About time."

"Yup." Kou nodded.

"What?" Tadashi froze, glancing between the two idiots.

"Finally getting your lazy ass out of bed, that's what," said Berg.

Tadashi's jaw dropped. "Excuse me?"

Kou hopped down from the stove. "It's about time you got some fight back in you." He crawled up Tadashi's PJs and up onto his shoulder. "We were wondering if you'd ever get sick of staying in bed."

"You're the ones insisting I stay in it!" Tadashi snapped.

"You didn't exactly fight us on it before," Berg said, smiling.

"Why would I fight you?" retorted Tadashi. "I was just recovering, and now I'm well."

Berg's brilliant grin grew wider. "I'm glad you're finally well."

Bastard. A warm fluttering in his chest immobilized Tadashi. Every day Berg was there, making him feel. Ever since they held hands after their fight, Tadashi's emotions flowed from him like a broken dam. He didn't like it, but yearned for the sensations at the same time.

"Are you just going to stand there?" Berg asked then pointed to the stove. "Or are you going to help?"

"Help, I'm going to help."

Kou chuckled, hugged Tadashi, then ran down him. He jumped on the bed and sat. "That means I get to supervise."

I give up. These two don't make sense together.

Berg put his shoulder to the stove. "Let's get this junker outta here."

Tadashi maneuvered next to Berg. The heat of the device radiated off it, but the metal was cool to the touch. No, Berg was the furnace. The large man's body heat rapidly consumed Tadashi. He leaned so his back pressed against Berg's chest. His eyes closed. With every push of the stove, Berg pressed into him. The only time he had been this nervous was when Berg brought up Tadashi visiting town and having dinner at his place. But that'd been a bad kind of nervous. This… this felt good. Exciting.

"Hm," Tadashi hummed.

"What?" Berg asked, his voice gruff.

"Hm?"

"I thought you said something," Berg replied with another grunt.

"Nope," Tadashi answered, his eyes opening once more. Embarrassment rose through him.

"Okay then. One more push and it's through the door," Berg said.

"Yeah, sure."

They pressed against the metal, chests heaving with exertion, and pushed. The stove tumbled out of the door and rolled into the courtyard. Tadashi turned, smiling. Berg's laughing gaze met his.

"We did it!"

"Yup." Berg grabbed Tadashi's hand and pulled him back into the shack. "Now to install the new one."

Tadashi frowned, catching his appearance in the mirror on top of his dresser. "I'm dirty."

A loud, jolly laugh from Berg drew his concentration away from his appearance. Berg motioned to himself. "So am I."

"I'm not even dressed." Gods, he'd jumped out of bed without a thought of getting ready for the day.

"We could take a bath, wash your clothes afterward. No point in making more dirty," Berg answered. "Besides, you'd better get used to it. There's a lot of fixing that needs to happen here. This place needs to be suitable for the living."

"Well..."

"It's not like I haven't seen you in your pajamas before, or in the all together," Berg said, chuckling. "Come on, let's get clean."

"I think I'm getting too used to you."

"Is that so bad?" Berg asked softly.

Tadashi didn't answer. Instead, he helped Berg shift the new, lighter stove in place. Then he helped install it, with Kou running around them handing them tools and helping reach the awkward angles their hands could not. In the end, they were all covered in black smudges. Kou was the worst off, looking more like a black squirrel than anything else.

"I do think a bath's in order," Tadashi said and flopped down on the floor. "I don't think we could get this off in the water basin."

Kou chirped, happy. "You mean we get to use the bathhouse?"

Tadashi flinched but nodded.

"Yay!" Kou ran around in circles all over them. "I get to have a bath! A real bath!"

"He's just a little excited, isn't he?" Berg laughed.

Tadashi grinned. He'd heard the sound many times over the last two weeks and loved... *liked it* more each time he heard it. Kou ran up Tadashi's leg and sat on his knee, slipping. Tadashi caught him.

"You're getting bigger," he observed.

Kou puffed up. "I know! I'm growing again!"

Tadashi rubbed his squirrel's head. "Yes, you are. Now, let's get the bath ready."

It wouldn't take long. He had maintained the bathhouse over the years, though he didn't use it. It seemed wrong to use a family bath with only really him needing to wash up. Plus, a lot of energy was needed to get the fire going to heat the water.

Not to mention getting the water from the pump to the bathhouse. They still needed to strip before… oooh! Berg naked. Maybe the washbasin would be easier.

"No," Berg said.

"No, what?" Tadashi asked.

"I know that look," Berg answered, shaking his finger at Tadashi. "You're finding all the reasons as to why we can't get cleaned up in the bath. I have been waiting years for a Japanese-style bath you're not allowed to put the kibosh on it now."

"Are you using me for my bath?" Tadashi teased.

"Yes, yes I am."

"Then no bath."

Kou stopped his satisfied purring. "What? Nooo!"

Berg pointed to Kou. "He is getting bigger. You can't really expect a washbasin to work for both of you forever. You need a working bath."

"Fine," Tadashi said, sighing. "As long as Berg fetches the wood."

"Already done."

Damn. "And we need to clean it."

Kou waved his paw. "I did this morning!"

They really were conspiring against him. "We have to get water in it."

"I hooked up the plumbing, we should be able to have it pipe into the bathhouse unless there's a problem with the well," Berg supplied. He rocked on his toes, hands clasped behind his back. He looked as smug as a cat.

"When did you do—?" Tadashi closed his eyes for a second before looking at Berg again. "That's what you've been doing in the mornings."

"Yup."

Double damn. Tadashi was all for the bath until he realized he'd be naked… with Berg… again.

Berg chuckled and patted Tadashi, pulling him out of the shack. "I promise you won't drown."

With a snort, Tadashi crossed his arms, following Berg with Kou scurrying after them to the bathhouse. "Who's dumb enough to drown in a bath?"

"Something you want to tell us?" Berg teased, his eyes dancing with delight. He pointed. "Or is there a reason you can't get in the bath?"

Triple damn. There really was a stack of wood.

* * * * *

Maybe the bath had been a bad idea. Berg didn't know where to look. Besides the false start of the water not pumping initially, the bath should have gone off without a hitch. Except there was one. Tadashi. His skin. His hair. His tail. All of it, out, wet and glistening. Drops of water formed on the thick fur and dripped steadily down onto the floor like the ones down Tadashi's bare chest.

Whatever had changed between Berg and Tadashi two weeks ago was becoming more evident day by day, and today it just smacked Berg in the face. Watching Tadashi sit down on the stool to wash carefully would be his undoing. Berg was grateful for the towel across his lap. Shame heated Berg's cheeks.

Looking was one thing, but continuing to dance with temptation was another. He needed to put distance between them. He was only a friend. Someone Tadashi could rely on, nothing more. He couldn't be. Maybe he needed to try to invite Tadashi down the mountain again. Or maybe invite people up. Inviting Tadashi to town hadn't seemed to work thus far, maybe he had to switch strategies… and stop ogling his friend.

"Um… you need the shampoo?" Berg asked, struggling to fill the silence.

"Yes," Tadashi answered as he reached for the bottle.

Their fingers brushed, and Berg nearly dropped the bottle. A hot spark jumped between them. Tadashi's startled eyes met his. Berg dropped his gaze, rubbed the back of his neck, and mumbled an apology.

A hush fell over the room. Tadashi worked his fingers into his hair as he washed it. Berg gawked, feeling a bit like a weird creepy guy, but watching the black locks sway and drip was mesmerizing. Until Kou slid in on a bar of soap.

"I found it! I found—what?"

The squirrel eyed them.

"Nothing," Berg and Tadashi answered together. They glanced at each other, then to Kou.

"Uh-huh." Kou narrowed his eyes then pushed the soap to Tadashi. "Here. It was next to the washbasin like you said."

"Thanks, Kou." Tadashi reached for the squirrel. "Why don't you let me wash you before getting in the bath?"

"Papa!" Kou whined, ducking out of reach. "I can do it."

"Fine." Tadashi plopped the shampoo bottle next to Kou. "I was just offering to help."

Kou sniffed, his tail swishing and bobbing. He turned away from Tadashi, then pushed against the bottle, tipping it over. It bounced against the floor before settling. Kou pulled on the cap to no avail. It was screwed on tight. His black eyes focused on Berg, ignoring Tadashi.

"Will you unscrew it?"

Berg nodded, waving Kou to him. Kou rolled the bottle over and Berg opened it with ease. Kou tried to climb up the bottle, but it tipped over, squishing him. Berg covered his laughter with a cough. Tadashi didn't manage it, earning Kou's wrath. He shot toward Tadashi, but not before Berg grabbed him and picked up the shampoo, setting it aside.

"Whoa there, Kou."

"He's laughing at me." The squirrel huffed. Kou squirmed, and being wet, he was hard to hold onto.

"So was I, but—ow! Why do you bite?" Berg switched hands and shook out his damaged one. "No biting!"

Kou's mouth quivered.

"Do you want to be seen as grown-up?"

The squirrel gave him a curt dip of the head.

"Then no biting and know when to ask for help," Berg explained, hoping to hell what he said made sense. "Even if you're getting bigger, part of being a grown-up is knowing your limitations."

Out of the corner of his eye, Berg noticed Tadashi nod in agreement, as well as the relief in his expression.

"Okay, Kou?"

The squirrel's tail fell and he nodded.

"You know I'm not scolding you, right?"

Kou looked away.

"I'm not, I'm just giving you some advice so maybe you and your papa can stop arguing so much." Berg ran his thumb over the squirrel's head. "You'd like that, yes?"

"Yes," Kou answered faintly.

"Here, you can used the shampoo while your papa... well—" Berg put the squirrel down and turned away from Tadashi. "Would you scrub my back?"

"Excuse me?" Tadashi exclaimed, a hitch in his words.

"Wash mine and I'll wash yours," Berg offered, thinking about how crazy he was. "That's how this works in Japan? Or am I wrong?"

"You're not wrong," Tadashi said. "Then, if I may."

The scrape of his stool echoed in the bath, and before long, rough cloth moved over Berg's back. He inhaled slowly and closed his eyes, willing the excitement in his body to go away. But everywhere one of Tadashi's long fingers touched his skin, the mark scorched into him. His breathing deepened as Berg fought to control it.

Tadashi's hands slipped down farther, getting closer to Berg's hips until Tadashi's lips and cheek were brushing against Berg. The man's breathing increased, the air crackling with an undercurrent of tension between them.

Berg suppressed a moan. He knew Tadashi had to feel it too.

"You're back is very... large," Tadashi said, a low rumble came from him as he spoke.

Berg nodded, unable to answer. Sparks danced across him from the sounds coming from Tadashi.

"And your chest… it's covered in hair."

"It's definitely a forest." Berg smiled, nervous. "I'm pretty sure small mammals could get lost in it."

Tadashi chuckled, and a finger slipped around to Berg's chest. A tug made his breath hitch slightly. "You may be right."

Berg grabbed the hand, not thinking, and held it to him. The warmth of Tadashi's long fingers seeped inside him, curling inside his chest.

Then the hand was gone, leaving Berg shaken and worn out. He turned around, locking eyes with Tadashi. His pupils were dilated, his chest rose and fell rapidly, and his nostrils flared. *He must be able to smell the desire coming from me.* Tadashi reached for Berg, but was interrupted.

"You know, I think I'll wash myself," Kou said, still rolling in the shampoo.

Berg blinked, then looked down at the little squirrel. "Let your papa make sure the shampoo is rubbed in well. We want you clean."

Kou's eyes flicked to Tadashi and then back to Berg. "All right."

"I'm going to rinse off," Berg said, scooting toward a bucket of cold water. Hopefully that would fix the fire ignited within him.

Kou scrambled over to Tadashi and perched on his knee. He turned when instructed, lifted his arms, and squirmed when Tadashi rubbed behind his ears. When done, he stared at Berg.

"What?"

Kou jumped off Tadashi and ran over to Berg. "Can I jump in?"

"Jump in what?"

"The bucket," Kou answered, staring at Berg like he was stupid.

"Oh, yes, go for it."

Kou whooped and jumped, splashing into the small tub. Ice-cold water hit Berg's legs and he yelped, scooting back. Kou bobbed up from the surface, grinning. He swam around and dipped under the surface a few times. Apparently satisfied, Kou reach the lip of the bucket and pulled himself up.

Kou jumped down then shook himself out before heading toward the bath. A wood float sat on the surface. Kou climbed aboard and pushed into the tub. Berg would've considered it weird, but since Alva's rescue, nothing had been normal.

"Thanks," Tadashi said, closer than Berg expected.

He glanced down to find Tadashi within a foot of him. "For what?"

"Helping me with Kou."

"Oh, um, no problem." Berg swallowed, his gaze focused on Tadashi's lips. They weren't too full, but they weren't thin either. Perfect really. "Need something?"

"I was wondering if you could scrub my back?"

With Tadashi's dark eyes staring up at him, there was no way Berg could say no, even though he knew it was a bad idea. "Sure."

He took the washcloth, soaping it up good before slowly sweeping it across Tadashi's back. His skin was firm and taut. He was also so pale he seemed to glow. The pink hue his skin took when the cloth pressed against him fascinated Berg.

With thoroughness and care, Berg cleaned Tadashi. When he reached Tadashi's tail, Berg stared, petting the bushy fur, pulling like he would with a cat. The slight vibration coming from Tadashi only confirmed that he liked it. That… Berg squeezed his eyes shut then slowly exhaled. Berg reached for the bucket.

"It'll be a little cold," he said.

Tadashi nodded and then shivered as Berg poured the cold water over both of them. He shuddered, feeling a fog lift. Reason grabbed hold and Berg scooted back.

"How about that bath?" he suggested.

Tadashi nodded, swallowing before his lips twitched. "Yeah, a nice bath."

He stood alongside Berg. Their arms brushed, Berg all too aware of the demon: the one next to him as well as the one inside him. They stepped toward the bath, only to fall back when Kou popped up.

"I'm done!" Kou announced, climbing out of the tub.

Tadashi leaned toward the squirrel. "Are you sure?"

"Yup." Kou climbed down and ran over to the door, darting out of the bath into the changing room.

Berg inhaled and held it, staring at Tadashi, who seemed as shaken as him. Another glance at the door confirmed they were alone, the only buffer between them gone.

And that, more than anything, frightened him. There were certain lines Berg could not—and would not cross—and if he stayed, he wasn't sure he'd withstand temptation. The last thing Berg wanted to do was hurt anyone. Tadashi. Freyja. Him. Anyone.

"You know what?" Berg shuffled toward the door. "I think I'm good."

Tadashi gave him a surprised look. "You sure?"

The poor man had no idea what was going through Berg's head. Like how he loved how the droplets trailed down Tadashi's chest. The way his hair clung to his body. All of it… invigorated Berg. And all of it wasn't allowed.

He smiled, despite the sadness looming inside him. No, it wasn't, and that's why he had to leave.

Chapter Eleven

Stepping into a bath had never been so hard. Berg sunk into the hot water and sighed. He had knots everywhere and could use some downtime. With all the animals deciding to have problems at once, Berg was run ragged. A sharp knock on the door came before Freyja stuck her head in. She smiled at him and settled down on the toilet. Freyja dropped her hand into the tub and wiggled her finger.

Their feathered touch against the water were all Berg needed. He reached for her hand and took it in his own, earning another grin. With a heavy heart, Berg attempted to return it in kind. He didn't quite make it. A crease formed on Freyja's forehead.

"Fowler giving you trouble again? Or Red?"

Good guess, but no. He shook his head. "They been bothering you again?"

Freyja shrugged. "Not really. Mr. Grahn saw Fowler pull me over yesterday and gave him an earful."

Berg winced. "Sorry."

"What did you do to piss him off?" she asked.

The answer wasn't so simple, and Berg wasn't sure he even had an answer either. Berg had danced around answering for weeks since the sheriff first rebuffed him, then promptly wrote him a ticket for loitering. Ruth interceded on his behalf, as well as other people in the diner, so it was quickly torn up, but still, Fowler gave him shit every chance he got. When he started on Freyja, Berg nearly lost it, going into the diner and kicking up a stink.

The town must have talked. Not unusual, but the fact that Mr. Grahn noticed the harassment… shit, Berg was in trouble.

The way Fowler and Red reacted spoke volumes though. Berg would put money on them being the reason Tadashi wouldn't leave the mountain. It made sense. They were the ones that started the rumors of monsters after the war. The ones who had every excuse under the sun as to why the fire marshal shouldn't inspect the forest and why the fire started all those years ago.

"Berg, love?" A stray strand slipped in front of Freyja's face as she tilted her head toward Berg.

"Sorry, just thinking."

"You've been doing a lot of that." Freyja didn't push, but Berg could see the worry plain as day.

"Yeah, I have. I'm sorry." He gave her hand a slight squeeze and let it go, settling back into the deep tub. "I think… I think Fowler and Red are the reason Tadashi and his family don't come into town unless they have to."

Freyja frowned. "Why's that?"

"The harassment started when I asked Fowler about why the Mizunos don't come down the mountain much."

Creases formed around Freyja's pretty mouth and her gaze sharpened. "They always were assholes, but now I definitely don't like them."

"Freyja!"

"It's true, and maybe there's a reason." Freyja tapped her lips with her forefinger. Then her bright eyes widened in triumph. "Wasn't there a bid from a set of developers years ago? Not the ones here now, but a set that wanted a hunting and ski lodge?"

"Shit."

Freyja waggled her eyebrows. "I bet that was around the time of the fire when we were in middle school."

Fowler and Red did have a distinct interest in the new resort owners. Not to mention the new developers wanted to get their hands on more land. A sinking suspicion filled Berg. At least he understood why Red had called for a survey of the mountain at the last town council even though Berg insisted it wasn't necessary.

Berg tensed, locking eyes with Freyja. "I bet that's why Red wants the survey, and the hunt, and the land property—"

Careful maneuvering had Freyja kneeling on the tile, placing her palm against Berg's chest. "You're so giving."

"Uh?"

"That's why I love you, you know."

Berg lifted her hand and kissed it.

"I still think you'd make a fine doctor. You're smart enough for it and have the heart for it."

"Maybe in the next life," Berg answered. "I find animals are less whiney."

Freyja chuckled and gave Berg a light kiss. "Yes, they are, but they can also bite."

"This is true."

"So, what are we going to do?"

"I have no idea." And unfortunately, it was the truth. Berg had no idea how to fight Fowler and Red when all he had were guesses.

"Berg." Freyja shifted, sitting on the edge of the tub.

"Hm?"

"What if…?"

"Since when are you timid?" Berg teased.

"What if the Mizunos had a party, you know, to celebrate the start of summer?" Freyja became profoundly interested in her nails.

"What did you do?" Because she did.

"Me?"

"Yes, you."

Freyja smiled. "I ran into Airi and the rest of the Mizunos."

"Uh-huh."

"They were in town to pay the property taxes."

"Okay."

"I happened to be there to pay ours," Freyja continued, finally lifting her eyes. "I also told them I was grateful for them putting up with you while you made all the renovations to their house."

Oooh! That conversation could go bad quickly.

"They smiled and thanked me for being so patient and them taking up all your time."

Okay, his heart could return to his chest where it belonged.

"I laughed and said they needed to hold a get-together, show it all off."

Terror. Utter terror rolled through Berg. Warning bells clanged in his head.

"They agreed."

"They did?"

"They said maybe not this upcoming weekend but next since it would be too short notice for anything now." Freyja radiated joy. And the more of it she exuded, the more Berg felt like frozen ice washed through his veins. "So I said we should invite everyone like old times."

"What?" Berg's throat caught. "What did they say?"

"That it was a great idea, and they invited us up to stay Saturday night to help plan."

The heat from the water was getting to him. "Are we?"

Freyja chuckled and shifted to give Berg another kiss. "I think your voice changed an octave."

"It just may have," he agreed.

"Trust me, this party will be a smash hit," Freyja said, patting his arm. "The townspeople need to be reminded what good people the Mizunos are. If we do that, the town will be on their side."

He hated when Freyja made sense with her evil schemes.

* * * * *

This couldn't be happening. Just... couldn't. No. Tadashi growled, his hair rising and fur sprouting. He dropped the cloth he'd been using to wipe down the floor in the shrine room.

His father put his hands up. "We thought we'd be welcomed."

"Why?"

"Freyja Engman, Berg's wife, she said you'd been making renovations," his sister answered. She gestured to the lights. "And you have."

"Yes," Tadashi ground out. He had enjoyed the last few weeks working beside Berg. He'd learned much. Enjoyed the company. Theirs. His family. Their company, he did not want.

"Why are you here?" Tadashi asked barely suppressing the urge to fight… or run.

"To heal."

Tadashi laughed, his voice cracking. "Heal? You want to heal? Now? After seventeen years?"

His sister stepped forward, arms outstretched. "You were so hurt… we thought it best to let you grieve."

He rebuffed her, his temper flaring. More fur erupted over his body.

"Akatsuki wasn't some stranger! He was my heart!" Tadashi barked. His family flinched. "He ate, cleaned, he worshiped, he bathed and slept beside us! You loved him like a son! Why would you not come home?

"Why weren't you here to help me"—his voice cracked—"help me say goodbye?'"

This time his mother spoke. "Would you have let us in if we did?"

"Yes!" Tadashi shook, tears streamed down his face, burning. "I needed you!"

"We had come," his father said softly. "You… chased us away."

"What?" No. They had stayed away. They had left him like Akatsuki had.

"You were in your fox form," his mother answered. "You… we had to protect your siblings."

"I attacked you?" The teeth that had been elongating stopped.

"You were so deep within your fox, Tadashi, do not blame yourself," his mother said quietly.

But that couldn't be true. They hadn't returned with him. Then they never came. They didn't. He would have remembered. He would have... actually, no.

"But we did," his sister said, her eyes so big, so wise, so full of understanding. "And we cried, too. We cried a lake of tears for Akatsuki."

Tadashi fell to his knees. The fur was gone.

"We've come back. Time to time," his father informed him. "To check. To help pay bills."

"But..." He had so many questions. It hurt. It all throbbed and burned inside him with nowhere to go. "Where did you go?"

"We've been close for years." His sister's sad smile tugged at his heart, twisting it a little harder. "We've missed home."

So had he. This hadn't been home, not without them.

Then his younger brother crouched down next to him. "Tadashi?"

Gods, when did he get so big?

Etsou shuffled back and forth on his feet. His gaze darted between their parents and Tadashi's like the nervous pup he was. "Can we come home now?"

There was no way to say no to that plea, the hope in Etsou's eyes. They'd work it out.

Some days, getting out of bed sucked. Other days, your heart was torn from your chest. And then there were the ones that shattered everything inside you. Then there were the days that gave you hope. Tadashi wanted today to be one of those. He'd had enough of the others.

"Yes, you can come home," Tadashi said with a large puff of air. Etsou launched himself at Tadashi. Tadashi managed to catch him. He let out a grunt, a really heavy one. Etsou had gotten big.

His brother's arms curled around Tadashi's waist. Etsou buried his face into Tadashi's chest. Tears wet his shirt. Etsou's muted sobs shook against him. Tadashi held his brother close, cradling him, loving him.

"I'm sorry. I'm so very sorry my anger kept you away," Tadashi whispered, holding his brother as close as he could. "All of you."

"We're together now," Etsou said. "That's all that matters."

It was.

"Papa?"

Oh gods, Kou.

He twisted around and saw his squirrel just on the inside of the entryway into the shrine room.

Everyone else had turned around, too. Etsou was struggling to get out of Tadashi's hold. He let go. His brother crawled on his knees toward Kou.

"What is it?"

Kou puffed up his tail. "It? I'm an 'it'?"

Oooh! Tadashi knew that look. He dove for Kou as his squirrel jumped at his brother. He crashed into the floor. A jarring sensation tweaked his knees and flowed up his elbows. He rolled, breathing heavily. He cradled Kou against his chest.

"Tadashi?"

He met his parent's gazes. His mother's eyebrows rose slightly. His father pointed.

"What do you have there?"

Tadashi stood. His back popped. His knees creaked. Some days… he felt old, worn. "Father, Mother, this is Kou, my son."

Wow. Tadashi never thought he'd see the day his parents were surprised.

"He's a squirrel," his dad said.

"Yes, he is," Tadashi agreed. His parents remained silent for a moment before his mom walked forward and placed a kiss on Kou's head.

"Welcome to the family, Kou. I always wanted a grandson."

Tadashi pulled his mom against him. "Thank you."

"Don't think you aren't explaining yourself later," she answered, hugging him back, chuckling.

Chapter Twelve

Until Tadashi, Berg never met an awkward moment he couldn't walk away from unfazed. Any one since he met the kitsune, yeah, they were all awkward. This one though. This one left the rest in the dust.

Freyja smiled as she helped scrub the floors. Hell, she *beamed* at the Mizunos, and Berg, well, Berg wanted to sink into the floor. That wasn't an option, but it'd be nice if it were.

Several times Kou showed up and Berg half expected the squirrel to say something to him but he didn't. The squirrel would watch, then scurry away, glaring. Berg anticipated getting bitten, but he just hadn't figured out when.

The wait was killing him.

Tadashi looked as though he swallowed a bug or several or a whole ant farm. Basically, he seemed as pleased about the situation as Berg was. The day needed to end. Quickly. But it had dragged out through the morning on into lunch, and now the smells of dinner wafted from the house into the shrine.

Once they arrived at the temple, Freyja and the Mizuno women immediately set everyone to work. Weeds were pulled, bushes trimmed, the last of the wiring done for the house, and the temple scrubbed down. They were now in the main temple room washing and polishing every surface, Freyja on one side of Berg, Tadashi on the other.

Every time his elbow bumped into one of them, Berg jumped or yelped, getting stares. From everyone. The Mizunos had to think he was nuts. Like a top, Berg was spinning and falling and soon he'd topple over. Tension coiled in Berg, knotting, twisting, and contorting until his chest felt like it would collapse under the weight.

"You're going to shine right through the wood if you keep rubbing that hard."

Berg whipped up his head. Airi stared back at him with a smile. He then looked back down at the floor. A perfect reflection stared back at him. Yup. Clean.

"How about you take Freyja to the house?" Airi suggested, her black eyes darting to his wife's stomach. "Dinner's ready and your wife should really sit."

"Afraid she's gonna pop?"

"Yes."

Berg laughed alongside Freyja and Tadashi, his first honest one of the day. "All right, I'll get her to the house."

"And Berg?"

"Yes, Airi?"

"Thank you." Airi leaned forward and stole a kiss on his cheek.

"For what?"

"For being you."

Now that wasn't cryptic at all. Out of the corner of his eye, Berg could see his wife nodding in agreement. Women and their silent communication, Berg would never understand.

"And for"—her gaze flicked to Tadashi then back—"for everything."

With an amused chuckle, Freyja answered, "It was our pleasure. I've missed coming to the temple. I always thought it was beautiful here."

"Me too," Berg agreed and stood. He glanced down at Freyja. "Need help?"

"Please." She reached out. He grabbed hold of her arm and supported her as she rose. "This baby may not be ready to come out, but I sure am."

"Soon," reassured Berg.

"Hopefully not too soon," Airi joked, winking. "We have the party next week."

Freyja nodded. "No way am I missing it, but with all this walking, who knows? It may help move this little guy along."

"Well, let's make it through dinner first," Tadashi said, ushering them along. "I'm starving, so you two must be."

Once they stepped through the doorway and the full onslaught of smells hit Berg, he had to agree. His stomach made its opinion known as well by rumbling loudly. Tadashi and Freyja laughed, his wife shaking her head.

"I hope you have enough food, this one eats enough for a wild bear." She patted him as she found a chair to sit at.

Berg pulled it out for her and took the one next to it with Tadashi squeezing beside him. Etsou and Airi sat opposite them while Mizuno and his wife took the head of the table.

Freyja pointed to the dishes. "Is this tofu? Oooh! Noodles! Ah, look at the fish. Oh? More tofu?"

Mrs. Mizuno nodded, her eyes sparkling with amusement. "We love tofu and our dishes tend to have it in them."

"Oooh!" Freyja wiggled in her chair. "I haven't had this since I was a kid!"

Berg smiled. "Happy?"

"Very," she responded. "*Arigato*, Mrs. Mizuno."

The smile across Mrs. Mizuno's face couldn't have been wider. "You're welcome, my dear. Now, everyone, dig in. And let me know if you need more rice."

There was a flurry of movement as everyone began eating. Very little conversation was made. They had worked long and hard so it made the meal taste that much better to Berg. Only when the frenzy died down did Berg realize he had finally relaxed and enjoyed himself. If only he'd been able to do that earlier.

Watching his wife as she chatted and ate, Berg knew why he hadn't.

"Do you?"

"Hm?" Berg asked when Freyja's bright eyes met his.

She shook her head. "Men, they never listen."

"What is it?"

"Do you think it'll be a success—the party," Freyja said.

The Mizunos were all watching him with keen interest.

With a brief nod, Berg said, "Yes, I do. Especially with Freyja helping by inviting everyone. Curiosity will bring a lot of people. Not many people believe the tales about monsters anymore. So I'm sure a lot of people wonder what condition the temple will be in."

Mizuno-san smiled. "Good. I want them to come. This is a place to gather and enjoy. It wasn't meant to be kept in solitude."

"I agree," Berg answered, glancing at Tadashi, whose gaze was unfocused and lost. "Company is always good to have."

"Oh dear!" Freyja gasped before laughing.

Berg jumped, and then surveyed his wife for what was wrong.

When her hand went to her stomach, Berg's quickly followed. Each thump against her belly sent a thrill through him. God, he couldn't wait to be a dad. It was one thing he'd been looking forward to. Freyja smiled up at him as they felt the baby kick. Her eyes shone brightly. Sometimes her love hurt so bad. Finding a grin inside him, Berg returned his wife's exuberance. Or, he hoped he did.

She was still smiling so he must have.

"May I?"

Berg shifted to find Tadashi standing next to them. His gaze was fixated on Freyja's stomach. She pushed back in the chair and took hold of Tadashi's hand. Freyja pressed it against her belly.

"Oooh! Wow," Tadashi murmured. "It's been so long since… he's strong. A fighter."

"Not you, too," Freyja moaned. She pointed at Berg. "He's convinced it's a boy too."

"He's right," Tadashi said.

Freyja shook her head. "How would you know? There's no way to tell until it's born."

Berg flinched but luckily Freyja was too focused on Tadashi to notice.

"Ah." Tadashi bit his lip before his expression brightened. "I'm a shrine priest. We know all."

The waggle of his eyebrows did Freyja in, and she began laughing. Berg couldn't help but join in as the rest did as well.

Once dinner was over, Mrs. Mizuno, Freyja, and Airi chased Berg and the guys away, telling them to wash the stink off. Berg acted affronted by the accusation but followed Tadashi and the others out. He'd sweat through his shirt hours ago and didn't want to go to bed grimy. At least it would be the four of them in the bathhouse and not just him and Tadashi.

There was no way Berg could feel temptation if Mizuno-san and Etsou were around.

"Should I get some wood?" And hopefully not sport any.

Etsou smiled. "I started the fire earlier."

"Oh, good."

Steam met them when they entered the bathhouse, immediately clinging to Berg and his clothes. He felt like he'd crawled through the inside of a pipe. They quickly undressed in the changing room, then wrapped their towels around their waists and made their way into the bath.

They scrubbed and chatted about what was left to do, and Berg was able to keep up conversation with Etsou and Mizuno-san without having to look directly at Tadashi. He wasn't sure what he would do if their gazes actually met.

"So when's Freyja due?" Mizuno-san asked.

Berg thought. The due date was any day now really. "Any time now. Hopefully she won't have the baby until after next Saturday though. I'd hate for her to miss out on it. She's been chatting about everyone coming up to the shrine like we used to."

Mizuno-san's dark eyes lit up. "I am too."

"Hopefully everything will go off without a hitch."

"I would like that as well," Mizuno-san answered. "What about you? Are you excited to be a father?"

"Yes," Berg agreed, his chest swelling. "It's one thing I've always wanted—children—and I'm lucky enough to get that."

"And a lucky man to have such a lovely wife," Mizuno-san added.

Berg cleared his throat and nodded. "She deserves better."

"You're kind," Etsou said, sliding over by him. "You made Tadashi happy again and we could come home."

Berg swallowed. That heavy feeling was pressing down on him again. He pressed the palm of his hand against his chest, hoping the throbbing would stop.

"Etsou," Mizuno-san called, his dark eyes a little too knowing for Berg. "Rinse off."

"But I was—"

"Now."

The boy scooted back to his stool, mumbling as he went, but did as his father told him.

"Neat trick," Berg said, forcing a chuckle. "You'll have to teach me so I could use it on my own kid someday."

The lines deepened around Mizuno-san's eyes as he grinned. "My pleasure. Anything you need. Because he's not wrong."

How did he say thanks? "I can't just stand by and watch someone who's hurt. That's all."

"You helped Tadashi because you have a good heart," Mizuno-san said. "The world could use more people like that. You would've made a good healer."

"I am, of sorts."

"A doctor."

"Freyja says that, too. Maybe the next time around," Berg said.

Mizuno nodded. "Maybe. Your wife's confidence in you is well deserved. Tadashi told us what you did for him."

He did? Berg whipped his head to his friend. Tadashi gave him a half wave. Berg focused on scrubbing his legs so he could finish up and rinse off.

"Thank you, truly." Mizuno-san bowed his head. "For saving my son's life."

"You're welcome." Berg couldn't stop staring at Tadashi, but he asked. "So you know I know?"

A rough chuckle fell from Mizuno-san. "Yes, but Freyja does not?"

"I haven't told anyone."

"You could tell her," Tadashi said. "She's your other half."

Unbelievable pain shot through Berg. He somehow managed to force a smile. "Sure."

An odd expression crossed Tadashi's face before he grinned. "If you're trustworthy, so is she."

"Thank you." It meant a lot, which reminded him. "I've been meaning to ask. Where's your tail? It's usually…"

"Out?" Tadashi supplied.

"Yeah." *That*.

"I've been more focused. Feeling better. So I have better control."

"Oh, good," Berg answered.

Etsou giggled. "Tadashi's lucky to have such an understanding human as a friend. Most people would've called us demons or freaks or worse. I hope I have as good of a friend someday."

Berg shrugged, growing uncomfortable with the praise. Mizuno-san must've picked up on his discomfort and moved the conversation onto getting finished up, for which Berg was grateful. He wasn't sure how good of a friend he was at the moment.

"Hey, you guys!"

Berg turned in time to see Kou running through a crack in the door.

"Me too, I want to take a bath too!" he yelled, which honestly, was more of a squeak. "I've had to hide all day because of Freyja."

"Can't stand not being able to chat my ear off?" Berg leaned down and picked up the squirrel.

"Do you know how hard it is to not talk when everyone else is?" Kou squatted on his hand, all puffed up.

151

"Sorry, Kou," Tadashi said, bending in to rub Kou's head. "Just a little longer, then you can run about like normal."

"You owe me for this," Kou complained, but he nuzzled into Tadashi's hand.

Berg smiled, hoping his relationship with his son would be just as good.

"Let me wash you," Tadashi said, picking Kou up. "The girls still need a turn."

"Fine, but don't expect me to roll over and beg," Kou chirped.

Everyone chuckled, then finished scrubbing. They rinsed off and crawled into the large bath. Berg sighed. Contentment bubbled up inside him though uneasiness still spun within. If he could let go, just a bit, relax. Not worry. There was nothing to worry about. He was doing nothing wrong. Berg closed his eyes and let his head fall back on the lip of the tiles.

"Relaxed?" A warm voice asked.

"Mm."

The lyrical laughter felt good against his neck. Goose bumps prickled along his skin. "You must be."

"Mm."

"Considering you fell asleep."

"What?" Berg jerked, regretting the sudden movement. His head went under the water. He sat up, sputtering and coughing. "Hell."

It hurt. So bad. Like a bubble had formed in Berg's chest and was pressing against his heart, choking it and him.

"Whoa." A hand pulled him up more. "I didn't mean to make you drown."

Tadashi's black eyes were the only thing Berg could focus on.

"You all right? Do you—should I heal you?"

"What?" Heal? He gasped, fighting for air. How much did he swallow?

Tadashi pressed his palm against Berg's chest. His eyes focused on where his hand lay. Berg stilled. A white glow emanated from his friend. The burning agony lessened. He could breathe. The soft light flowing from Tadashi, his look of determination and concentration made it hard to focus on anything but him.

Panting, still confused, Berg gaped at Tadashi. He'd forgotten Tadashi could do something like heal him. But there was something else calling his attention. Apparently, Tadashi wasn't focused because there was white peeking out from under his towel.

"You have two tails."

"What?" Tadashi turned in a circle, trying to look at his ass.

Berg died. He just did. He couldn't stop the laughter if he tried.

Wide eyes met Berg's gaze. "Why are you laughing?"

"Because you're turning around in circles like a dog."

A loud growl filled the room. "I am *not* a dog."

"Don't tell that to Alva."

Tadashi's ears perked up. "She's well?"

"Yup, and happy as can be." Berg waved Tadashi closer, curious. "Now stop moving and let me look."

Tadashi grumbled but spun around. Berg lifted the towel, only to have Tadashi thump it back down. The fox glared at him.

"How else am I supposed to check your tails?"

"Oh, uh, go ahead then." Tadashi's muscles were flexed, hands fisted at his sides.

Lifting the towel once again, Berg confirmed his suspicions. Two tails flicked back and forth. He reached out and stroked them. Yup. No mistaking it, there were two luscious tails. The thick white fur felt wonderful in Berg's hand. He tugged, not hard, but with enough force to check if they really were attached. They were. Berg still had trouble reconciling that Tadashi had a tail sometimes.

"Well?" Tadashi asked, his voice hesitant, wobbling.

"Definitely two tails."

A yip of happiness was not what Berg expected. Neither was the blur of activity as Tadashi spun around again. The cries of joy. Or Tadashi whipping his towel off, giving Berg a show. Tadashi cradled his tails, tears streamed down his face.

"So, you're happy then?"

"Yes," Tadashi whispered, rubbing his face in his tails.

Wasn't two tails weird? But… Tadashi wasn't a normal fox. He was a kitsune. Berg racked his memories for the stories.

"You could have up to nine, right?"

Tadashi nodded. His eyes closed. Grief clouded his face. He pressed the tails tighter against him as if he believed they'd disappear.

"I'm sorry." Berg had said something wrong. He just didn't know what.

Tadashi shook his head. "I'm just happy to have another back."

"So…" Berg lost his thought, unable to push more past his lips. Tadashi used to have more. Why'd he lose them? But with the atmosphere the way it was, Berg didn't think he could ask.

A knock at the door made them jump. Then a silky voice flowed through to them. "Tadashi? Did you wake Berg?"

"Yes, Mother." Tadashi gulped a few times, steadying his voice. "He's getting out right now."

Berg didn't waste any time and stepped out. "Sorry."

He didn't know why, but he kept feeling like he had to apologize. Tadashi waved him off and picked up his towel. Berg watched in fascination as the tails began disappearing. Seeing Tadashi with no tails seemed odd. The man seemed incomplete without them.

When Berg lifted his eyes, Tadashi was giving him one of those odd smiles again. "Let's get out of here before the girls burst in."

Good idea.

"Let us get out," Tadashi shouted toward the exit.

"Leaving!" Mrs. Mizuno called back.

As Tadashi pushed open the door, the last of his tails finished disappearing. *Tails.* Huh. A seed planted inside Berg's mind. There was something important Berg needed to remember, something besides the fact a kitsune could have more than one tail.

* * * * *

The pale moon lit the veranda around the shrine, giving Tadashi a good view of Berg sitting on the railing. His head lay back against one of the supports as he gazed over the courtyard. He looked handsome in his *yukata*. Not wanting to interrupt Berg, Tadashi waited, hoping for an opening. Like one with Berg returning to his room.

Today had been… *odd*. Besides the day Berg installed the new stove in the shack, Berg had been laidback and easy to spend time with. Many times Tadashi had found them in close proximity to each other, arms brushing, fingers touching as they worked.

Until today, Tadashi had almost forgotten Berg was married. Seeing Freyja with her swollen belly had been a bit jarring. Then Berg had been rigid, tense, and had made little eye contact until they were in the bath with Tadashi's family. Not that Tadashi had been any different. He'd been angry at himself for falling in love with a man who couldn't be his. Plus he felt stupid. Poor Berg. Always so kind, giving. The man probably didn't know how to tell Tadashi to back off.

With a deep longing to return to the usual rapport between them, Tadashi had sought Berg out, only to discover his scent leading away from the house and to the temple. It was a nice view. The black shadows of the trees swept over the mountain lit up in silver by the moon.

Inhaling once, Tadashi found the resolve to talk to Berg. He pushed away from the shadows and began walking toward his friend. Just then, Berg pushed away from the railing and walked off the veranda out into the yard. He swung around the side of the temple, disappearing from sight.

Tadashi followed, drawn to Berg and unable to stay behind. When he saw Berg staring at the path leading up to the bluff, Tadashi had to choke down a quick indrawn breath. He waited to see what Berg would do.

His friend pushed some low-hanging branches aside and stepped onto the path. Tadashi's heart hammered hard. He could follow. It'd be obvious he did though. He couldn't just pretend to run into Berg like at the shrine.

But they needed to talk. Whatever was going on between them, they needed to stop dancing around it.

Decision made, Tadashi followed Berg. He stepped carefully, not wanting to scare his friend. The walk was slow. Berg stumbled more than once over tree roots, but eventually, he made it to the top. He stood, staring out over the valley.

Tadashi slipped next to him. Excitement fought against sadness. Confusion tumbled with contentment. He wanted to be here with Berg but wanted to run away. A solemn air hung in the night.

He jumped when firm flesh met his fingers. Like the day Berg refused to leave his side, Berg's large hand surrounded Tadashi's. Its heat sank into him. Tadashi didn't speak. Didn't want to break the spell Berg was under. A steady spark flowed between them, reassuring Tadashi.

It couldn't last forever though. A sharp wind blew, kicking up their *yukatas*, and Tadashi had to let go of Berg's hand to keep his together. Otherwise, he'd be giving Berg another show. One a day was more than enough. He still couldn't believe he danced naked in the bath like that. Another tail growing had to have short-circuited his brain.

"You all right?" Berg stepped in front of him, blocking the wind.

"Yeah, just surprised."

"Cold?"

Tadashi shook his head.

"It's breathtaking, the view."

"Yes." Tadashi stood, letting go of his clothes. He patted them down. "I had always found it calming to come here."

"You come here often?" Curiosity filled Berg's voice, though its deep roughness came through more than usual.

"I used to… with Akatsuki."

"Mm." Berg stepped away, allowing Tadashi to overlook the town.

"It was one of our favorite things to do together." Why could he share his memories so easily? *Because it's Berg.*

"Tadashi?" Berg breathed in and paused, as if he had to think about what he wanted to say. "Who was Akatsuki to you?"

If it had been anyone but his family, Tadashi normally would've ignored such a question. Berg wasn't just anybody. "My lover."

"Oh."

Nothing more was said. Tadashi stood next to Berg, overlooking the town, waiting. A tight knot fluttered in his chest. Would Berg walk away from him now?

"So that's why his death hurt you so much."

Gods, the ache inside him. "Yes."

"I'm sorry. I really, truly am." Berg took Tadashi's hand again.

"Me too."

"I could've sworn we've had this conversion before."

Tadashi chuckled sadly. "Sort of."

"You loved him a lot, huh?"

"Yes."

"Must've been nice," Berg said wistfully.

"You have Freyja." She loved him clear as day.

"I do."

Once again, a lull hit their conversation. Berg sat on the bluff, Tadashi following him down. Their hands never once untwisted from each other.

"You know…" Berg's voice trailed off, but Tadashi waited. He knew Berg had more to say. "All those years ago, Red and the Sheriff claimed a multi-tailed monster hunted down their friends and slaughtered them."

Tadashi's heart pounded. He went rigid. He tried to pull his hand away, but Berg held on.

"The town wrote it off on them being drunk and seeing Shane's dog attack their friends." Berg inhaled sharply. "But with the fire and different sightings, Fowler and Red insisting on a beast, the town gradually believed some mutated wolf roamed the mountain.

"But that was you, wasn't it?" Berg asked, but he didn't wait for an answer. "You did attack their friends, didn't you?"

Berg sounded positive in his assumptions. Tadashi closed his eyes. "Yes."

"Why? Akatsuki was... he had..." Berg shook his head.

"Fowler sent Red and his friends up to chase me off the mountain," Tadashi said. "They wanted the land. I ran them off but they came back. They were going to hurt me, kill me and, quite possibly Kou, in the process. I had already lost Akatsuki because of the men of the village. I wasn't going to lose my home. I'd been hurt. Angry for so long. I snapped."

Berg's shoulders slumped a bit, the tension surrounding him released. "I'm sorry."

"Not your fault."

"Doesn't matter. I liked Akatsuki," Berg shared. "He was a gentle man. One of the influences in my life that made me a vet."

A sting inside Tadashi's chest grew tight.

"So you retaliated against them when they came back?"

"Huh? Oh, yes." Tadashi rubbed the ache on his chest. "I lost myself to my fox. Hunted them down. It was a while before I was forced to come back to myself."

"What happened?" Berg turned to him. His eyes focused on Tadashi.

He gulped, his throat swollen and hard to work. The words came out in a rasp. "I... I killed Kou."

"I'm pretty sure Kou's alive."

"Now."

"Is this why you said he's a demon squirrel?"

"Yes." Tadashi blinked, his eyes stinging. "I had to give part of myself to save him."

"Explains a few things," Berg answered seriously.

"It does," Tadashi agreed, smiling. "There had been a faint heartbeat. His soul was still attached to his body. I gave him some of my light so he could live. In the process, I made him like me."

"Is that how you lost your tails?" It was an honest question and not a bad assumption.

Regret ripped through him. "No."

"Then how?" Berg's plea wrapped around Tadashi's heart; he was struggling with something, but Tadashi didn't have a clue as to what.

"For the killings." Tadashi's voice faltered. He had to make several attempts before he could speak. "I lost my tails when I went feral and killed those men."

Berg didn't let go of his hand, but his breathing increased. Tadashi could smell the nervousness from Berg spiking in the air. He tried to shake his hand loose again but Berg, being the stubborn ass he was, didn't let go.

"I think they're after the land again."

Um.

"Red's been chomping at the bit to bring a search party up here to check for the 'wolf-dog' hybrid." Berg pressed his lips together. "He hasn't liked my reports that nothing's been amiss. I also heard he made an inquiry into whether you and your family been making your payments on your property taxes."

A growl escaped Tadashi. Berg shivered. "Those bastards."

"They can't touch you," Berg reassured him. "Your family has never missed a payment. And it's a shrine. This party could help, too. Remind the town why everyone loved coming up here to celebrate different holidays."

"You think so?" It was hard to believe, especially after everything he'd been through.

"Yeah, and besides, you've got me on your side." Berg winked. "If the town wants their animals looked after, they need to keep me happy."

Tadashi laughed, hard. "I guess that's true."

"True enough."

"I'm glad you got one of your tails back."

Berg really jumped tracks a lot tonight.

"How many did you have?"

"Nine."

"Wow," Berg answered in awe.

Tadashi preened.

"I hope you get them all back."

"Someday," Tadashi agreed. "It'd be nice."

Berg squeezed his hand. He turned back, watching over the valley. Tadashi watched Berg. The man's chest hair popped out from the *yukata* as his chest rose and deflated, and he leaned on the other hand to support himself. Tadashi didn't want the night to end.

"Can I see?"

"See what?"

"Your fox," Berg answered. "Or is it rude to ask?"

"Not for you."

Quickly, Tadashi stripped down. Berg's intense gaze nearly burned his skin. Just as speedily, he was in his fox form before other parts of his body betrayed him. They needed to talk but that could wait a little longer, and he needed to regain some control. If he was in his fox form he could find his center again.

But when Berg buried his hands in Tadashi's fur, he forgot everything. All he could do was feel the strong hands stroking up and down his sides, tugging on his fur, and sliding over his head. The second Berg got to his tails, it was game over. Tadashi leaned down, sticking his butt in the air. Berg pulled and petted, using his other hand to rub Tadashi behind the ears.

Tadashi's change came so suddenly it surprised even him. One second he was a fox on all fours, next thing, he was naked in Berg's lap, pressed against his friend's chest. Berg buried his nose in Tadashi's neck. His strong arms held Tadashi with astonishing gentleness.

There was no way Berg couldn't not notice how hard Tadashi was. His length was pressed against Berg's stomach. But Tadashi didn't rub like he wanted to. The moment seemed like it would break if he made any move.

Berg eased Tadashi away from him. His hands moved to Tadashi's face, tracing over it with his fingers. His intense gaze stayed locked on Tadashi.

"Hm," Tadashi groaned. "Berg, you're killing me."

Berg gave him a weak smile and pulled away.

Tadashi whimpered.

"I'm sorry, that was dumb."

He shook his head.

Berg's voice cracked. "I can't, Tadashi."

"Why?"

"Because I won't hurt my wife like that. Or you."

Berg's statement was like cold water poured over Tadashi. He blinked a few times. When had his breathing become so ragged?

"We should go back," Berg said then stood.

"Wait!" Tadashi grabbed Berg's hand. "Please."

"Would I be the man you care about if I kissed you? When I'm already committed to my wife?"

An unfamiliar but recognizable ache split Tadashi's chest. "No."

"Then we need to get back," Berg answered quietly, his words gravelly, as if he was struggling to speak. His shoulders slumped, as if the world was crushing down on top of him. Suddenly their talk from the first time they held hands clicked.

"You said... you said you knew what it was like to feel different."

With a sigh, Berg crumpled to the ground. "Yes."

Tadashi scooted close. He reached out, tracing Berg's jaw. "You said you knew what it was like to be hunted as a freak."

"Yes."

"To lose everything you care about."

The next "yes" was barely a puff of air.

"It's not wrong to want to kiss me."

"It is in my world, Tadashi."

He knew that. He did, but Tadashi couldn't let it go. "It's why you look so lost sometimes. So pained."

"I can't be…" Berg closed his eyes and removed Tadashi's hand. He pulled his long legs up and circled his knees with his arms. "Maybe someday in another time, another place, another life, I could've been me. Not now. My kind aren't accepted. For me to live in my world, to be with my family, I have to be the person I am. The man and husband people expect me to be."

It wasn't fair.

"I made a commitment to my life, to Freyja," Berg said. His voice shook. His hands trembled. "That's all there is for me. I won't betray that."

"Even if that means denying who you are?"

"Like you wouldn't know anything about that?" Berg snapped, his eyes opening again.

They hurt. The words. And they were true.

"Do you love her?"

"As best I can." Berg sighed again. "Like I said, she deserves better."

"You could—"

"I won't be like Red or Fowler, it ain't right," Berg interrupted fiercely, almost in a growl.

"What?" Tadashi didn't understand.

"They're like me. They're… lovers. They have girlfriends, heck, Fowler is even talking about finally settling down with a wife, but they're with each other." Berg gulped hard. "I won't do that to Freyja."

Tadashi felt like scum. How could he even… to put Berg… he just… *wanted*. Berg was so close. Right there. And yet…

I can't have him.

"Please." Berg knelt and put a hand under Tadashi's chin, raising it. They were within a hair's breath of each other. "Please understand. I know… I feel… so much." Berg pressed a palm against Tadashi's chest. "So much. So much more than I ever thought I could. And… it has to be enough as it is."

Tadashi grimaced as pain laced through him. For his, and for the hurt he saw in Berg's eyes. It tore him up. He was finally able to feel again, and when he thought joy was possibly within his grasp, it was ripped away.

"I wish things could be different. I do," Berg croaked. "I have no place in this world."

A stray tear rolled down Berg's cheek. Tadashi wanted to be angry. To yell. To call Berg a coward.

Berg's eyes searched his face. "I wouldn't be me… if this became more. No matter how much I want it."

He wouldn't. Gods, Tadashi knew he'd be ripping Berg in half, making him less than what he was. Tadashi wouldn't be responsible for crushing Berg that way.

"The world's not fair," Berg said quietly. He pressed his forehead against Tadashi's. "To put everything I want in front of me, only to know I can never have it."

"Yeah."

"I'm sorry, Tadashi."

"I know."

"Will you forgive me?"

He fought the tears back. "Of course."

Chapter Thirteen

The party was loud and obnoxious, but it was a success, and that was more important than Berg's discomfort. Freya waddled to and fro talking to anyone and everyone, hovering like a mother hen. She soon would be.

Airi waved from across the courtyard, and Berg used it as an excuse to extricate himself from all the mothers giving advice to them.

"Everything all right?" she asked once he got to her. She bounced on her toes, her gaze flickering over the room.

"Yes?" Berg frowned. "Are *you* all right?"

"What? Oh, yes, everything's fine." She laughed a little too forcefully. "You looked like you could use a break, that's all."

"Has someone been causing problems?"

"No, not at all," she protested too loudly.

Berg scoured the grounds. A general hum of excitement crackled in the air. People milled about looking at the different street games and foods set out on the tables. Laughter was abundant.

All seemed well.

Then why did Airi look like she was about to crack her face in two with her smile?

"Airi, what's wrong?"

She bit her lip. Airi's dark eyes rounded and focused on Berg. He could see a thousand thoughts cross her mind.

"I'll help if you'll tell me what's wrong, Airi," offered Berg.

She huffed, a strand of her hair blowing up before falling back down on her forehead. Her mouth quirked to one side and her fingers fidgeted. The urge to shake her so she'd 'fess up to whatever was making her worry was hard not to listen to.

Airi looped her arm in his and began walking around the courtyard, stopping to talk to excited villagers, offer suggestions, and… and she squinted a lot. Carefully watching the ground.

Berg followed her gaze and saw nothing except for a squirrel. But he wasn't surprised. With all the food around, a squirrel or two were bound to show… a *squirrel*. A really big squirrel. Berg paused, a buzz rang in his head as his mind played catch up. He grabbed for Airi as she stepped away from him.

"Where's Kou?" he asked quietly.

She stiffened, giving him the only answer he needed to know.

"To your right. At your three," he told her as he began pulling them in Kou's direction.

Her gaze swept to where Berg indicated, and she exhaled. "We have to get him."

"What's he doing here?" Berg whispered, urgent to get to the little squirrel before he did something everyone would regret. "I thought he was supposed to st—"

"He got upset he was missing the action," Airi interrupted. She motioned for Berg to stop. "He's never been around people before Tadashi, then you, then us. He was mad he couldn't at least look. He and *nii-san* argued, and then he bit Tadashi and ran."

"Again with the biting," Berg moaned.

"He's still a squirrel. He felt threatened." Airi sucked on her lip. "He is technically prey to us."

"Still, it hurts."

"Agreed."

"Got you too?"

An impressive growl fell from Airi. *Better to leave it alone.*

"We going to box him in?"

"Think we can do it on our own?"

"Maybe…" Berg searched the party for Freyja. He saw her with yet another group of people surrounding her stomach. He waved, hoping to catch her eye, and yelled. "Freyja."

She turned immediately, beaming. She did that a lot lately. Alva was next to her, the little girl's hand in his wife's. He waved her over.

Airi's eyebrows rose. "You told her?"

"No, not yet, but she won't ask questions." Berg was still trying to figure out the how part. And with how things were with Tadashi, he didn't want to rock the boat. "Besides, he'll know he can't talk to her. So hopefully he'll try to get away from her and I can grab him. Hey, sweetie."

"What is it?" Freyja asked, huffing. Were her cheeks red?

"Everything okay?"

She nodded and pressed a hand against her belly. "Just gas."

"Well… we have to catch that squirrel." He pointed and Freyja's gaze followed.

"Which way do you want me to walk?" she asked.

That's my girl. He pointed. "Airi and I will go to there and there, you come at him from this direction. Drive him to me."

The girls nodded then moved out. Berg circled around, hoping the oak tree would give him enough cover to surprise the crafty squirrel. Crouching down, Berg leaned out to see how successful the girls were being. Kou was headed right for him. Too busy looking over his shoulder, Kou didn't even notice when Berg dove for him.

The shock didn't last long. Kou let out a panicked squeal, then bit. Hard. So fucking hard. It made the bites from when Kou thought Berg killed Tadashi seem like love nips.

"Ow. Hell. Ow." Berg hopped around, still holding Kou close to his chest. "Stop it, Kou! Right now!"

The squirrel stopped his assault. He rolled so he could face Berg. Kou squinted, getting that look like Tadashi's. Assessing. Like he was trying to decide to disembowel Berg or not.

Freyja and Airi ran up to him. Freyja bent, hands on knees, out of breath. Airi tilted her head, trying to get a look in Berg's hands. "Did you get him?"

"Am I bleeding?"

Her lip twitched. "Yes."

To Kou's credit, he still hadn't said a word. He was chirping like mad, his tail vibrated, his fur on end.

Berg was a dead man. Kou would bite him to death in his sleep. Berg could see it in his eyes.

Freyja's cry interrupted their staring match. "Ugh! Oooooo! That's not gas. Ahhhhh."

"What?" Panic rose in Berg. "What's wrong?"

Airi pointed down.

Was that a puddle?

"Ew."

"Berg!" Freyja's furious gaze locked onto him. "Considering you put your arm up horses' vaginas on a regular basis, I should not hear the words 'ew' out of your mouth!"

But that had been Kou! "Yes, dear."

Airi took Freyja's arm. "I'll take her inside to my parents. You get Dr Franson. I last saw him by the dessert table."

"Right." Berg spun around.

"Get my brother to help you!" Airi yelled. Freyja had a confused expression but allowed Airi to pull her away. "And get K—the squirrel inside!"

Better do that first. Berg went around the back of the temple, ready to drop Kou off in the shack.

"Is the baby coming?" came the small inquiry.

Berg looked down at Kou. "Yes."

"I want to see it."

"I'm not sure I want to," Berg admitted.

"But it's your baby."

"Yes, but Freyja—"

A loud thump stopped Berg midsentence. He had just gotten around the shrine about to step next to the shack. Two large figures were leaning against the none-too-sturdy wall. Instinctively Berg pressed against the wall and put a finger over Kou's mouth. The squirrel trembled in his hand.

"Leslie…" a man whined.

Who? Then Berg remembered it was the sheriff's first name. Which meant the man had to be—*fuck.* Now Berg really didn't want to be seen. He shuffled back.

"Please, Leslie," Red begged. "I'm tired of waiting."

So did not need to know this or hear this.

Silence met with Red's plea. Walking away would've have been the smart move. However, a soft noise, a low rumble, caught Berg's attention. He leaned forward, peeking, and got the show of a lifetime. Certainly not something he expected to ever see.

Fowler had Red pinned against the shack and was kissing the other man within an inch of his life. Goes to show you one should never make assumptions about people. Berg had *known*, but seeing it was a whole other ballgame. Groans, grunts and a contented sigh later, the two men had their foreheads pressed together, the moment so intimate, so tender.

There was no way Berg could look away. Jealousy kept him rooted to his spot as much as curiosity. It was all he couldn't have with Tadashi. He wanted to know why those two showed up. Yes, he expected Freyja to invite them, but he didn't think they'd actually come. No one did.

"This'll have to do until we get back," said Fowler, his voice scratchy. "'Sides, we have work to do."

With a thunk, Red's head dropped back and he spoke, his words slurring, "Th-they weren't all s-s-supposed to-to be here."

"Well they are." Fowler exhaled slowly. "The Mizunos just make things a bit more complicated."

"They haven't lived here in years."

"Well, they're here now."

Red huffed. "You think it'll work?"

Tender fingers met Red's lips, Fowler staring down at his lover. "It has to."

"But…" Red shook his head, slumping. "Y-you know I hate those Japs."

Fowler cradled Red's face in his hands. "I know, Red. I know."

"When we were fighting, back in the war, they wouldn't stop." Red's tone softened. "They just kept coming and coming. I thought I'd die there."

"The Mizunos aren't some kamikaze soldiers. They're priests," Fowler said, his voice firm as he slipped his arms around Red's waist. "They'll scare off, we can buy the land cheap, and then sell it to those developers. It'll work this time. The rain that stopped the fire was a freak occurrence, as was that monster."

It was them? The fire, all those years ago? God, Berg wanted to pummel the men.

Red nodded. "A-and then we can leave this god-forsaken place."

"Yes, then we can leave." Fowler leaned back and cupped Red's face with one hand. "You want to move up north, right?"

Red nodded.

"Cabin just for us?" Fowler trailed his hand up and down Red's side.

"Yeah."

"I'll be able to take care of you, stop the nightmares."

"I'd like that, Leslie." Red sighed, dropping his head against Fowler's chest.

"Me, too, Red. Me too."

The men held each other, their quiet breaths loud in Berg's ears. His head buzzed, Berg's mind in overload.

"Well." Fowler straightened, and frowned. "Let's sober you up. You're weaving more than a sailor out at sea."

"'Kay, Leslie."

The sheriff pulled Red up, dusted him off, and made sure he stood by wrapping one arm around Red's waist. "Let's get you to the temple steps."

"'Kay."

"Come on, walk straight."

"I am!"

The men continued arguing as they walked from view, oblivious to Berg. He didn't move even when he couldn't hear their voices anymore. What could Red and Fowler do to scare off Tadashi? And how did they know the rest of the Mizunos hadn't been living at the shrine?

"Berg!"

He looked down. Kou was still sitting in his hands, his little paws out. "Oh, sorry Kou, I-I forgot about you. I'm sorry."

The little squirrel shrugged. "It happens a lot."

"It shouldn't."

Kou glanced away from Berg, his eyes filled with anxiety. "Are they going to hurt Papa?"

Shit. Fowler and Red. "No, Kou. I won't let them."

"We need to get the doctor first," Kou said. "Then talk to Papa."

"Freyja!" Fuck, Berg was just making a mess of things. "Right. Here, just get in my pocket, and don't talk to anyone no matter what!"

"I won't," Kou answered as he climbed up into Berg's breast pocket in his flannel. "I'll be good, promise."

"Great." Berg took off, going around the temple the way he came. The last thing Fowler and Red needed to see was him coming out of the same place they did. A shudder went through him at the thought. He was afraid of what the men might do in response considering how Fowler went after him when asking why he thought the Mizunos didn't come to town.

Berg ran through the trees and made his way to the dessert table. Dr. Franson was nowhere to be seen. He asked the ladies helping themselves to the small delights. They pointed him toward the craft table. At the table, the people pointed Berg to the games area. When Berg arrived, he decided Dr. Franson was a ghost. The man was impossible to find.

"Hey, Berg," a man called.

He spun around.

Dr. Franson smiled at him. "I hear you're looking for me."

"Yes!" Berg grabbed the doctor. "Freyja's in labor. Her water's broke."

"Whoa there!" The good doctor pulled back and Berg almost growled at the man. "I need to get my bag."

"You brought your bag?"

"Have you seen the size of your wife?" Dr. Franson asked, raising a brow.

"Point taken," Berg agreed. Freyja was huge.

"All this walking up and down the mountain probably helped things along finally," Dr. Franson said as they changed direction. "It'd be nice to get a road up here, make things easier for us and the Mizunos."

"Yeah, I suppose."

"It's nice to be able to come back after so long, but my old knees can't take the hike." Dr. Franson gave Berg a wry smile. "And if they're really opening the temple back up, it'd be nice for people to be able to come and go."

The doctor had a point, but Berg had other fish to fry at the moment and the doctor really needed to help Freyja. "Listen. I have to find Tadashi and then I'll be right back to help you with Freyja."

"Of course," Dr. Franson said. "Do you know where they took her?"

"The house," Berg answered. "Thanks, doctor."

He ran off without waiting for a response. Berg had to find Tadashi. He didn't know what they'd say. They hadn't spoken much since the night on the bluff. Yes, they worked together, but a gap had grown between them. It hurt. An ache burrowed deep inside Berg, but it was for the best. He knew that, he really did.

Too bad it hurt so bad.

People began laughing as he worked his way around the courtyard looking for Tadashi and Etsou. First the doctor, then Tadashi, people were putting two and two together, getting five, but coming up with the right answer anyway. People were starting to ask after Freyja, her departure and the doctor's already having made the rounds.

172

"She's finally having the baby, huh?" asked someone, who, Berg wasn't paying attention.

"Yup, now I have to—"

"Tell her good luck."

"Sure," Berg answered half-heartedly. He had to find Tadashi before something bad happened. His heart beat out of control as if he knew something would. Berg couldn't explain it. Just a feeling, but he could taste the charge in the air.

To his surprise, Berg found Tadashi in the main temple room, telling stories to an enraptured audience. Etsou was sitting in front, which explained why he couldn't find the youngster either. He was just as engrossed as everyone else. The fluid movements of Tadashi's arms, the delight on his face and his careful steps to and from the audience were like a dance, captivating everyone, including Berg: the tale of two lovers—a kitsune and her human lover—torn apart by their families.

He listened to the old story, unable to interrupt without drawing attention. A story from before anyone here was born. A story he felt Tadashi knew from personal experience. He didn't know why, but Berg was absolute in his conviction Tadashi had lived the tale he weaved for the townspeople.

With one final flourish of his hand, Tadashi stopped, frozen in place. The story at an end, as the ill-fated lovers triumphed over evil. Everyone gasped before erupting into loud cheers and clapping. Tadashi stood, blushed, and bowed. He rose with an uneasy smile.

Their eyes locked. Tadashi's grin faltered, replaced by grief. Berg stepped forward. He wanted to fix it. He wished to the gods to take away Tadashi's pain. A hurt he had put there. As he went to Tadashi, everyone else decided to as well. The crowd stood, rushing Tadashi.

They circled around him, the tide taking Tadashi out of the room and down into the courtyard. Berg followed. He had to talk to Tadashi before it was too late. Red and Fowler had something nasty planned. Berg had no idea what, but it wouldn't be pleasant. Berg pushed through the crowd, determined to pull Tadashi away.

"Hey!" yelled an all-too-familiar voice.

Berg stopped his quest for Tadashi and spun around, looking for Red.

"Hey! Jap!" Red shouted, weaving as he held onto the railing of the shrine's steps. "Come 'ere, you bastard!"

Berg was stuck. He wanted to go to Red and shut him up, but his instinct was to go to Tadashi to protect him from the bigoted asshole.

"H-how dare you take Alva, you fucking pervert!"

What?

Everyone in courtyard gasped collectively, which was followed by silence. People's heads volleyed between Red's belligerent expression and Tadashi's wide-eyed shock. Then Fowler showed up.

No.

"Something wrong, Red?" the Sheriff asked, looking way too smug for his own good.

"Yes!" Red swung around, nearly falling down the steps. Fowler caught him and steadied Red.

"Careful there, friend." Berg noticed Fowler put a hand to Red's lower back.

"I'm fine!" Red shrugged the sheriff off. "But that bastard needs to be arrested!"

"Oh?" Sheriff Fowler's gleeful gaze focused on Tadashi... who was now standing next to Berg, looking up the steps with a thoughtful expression.

When did he move?

"Yes," Red slurred. "That bastard kidnapped Alva!"

More gasps filled the courtyard. Angry expressions turned on Tadashi. *Whoa.* No. Alva went missing from the birthday party.

"My brother did no such thing!" Etsou yelled, surging forward. Tadashi dove for him, catching Etsou before he got up the stairs. He pushed his brother behind him.

"He took her!" Red insisted. "The pervert stole my niece!"

Fowler took out a pair of handcuffs and his gun.

"Wait a minute!" Berg shouted, stepping between Tadashi, his little brother, and the sheriff. "You can't just accuse a man of kidnapping. Especially one who wasn't even at the birthday party."

"How do you know he wasn't there?" the sheriff queried.

"Since when have the Mizunos come off the mountain except to get supplies or pay their taxes?" Berg answered, his chest heaving, pain lacing through him from the inside out. "Think about it, someone would have noticed the Mizunos at the party."

Fowler and Red scowled, then looked at each other.

This couldn't be happening. It couldn't. Tadashi wouldn't hurt a little girl. Hell, he *protected* Alva. Not that anyone would know. Tadashi had been a fox, although it was a small problem to reveal that tidbit of information to everyone.

"I bet you Alva doesn't even recognize him," Berg said, inspiration hitting.

"How could he not know about a little girl on the mountain?" Red asked, stumbling forward. "And they do come down time to time. You've seen them in town just as much as I have."

"How *could* he know? Or any of them?" Berg shot back. "Did you see them in town that day? Were taxes due or supplies being sent up? No. They weren't.

"And how could they know about Alva? Do you see a telephone line anywhere here?" Berg motioned to the treetops. "No, no line. They *just* had electrical installed in the house from the old lines."

Red sputtered.

"Show Tadashi to Alva. See how she reacts," Berg insisted. It was rash, but the best option he had to get public opinion on their side. A hand dropped on Berg's shoulder. He glanced over to see Edwin and breathed a sigh of relief. Hopefully he could talk some sense into his brother-in-law.

"Maybe he's right, Red," Edwin suggested. "Accidents happen. You understand all about that. Alva could've easily wandered off. People always say don't turn you back on your kids; they'll make a mess in less than a minute when you do. I'm just lucky Berg found my little girl as quickly as he did. And I have seen nothing but goodness from the Mizunos tonight."

A thin line formed on Red's face as he pressed his lips together. His face had blossomed into a scarlet color. His left eye twitched. Tadashi was whispering in Berg's ear, begging him to keep quiet.

"Show Tadashi to Alva," Berg pleaded. Tadashi grabbed hold on him, hissing in ear to quit. "Besides, have you heard her say she saw anyone besides that dog?"

Red shook his head, hands fisting at his side.

"She talks about the dog all the time now, doesn't she?" Berg drew closer to Red. "You'd think if she saw someone, she'd talk about it."

"Maybe not," Red snapped, his fists rose. "Maybe she's too traumatized."

She wasn't the fucked-up one. Red had the problems.

Sheriff Fowler pulled Red back, his glared at Edwin. "Get your daughter."

Edwin pushed through the crowd that had gathered. Berg watched as Jean Ann and Alva met him halfway. Edwin picked up his little girl, cuddling her to his chest, and came back to the shrine steps, using himself to block Tadashi from view. Edwin talked quietly into Alva's ear, then put her down, facing him.

"Okay, honey, here we go." Edwin stepped out of the way.

Alva's confused blue eyes darted around before landing on Tadashi. The biggest smile crossed her face and she dove forward. Everyone jumped to catch her.

"Doggie!"

Tadashi caught her, and she giggled.

"Doggie!"

Fuck, that's uncanny.

"Nope, no doggie, just Tadashi," he replied.

A confused frown twisted up Alva's pretty smile. "Doggie."

"Nope," he said again as she buried her face in his shoulder and hugged him.

Berg turned to the sheriff, Red and Edwin. "Does that look like a scared little girl to you?"

Edwin seemed optimistic. Red and Fowler crossed their arms. Berg surveyed the people in the courtyard. Cautious skepticism met Berg's gaze. Unfortunately, Red had planted a seed. One that everyone would be talking about. Somehow Berg had to dispel it completely, or it would haunt Tadashi and his family forever.

"Alva, honey," he said.

She turned to him.

How do I word this? "Look at Tadashi's face. Have you ever seen his *face* before?"

She turned, analyzing Tadashi with the wonder of little girl. Her little hands pressed against his cheeks, pulled on his hair and lips, and yanked on his ears. Tadashi let her, holding her and only grimacing when she yanked on him.

Alva frowned. "No."

"No what, Alva?" Berg pushed harder.

"Not his face."

Thank the gods. "So you haven't seen it?"

She shook her head.

"What about him? Have you ever seen a man who looked like Tadashi?"

"No." She sounded disappointed. Poor girl. Berg, however, was thrilled. "No man like Tadashi."

A whoosh of air was let out as everyone breathed out in unison. The anger in people's faces had lessened. Hopefully everyone would write off the incident as one of Red's drunken rants.

"Let her go."

Berg turned. Red shook on the steps, Fowler struggling to keep hold of him. Red's eyes were wide and furious.

"Let my niece go, you fucking Jap."

Shit.

Tadashi leaned down, but Alva continued to hold on. He desperately, but gently, pushed at her fingers and tried to reason with her. "Alva, let go, sweetheart."

Edwin agreed. "Yes, honey, let the nice man go."

Red began shouting. He fought Fowler so much the sheriff had to sit back to keep his hold on Red. Alva whined, burying herself in Tadashi's robes.

Berg shot a worried look to Edwin. He wrapped his large hands around his daughter. "Let go, honey. We'll go visit the desserts, okay?"

"Yes, desserts," Tadashi said. "My sister made some wonderful desserts, have you tried them?"

Alva shook her head and peeked over her shoulder.

Her dad smiled. "Let go, and we'll get a nice treat."

She finally did. Just in time. Edwin swooped her up the minute Red broke free from the sheriff.

Tadashi met the full brunt of Red's attack, knocked over on his back as Alva cried out, reaching for him. Edwin kept walking, calling to Jean Ann, as some of the others began herding the other children away. The men called out to Red, but Berg could see he was beyond reason. Etsou watched, frightened, jumping forward and back as Red and Tadashi tumbled on the ground.

"Etsou, you have to get out of here!" yelled Berg as he grabbed the kid, pushing Etsou toward the crowd. "You have to go now!"

Etsou shook his head and reached for his brother. A circle had surrounded Red and Tadashi: the men trying to separate the men, but unwilling to get hurt. Berg shoved the kid in someone's hands.

"Get him outta here with the rest."

"Sure thing, Berg. Shit!"

Etsou ducked out of the man's hands and into the crowd. Berg pushed his way into the circle. Red was on top of Tadashi, pounding him.

"No!" Etsou cried, rushing forward.

His yell distracted Red enough to stop, and Tadashi took advantage of it to push the man off him. Tadashi stumbled up, panting and bleeding.

"Stay back, Etsou!"

His brother whined, low and fox-like.

"Listen to him, Etsou," Berg said. "I'll help him."

Etsou retreated to the front of the crowd.

Red weaved around Tadashi, shuffling forward then back, pushing him, and repeating the move over and over again. The movements seemed like a drunken plan but Red did it with such concentration it couldn't be. When Berg's foot hit something hard, he glanced down. The temple steps. Red's movements had brought the circle back to the shrine. The question was why?

With a cry, Red lunged at Tadashi, tackling him. Etsou screamed and ran forward, Berg on his heels. He grabbed the kid and watched in horror as Tadashi rolled back and forth with Red, all the way to the steps. Red sat up, once again victorious, and leaned forward.

Berg let go of Etsou and ran forward.

Red yanked Fowler's gun away from him. Etsou's startled cry-howl pierced the air. Berg dove, slamming into Red. The gun went off. Fowler's scream filled the air. Berg looked up, seeing Fowler twisting on the ground, holding his leg.

"No!" Red jumped up, bending over the sheriff. "Leslie. Leslie, you all right?"

The man was going to bleed to death and despite being a total scumbag, he didn't deserve to die on the temple steps. With shaking legs, Berg stood up, pulling Tadashi with him. Tadashi gathered a crying Etsou in his arms, shushing him and cooing in his ear. Berg faced the crowd.

"Someone get Dr. Franson; he's in the house with my wife," Berg ordered, and a half a dozen people peeled off the crowd in a run toward the house. "The rest of you get the women and children away from here."

More people ran in the opposite direction, calling out to the others. Berg turned around, finding the sheriff still writhing on the steps. Red slowly stood, rolling his shoulders as he did, standing straighter than Berg had ever seen him do. His head turned, death in his eyes, focused entirely on Tadashi.

"No!" Berg shouted.

Tadashi's head snapped up.

But the gun was already leveled at him.

Red splattered across Tadashi's left shoulder as a boom echoed down the mountain. He crumpled to the ground, Etsou crying out. Berg lunged, hitting Red square in the stomach, satisfied when he heard a loud crunch.

They went down, Red cussing and shouting, but not giving up. They tumbled, rolling, hitting wood and floor. Red lifted a knee and got Berg in the nuts. He doubled over, gasping, eyes closed. Pain like never before shot through him, and Red pushed him off.

Berg forced his eyes open. They were back in the main room of the temple. *How did we get here?*

Red swayed on unsteady feet.

"Don't," Berg said. "Please don't."

Red turned around and laughed. "You some Jap lover? Is that what you are?"

"I respect life and the people in it," Berg ground out. "The Mizunos have been here for generations. They're as American as you or me."

"No they're not!" Red yelled. "They never will be!"

"They will if you let them!" Berg shouted. He pushed to his knees and sat up. God that hurt. He didn't want to move. Ever again. But it didn't hurt nearly as bad as the thought of losing Tadashi.

"Fucking Japs," Red swore, spinning back around. "If they just left, that'd solve everything."

His arm rose again, gun in hand. He glanced back at Berg and smiled. "Say goodbye to your friend."

A small voice cried out, "No!"

Berg jerked, startled, then looked down. Kou was still in his breast pocket, squirming his way out of it more like. Oh no.

"What is that?" Red was now stalking toward them. "Did that squirrel just talk?"

"No," Berg insisted and pulled Kou out of his shirt. He set the squirrel down and nudged him with his foot.

"Yes it did."

"Nope."

"That fucking squirrel talked!"

Berg shook his head and pushed to his feet. "I think you're a little drunk, Red. Give me the gun, and we'll take you to the hospital with Leslie."

Red's head swiveled in the direction of the sheriff, concern plain as day on his face. Then his expression hardened.

He turned back to Berg. "Those monsters don't belong on the mountain."

"There's no monsters here, Red. None," assured Berg. *Except maybe you.*

Red swallowed, eyes bloodshot. He shook. Men gathered in the entrance behind him, but Berg doubted Red had noticed. He was fixated on Kou. Berg took a step toward Red.

"Stay away!" he shouted, his pitch wavering unnaturally high. "Stay the fuck back!"

The men retreated down the steps. Damn. Everyone was afraid of the gun.

Little claws poked through Berg's pants. He cast his eyes down and saw Kou clinging to the back of his leg, shaking almost as much as Red.

"Red, please," Berg pleaded. "Give me the gun."

"No!" Red spun around making more people scatter. "Get away!"

The man was a menace.

"You're scaring your friends, Red."

"You're not my friend!" he yelled back.

"No, I'm not, but people here are," Berg said.

"No!" Red stumbled back toward Berg. His eyes were vacant, lost, like he was somewhere else. Maybe he was, Red never really came back from South Pacific. Not all of him. "Liars!"

Tadashi was now on the steps, slumped over on the railing, but determinedly pulling himself up anyway. A growl came from his direction. The sound was loud enough to catch Red's attention.

Red swayed. "Everyone stay away! You fucking Japs won't kill me!"

Berg ran for Red. He could feel Kou thump against his leg as the squirrel hung on.

Red's arm rose, aiming for Tadashi. Etsou sprang out from nowhere, knocking Red back. But he was small, so small compared to Red. Red grunted, but managed to keep himself upright.

"Fucking kid!" He pointed the gun down. "All you Japs are—"

"No!" The gun went off again as Berg slammed into Red.

Etsou screamed. Berg yelled, tears pooling in his eyes. He'd been too late. A kid. Red shot a fucking kid.

He wrestled Red, angry and determined. But Red fought with the same frenzy he did, his hold on the gun still firm. Then, out of the corner of his eye, Berg saw something.

"Etsou!" Tadashi limped toward his brother.

A hand rose from where the boy lay.

"Thank the gods." Tadashi cradled his brother's hand against his cheek and then shifted his gaze toward Berg and Red.

His eyes flashed, elongating, no longer human.

A punch to the side of his face made Berg yell out. His ears rang. Red laughed and shimmied out from under him and pointed the gun, but not at Berg.

His aim was off. Berg twisted around. *Tadashi.*

"Fucking Jap, bastard, why can't you just die?"

Berg jumped, and Red pulled the trigger.

A bubble popped inside him. Berg coughed and fell to his knees. Shouts thundered in his ears, and Berg watched as Tadashi slammed into Red, jarring the gun out of his hands. It skidded across the floor. Berg coughed again, this time something wet falling from his lips.

One of the men scrambled to the gun and picked it up, holding it in the air. "Stop, Red! Just fucking stop!"

Berg turned, his chest heavy. It was hard to get air. Everything burned. Tadashi rolled off Red, who was whimpering, curled up in a ball. Men from town dashed over to Red with rope. But Berg wasn't watching them. All he saw was Tadashi running to him.

"No!" Tadashi grabbed Berg. "Gods, no!"

"Ta—" Berg coughed. It hurt to talk. He put a hand to his chin, then observed his fingers. Was that blood?

"Lie down, just lie down."

He did, blinking. God, it was hard to keep his eyes open.

"Please, no, you can't do this!" Tadashi looked up. "Where's the doctor?"

Do what?

"No!" Tadashi's warm hands pressed against his chest.

"Papa!" Kou crawled out from somewhere. "If we get him to Freyja, you can put his light inside the baby."

"Hush," Berg gargled out, worried people would notice the talking squirrel. Besides, Kou was not talking sense.

"I need to pick him up," Tadashi said. He turned and desperation laced his plea. "Help me get him to Freyja."

The man must be nuts, he couldn't lift Berg.

A voice overhead agreed. "You can't risk moving him, Tadashi."

"Wh-wh—" More liquid spilled from his mouth. Berg choked. The edges of his vision blurred in and out. He couldn't get enough breath.

"Then where's the doctor!" Tadashi yelled. Tears were falling from his eyes. Berg reached for him. He didn't want Tadashi crying. He'd cried enough.

"Tadashi!" A woman's voice cut through all the men's voices. "Tadashi! Berg! I have—oh my gods."

Airi's face loomed over Berg. Why was she here? Her head rose as Tadashi let out an anguished wail, joined by another smaller one.

"I'm too late. I can't do it now." Tadashi's head fell onto Berg's chest. His fingers curled into Berg's side. Warm and hard, digging in deep like they'd never let go. His hot tears joined the heat building inside Berg. "I—no!"

Tadashi rose and pressed his hands against Berg's chest, determination in his eyes. Airi shouted. "Stop!"

"I can't."

"You must."

I'm dying, Berg finally realized. His breath rattled in and out of his lungs. His ears hurt, as did his throat. The bubble inside him pressed everything out. It was his blood he had seen. Tadashi knelt back, his eyes filled with sadness, tears still staining his face. His mouth opened and closed as he shook his head.

A cry, not from Tadashi, made Berg roll his head to his side.

A wee babe wrapped in a blanket was bundled in Airi's arms. He tilted his head back. She smiled down at him.

"Meet your son, Per."

Berg smiled. He knew he'd been right. Pain burst through his chest, causing his own tears. "Ah!"

Tadashi leaned over him. His face hovered just above Berg's.

"Oh! Ah!"

"Berg."

His name was so soft on Tadashi's lips. So much agony filled one word.

Berg stared at Tadashi's dark eyes and saw the fox lurking just beneath their depths, anger building inside the beautiful man. He pressed his palm against Tadashi's chest.

"Love."

Confusion replaced the anger.

Berg pressed harder, his chest exploding. "Love. Always love." Gods he hoped Tadashi understood.

Wet drops fell on his cheeks. Tadashi's pained eyes stared at him, sobs falling from the fox. His hands once again covered Berg's heart, and he whispered the two best words Berg had heard in his life into his ear.

"Always love."

Part Three
Still Here

Chapter Fourteen

His reflection in the mirror—the spitting image of his Grandpa Berg as his Nana Freyja would say—showed Dag's unease plainly. The letter in his hand felt like a stone, ready to crush him depending on what it said. Either way, his life was about to change forever. He had been waiting, working, and praying at the shrine for this moment but now that the letter had arrived, he wasn't sure he could open it.

Dag knew the answer. He'd passed all phases of the application process with flying colors. At his final interview, they practically offered him a spot then and there. They couldn't say anything of course, but their actions spoke loudly. The handshakes and the thumps on the back reinforced his assessment of the situation.

A situation, a problem really, he had created for himself.

Tadaaki had been hurt once when they were kids and it frustrated Dag not to be able to help his friend or make him better. If he'd been a doctor, he could've helped Tadaaki. Dag could've done something to make Tadaaki stop whimpering in pain, but he'd been just a kid, unable to do anything. All he did was hold onto Tadaaki and cry, scared and wondering when an adult would show up to help them.

That one moment changed Dag's whole life. It was the reason he worked so hard in high school and college, the driving factor behind him seeking out the best medical school he could. To become a man who could protect Tadaaki from pain—except Dag was the one in pain. An insufferable ache burned in his chest because he knew… he really did know Tadaaki didn't need a protector. That had been made clear many times over.

Didn't stop Dag from wanting to, though.

An overwhelming urge to throw up struck without warning and Dag leaned over the sink, huffing and puffing as pain from the stomach cramps blanked out all thoughts. He fought back the bile and the frustration building inside him. He was supposed to be celebrating, be happy his career choice was going the way he wanted it to.

A crinkle and a flash of white caught his eye. Dag's gaze turned to the letter in his hand.

He stared at the envelope. If he opened the letter, Dag would have to face the truth. He wasn't sure he could.

The finality of being accepted into the medical school of his choice was here, and all Dag wanted to do was run back to Tadaaki and forget. At least at the shrine Dag would have the comfort of his best friend one more time, even if their time together was limited.

Now everything would change.

If he opened the letter, he knew his time with Tadaaki would turn to a weekend here or there, celebrating Obon would be a memory, and Tadaaki's and Dag's paths would veer even farther apart.

Would Tadaaki forget his face? Would they only say hello in passing? Those were Dag's greatest fears. To be forgotten by the one person who meant the most to him.

Too bad Dag didn't mean the most to Tadaaki.

"Whoa there," Jules said, his face filling the mirror behind Dag. "You all right, man?"

"Yeah," Dag answered, lying through his teeth.

The look on Jules face said he knew it, too.

"I'll be fine."

"'Kay."

"Really."

"I believe you," Jules answered, but he crossed his arms and lifted one brow, calling bullshit without saying so.

Jules's dark gaze went to Dag's hand. He narrowed his eyes, reading the label. Dag dropped his hand and pushed away from the sink. He slid around Jules and walked back into his room.

Boxes were strewn across the floor. Suitcases had been packed and lined up. Hell, Dag had even vacuumed the carpet. He didn't think he'd done that all year. His computer was put away in its carrying case and his iPhone was plugged into the wall. Fortunately, the bed was still made and nothing had been thrown on top of it. Dag collapsed on the edge of it, head in hands, elbows on knees.

He had to be happy. He had one more night here before he went home for the summer. *One*. Dag had one summer left before he and Tadaaki became strangers.

The bed dipped. Dag cocked his head and looked at Jules. The scowl on Jules's face didn't suit him. It was too serious. Dag opened his mouth to rib Jules but got cut off.

"It's not healthy."

"Excuse me?"

"Pining over a straight boy, one that will never love you back, is not healthy," Jules said.

Dag groaned. He so didn't want to have this conversation again. They'd had it a million times. Well, maybe not a million, but a lot.

"I know you don't want to hear it, but it's time you let that boyhood crush go." Jules placed a hand on Dag's thigh. "You deserve to be happy and with someone who cares about you back."

The gentle tone coming from Jules felt odd. Dag frowned and studied his friend. Jules's dark hair obscured his eyes, but his jaw clamped tight. His neck and chest were flexed and rigid. The knuckles on Jules's fingers were white, his grip on Dag increasing as the pause between them deepened. All of it screamed anger and hostility, two emotions Dag never saw on Jules.

"What's wrong?" he asked, worried and a little scared.

"What's wrong is that you've spent our entire college career pining after a guy who doesn't give two shits about you," spat Jules, flicking one wrist dismissively.

"Hey—"

"And I'm tired of watching you hurt over him."

191

Dag's rising temper cooled. Jules sounded so defeated, upset *for him*. Dag couldn't be angry with his friend for wanting him to be happy.

"I'm the stupid one who can't let go," Dag said then breathed in, trying to steady himself. "If I'm hurting it's my own fault at this point."

Jules nodded, and thankfully, didn't press the issue.

"So, you want to help me finish cleaning before I head home tomorrow?" Dag asked, hoping he could change the subject.

"Were you accepted?"

Huh? What? Jules nodded down. Dag followed his friend's gaze. Oh, the letter. "I dunno. Haven't opened it."

"You were pretty sure they'd take you."

"Yeah."

Silence drew out between them but Dag didn't make any move to open the letter. Jules finally shook his head, sighing, probably guessing Dag wanted Tadaaki to be the first to know.

"I hope you get everything you want at Berkeley," Jules offered, giving Dag a smile.

"Me too." Except he couldn't bring the one thing he wanted. Tadaaki.

Jules stood, offering Dag a hand. "Come on, let's see what's growing in your fridge."

"Nah, I thought it'd be more fun for the landlord to find a new pet."

Laughter broke up the awkwardness that had filled the room. Jules's wide smile was genuine and acted as a balm to Dag's bruised spirits.

"You gonna be okay?" Jules asked.

Dag stood. "I will be."

He somehow had to face the summer, which meant he'd have to face Tadaaki. If he was truly going to succeed in his new life, he'd have to let the old one go. He knew that. Known it for a while really.

He just didn't like it. Not that he had to, but letting go would make things easier. The letter had been the reminder that it was time for him to grow up, and didn't that just suck?

It was time. For the sake of his heart, Dag needed to move on. Now if he could just convince his heart what his head knew.

Jules wrapped an arm around his waist as they made their way out of the bedroom and to the kitchen.

"It's going to be okay."

"I hope so."

* * * * *

A rustle made Dag twitch, his brain partially aware movement was happening in his room.

"Rise and shine!" his mom sang.

Bright sunlight burst in through the windows just as Dag opened his eyes. "Ahh! Crap. Mom!"

He threw an arm over his face but his eyes already burned.

She chuckled and swatted his feet. "You got in really late last night. I didn't have the chance to say hello."

"So you thought it'd be fun to torture me first thing in the morning?" He just wanted to sleep. Was that too much to ask?

"Your dad needs help in the barns."

Apparently so.

"Up and at 'em. I got breakfast made."

"You have way too much energy for an old person."

That earned him a butt swat.

"That's child abuse," Dag teased.

His mom huffed. He imagined she had rolled her eyes at him, too. "I'll give you child abuse."

Dag heard the clank of ice cubes and sprang up in bed. "I'm up. I'm up. I swear to the gods, I'm up."

His mom cackled. She held a pitcher of ice in her hands. Dag snarled at her, but she seemed to think it was funny because she laughed harder.

"Please don't freeze me."

"I made waffles."

Bribes worked. "Pecan?"

"Yup. Nice and warm too."

"Do we have brown sugar?"

"Are you my kid?"

Dag smiled. "Dad insists that I am."

His mom's bright blue eyes sparkled and she grinned. "Then maybe that's why you're so smart, because he's sure not."

Dag stepped off the bed, inching along the wall while keeping an eye on his mother. "Don't let him hear you say that. You might make him cry."

"I never make Per cry."

"That's not what Nana Freyja says!" Dag sprinted out the door before his mom could catch him and practically dove into the bathroom. He'd experienced ice torture one too many times to think his mom wouldn't follow through on that one.

He quickly got his business done and was at the table eating his fill of waffles when his dad walked through the back door. His mom leaned into his dad with familiarity, getting a hug and a peck on the check in return. His dad cuddled against his mom and held onto her for a minute. Dag chuckled at his parents' behavior, finally getting noticed in the process.

"Morning, Dag." His dad sat down, grinning at him. "You got in late."

"Yeah, I overslept yesterday." *Because I stayed up the whole night since I was nervous about the letter and seeing Tadaaki again.*

"As long as you drove safe, that's all that matters."

"I did."

"Alva, honey, are there any more of those waffles?" his dad asked, leaning back in his chair.

His mom reached around, placing a plate of piping hot waffles in front of his dad, getting another kiss from him. Dag watched, longing for the same thing, wanting the same kind of loving relationship his parents had. Someday. Maybe. When he could stomach the idea of that person not being Tadaaki.

"You okay, son?"

Dag met his father's troubled expression. "Yeah, fine. Just a long drive home is all."

For a minute Dag thought his dad would argue, but he just nodded. "You don't have to help in the barns if you don't want to. I can have one of the part-timers come in. I need to get to the clinic anyway."

The veterinary clinic was twenty feet from the kitchen, seeing as it was in their house but Dag appreciated his dad giving him an out.

"Okay, thanks." He rose, grabbing his plate, but was stopped.

His mom had a handful of his shirt. "You sure you're all right?"

Why did everyone keep asking him that? It's not like he was dying, though it kind of felt like it.

His dad spoke up. "You hear anything about school?"

Ah. Maybe that was it. "Yeah, but I don't want to say anything yet."

Their expressions darkened, obviously taking his answer the wrong way.

"I want to talk to Tadaaki first." Dag forced a smile.

His parents' faces changed to ones of understanding, both of them nodding in sync. His mom gave him a pat. "I heard he's doing a blessing today over at the Grahns'."

"Yeah?"

His dad chuckled. "It's the annual blessing, the one the old geezer's insisted on every spring since I was born."

"Ah." Dag joined in his dad's amusement. Apparently they had had a heifer that kept getting sick until his dad had been born at the temple and it miraculously healed, never getting sick again. The old Mr. Grahn insisted it was because the Mizunos opened their temple to the town again. "Poor Tadaaki. Why isn't his dad doing it?"

"Etsou had a blessing for a family," his mom answered. "A granddaughter or something."

"Ahh. Okay. Makes sense." Dag squatted down by the door and grabbed his shoes. "I'll try the Grahn's, then."

His heel slipped into the second shoe, and then Dag pushed open the door to the back porch. A huge-ass dog bounded past him and began running around the table. Dag frowned. He hadn't remembered seeing a dog like that—

"Alva..." His dad's face was pinched.

Uh-oh.

"Yes, Per?" His mom's voice sounded sweet like honey.

"Whose dog is this?"

Shit. Dag turned, hoping to make it out of firing range in time.

"Why, dear."

Dag shook his head. When would his mother learn?

"It's ours."

"Alva." The restraint in his dad's voice was not a good sign. "I said no more dogs!"

"Hey, Dag!" his mother called, ignoring his dad.

"Yeah?"

"Thank Aunt Airi for the sweets."

"Okay, Mom."

His dad frowned. "What sweets?"

"I am not involved." Dag took off for his beat-up old car at a run.

Chapter Fifteen

The warm air blowing in from the teashop was a welcome relief. All morning, Dag had been one step behind Tadaaki and couldn't seem to catch up with him. Being May, the weather still held a chill even in the valley, and Dag needed to warm up.

Familiar faces called out and people waved to him as Dag walked up to the counter in Rei's Tea Europium, and put in his order. He carefully carried the teapot and cup to a chair and sat down. He dipped the tea strainer into the water and sat back, waiting for the tea to brew.

Carina and Tait stopped by for a few minutes. Too energetic for Dag. They wanted to know when everyone would be getting together now that he arrived in town, and by the way, where was Tadaaki? Dag had to beg off from any shenanigans the two were up to. Exhaustion had worn him down mentally and physically.

Dag needed today to be over. He needed to face Tadaaki, tell him about med school, and finally let go of his unrequited love. It had to be today. Tadaaki had always managed to deflect the subject, making his feelings known without saying as much to Dag.

Tadaaki was kind to a fault, never wanting to hurt anyone. The problem was, Dag did hurt. His pain was because of Tadaaki's kindness.

He needed to let it all go. Dag stared at the teapot, watching steam rise. The question was, could he really do it?

"Dag."

Someone shook his arm.

Dag blinked, the lights hurting his eyes as he opened them. When had he closed them? Nana Freyja stared down at him, the corner of her lips pulled up into a smile. "Tired, dear?"

"Nana." Dag reached around her for a hug. She squeezed back.

He let her go and surveyed the shop. Someone had put a blanket over him and the clock showed it was closer to dinnertime than lunch. Wow. He had slept through the lunch rush.

"You were snoring," she said as she sat down across from him.

"Was not," he replied, defensive and a little embarrassed he fell asleep.

She chuckled but didn't say anything more. Instead, Nana picked up a mug, handing it to him. "Here. I got you some fresh brew."

"Thanks, Nana."

"So what's got you so worn out?"

"Looking for Tadaaki."

"Ah, yes. I heard you two were playing leapfrog."

He stared at Nana. What a weirdo, but he loved her. "Something like that."

"He's at the school now," Nana said, "but he's supposed to go back to the temple soon. Airi probably wouldn't mind—"

"Dag!"

Nana Freyja and Dag turned to find Mr. Mizuno standing over them, a huge smile on his face.

"Long time! Are you back for the summer?"

"Mr. Mizuno." Dag put his tea on the table and stood, waiting while they all shuffled so Tadaaki's dad could sit down. "Yes, I am."

"Good. Tadaaki has been bouncing off the walls the last couple weeks waiting for you to get home."

"I doubt that." Tadaaki was probably busy chasing after Kou.

"He's missed you," Mr. Mizuno answered, his voice softening. "We've all missed you."

"Sorry I've been gone so much."

Mr. Mizuno pointed between him and Nana. "We all know how hard you've been working to get into medical school. We understand."

"Yeah. Still…" Dag didn't know what to say. They had all been so supportive and he just wanted to say fuck it all. All because he was acting like a five-year-old throwing a tantrum because he couldn't get his favorite toy.

"Trust me. I'm just glad you're home. Tadaaki hasn't been this happy in a—" Mr. Mizuno stumbled over his words before shaking his head and chuckling. "He's just happy you're home. Why don't you go on up to the temple and wait for him? He'll be there soon."

Dag glanced at Nana, checking with her.

She waved him off. "It's fine, Dag. Go on. Etsou and I have catching up to do."

"Are you sure?" She had that sad look again. Every time medical school came up, she got it. Dag wasn't sure it was okay to leave her.

Nana Freyja shook her finger at him. "Get going before I have your backside."

"Leaving."

Dag hustled out the door, excited to finally get to see Tadaaki again. The last thing he heard as he left was Mr. Mizuno commenting to Nana how much he looked like his Grandpa Berg.

* * * * *

Bored and tired of waiting, Dag swiped his finger across the screen of his iPhone. Another bird flew and smashed into the wood structures and pigs popped. Level after level he'd been killing the damn things, and he was starting to get pissed. Mr. Mizuno practically shoved him out of the teashop, okay he didn't quite do that, but he said Tadaaki would be home, Dag drove up the mountain just so he could finally tell Tadaaki about Berkeley… and say goodbye.

Of course, two hours later, Dag was convinced Tadaaki wouldn't be home any time soon. He sighed.

"Uh-oh, young man."

His nose got tweaked, and Dag looked up and smiled at his

'adopted' great-aunt Airi. Her steel gray hair was tied up tight in a bun, but the laugh lines around her eyes gave a youthful quality. She bent toward him, cupping her hand to her mouth.

"Something bothering you?"

Dag glared at her and got another bop on the nose.

"Don't you sass me, young man."

"Sorry, Aunt Airi." He rubbed his sore nose.

"You going to tell me what's upsetting you?" she asked again, sitting down next to him this time.

"Just wished Tadaaki was here."

"Ah." She nodded. "Have you texted him?"

"Yes."

"How many times?"

"Like twenty."

She smiled. "He'll get home soon. He's always happy to see you, you know that."

Dag nodded. She was right of course. Ever since he was six years old and got lost at an Obon festival where Tadaaki had found him, they'd been inseparable. Now... that was going to change. Permanently. Airi reached over and patted Dag's hand.

"Has your mother seen you yet?"

"Yes, and she said to send her thanks for the sweets."

Aunt Airi laughed. "Alva always had a sweet tooth."

"And a love for dogs," Dag replied, grinning. "She brought home another one this morning."

"It's a good thing Per's a vet and loves animals." Airi chuckled. "Almost as much as your grandfather."

"So everyone tells me." Dag laughed. "Dad almost blew a gasket this time."

"How many does that make?" she asked, her dark eyes lit up mischievously.

"Fifteen. It's a good thing we have a farm, otherwise we'd have nowhere to keep them all."

Airi reached over and patted Dag again. "You're probably right."

He nodded, wondering if this new dog was last straw that would break his dad's back. He hoped not.

Pushing up, Airi groaned.

"You all right?" Dag dropped his phone into his pocket and stood. He helped Airi the rest of the way to her feet.

She smiled. "Always so kind."

"Kindness is easy," Dag replied. She began to walk away when a thought struck him. "Hey, Aunt Airi?"

She turned, eyebrows up. "Yes?"

"You know my grandma well, right? You're her best friend."

"Yes…" she answered slowly.

Dag crossed the living room. "Nana Freyja always talks about Grandpa Berg and my dad and how proud of them she is in regards to their veterinary skills, but… "

"But what, dear?"

"It's nothing."

"Dag, you know me, ask."

He held his breath for a moment. Could he really ask? It all seemed so silly. "But she gets this sad look on her face whenever I talk about going to medical school."

Airi frowned.

"Have I disappointed her?"

Airi's jaw dropped. "How could you say that?"

"Well, my Dad and Mom always wanted me to go to vet school like him." Dag swallowed, his throat getting drier by the second because really, it was foolish to think his grandma loved him less for wanting to be a doctor. "So did Nana."

"Oh, Dag, is that why you've been so moody this afternoon?"

Uh, no, but he wasn't about to admit why to his great aunt so he nodded.

She swept Dag up in a hug and rocked him in her arms. "No, my dear boy, you haven't disappointed Freyja."

For the first time in months, Dag relaxed. He allowed his weirdo aunt to sway him in her arms and just felt the love rolling off her. She petted his hair, rubbing behind his ears like his dad did with dogs. Dag laughed and stepped out of Airi's arms.

"I'm not a dog!" he teased.

"You're a young pup to me," she replied, grinning. She ruffled his hair.

He stuck out his tongue.

Airi sighed, then gave Dag a strange look. "Freyja gets sad because she always said your grandpa Berg would've made a great doctor. He cared about people as much as you do, Dag."

Wow, um, how did he respond to that? No one had ever told him before.

"You also look like a younger version of him."

Yeah, Dag could see that. Lots of photo albums with his grandpa were at his Nana's house, and the resemblance was uncanny. It had unnerved him from time to time.

"You…" Airi tilted her head to the side, much like some animal would when assessing a human. "You are a lot like your grandfather, so she's probably remembering him when she looks at you."

Dag pressed a hand against his chest. No wonder she looked so sad, but how could he fix it? Should he stop going to her house?

"No."

He glanced at Airi.

She shook her head. "Your grandma loves you. It would break her heart if you stopped visiting her."

"It's creepy when you do that," Dag answered, but agreed whole-heartedly. He'd miss his grandma's stories.

Airi laughed. "I think it's fun."

Dag gave an exaggerated shudder.

"Oh, stop."

Giving Airi a wink, Dag sat back down. "I just don't want to make her remember the sad things."

"There were lots of good times, too," Airi replied, joining Dag again. "And the right people were punished for what they did and got help."

"Where did my great-uncle Red go?"

The question must've taken Airi off guard because she gaped a moment before recovering.

"No one has ever told me what happened after he was released from jail."

"Ah, well, I don't know—"

"You think anyone else will tell me?" interrupted Dag. Why knowing suddenly became so important to him, he didn't know; he just knew he needed an answer.

Airi bit her lip, apprehension written all over her. "Well, you see, dear, it's not a simple answer."

"Tell me, please."

She rubbed her temples, then sighed.

Victory!

"What I say doesn't go beyond these walls?" She pointed at him.

"Agreed."

"Okay." Airi took a deep breath in, then slowly let it out. "Your great-uncle Red was your mother's uncle."

He nodded.

"And your dad is Berg's child."

"Yes."

Where is this going?

"Are you giving me a riddle, Aunt Airi?"

She closed her eyes and shook her head. When she opened them, they were a little wet but clear. "Just trying to get you to connect the dots, but you must be only book smart."

"Excuse me?"

"When Red came back… there were issues."

"When was he released?" A sneaking suspicion filled Dag.

"When your parents were about your age."

"You mean when they first started dating."

She nodded. "I don't think he knew who Per was..."

"Did he figure it out?"

"It was decided he should move away before he could."

"Because?" The hair rose on Dag's arm.

"We were afraid he'd kill Per."

"Fuck."

"Dag! Language!"

"Sorry, Aunt Airi." He dipped his head. Still, curiosity won out. "Where is he?"

"If he's still alive—" Airi grimaced. "Which is possible, he'd be in Alaska with Old Sheriff Fowler."

"Alaska?"

"Yup."

"You really think he's still alive? He was a lot older than Nana Jean."

"It's possible, but even if he is, the sheriff knows Red isn't allowed to come back." Airi shuddered. "He was given a... *warning*... as to what would happen if they did."

"A warning?"

"My brother, Tadashi, gave it to him."

"That's right, he and Grandpa Berg were close friends, weren't they?"

"They were."

"Oh, uh, sorry." He hadn't meant to bring up so many bad memories; guilt washed over him. "You must miss them."

A flicker of something crossed Airi's face before she smiled. "Tadaaki fills his shoes, uh, well."

"Is that a nice way of saying those two are alike just like me and my grandpa Berg?" Dag grinned.

"In a way."

They sat in awkward silence for a moment as Airi considered him, her sharp eyes watching him astutely. Dag squirmed under the weight of her stare. He'd never seen her look so serious before, and he wasn't sure how to respond. Maybe he'd pushed Aunt Airi a little too far. Gods, where was Tadaaki?

"Is he still here?"

Dag and Airi jumped as Tadaaki burst through the door, looking about frantically. When Tadaaki's gaze fell on Dag, a smile bloomed. His long black hair stuck to his face, sweat dripping down his chest and under his arms. He was breathing heavily, and Dag swore he'd never seen anything more handsome in his life.

With a nervous laugh, Dag smiled. "Hey."

"Is everything okay?" Tadaaki scoured the room as if some ghost was about to pop out and scare them.

Dag laughed. "Yeah."

"But your messages, they said to come home, that it was urgent!" Tadaaki pulled out his phone and shook it. "Etsou even called me. He said it was important."

"He's your dad, and he likes me."

Tadaaki scowled. Airi laughed. Dag glanced between the two. Why did they always laugh when Dag pointed out the obvious? The look they shared when he said things, like now, annoyed him. Dag always felt he was missing out on some inside joke. Tadaaki mumbled, then huffed.

"Did you run up from the parking lot?"

Tadaaki's scowl deepened. "Yeah, we really need to consider an escalator instead of stairs."

"You'd ruin the beauty of the temple," Dag admonished, the corner of his mouth turned up. "Lazy bum."

Tadaaki sputtered. "L-lazy?"

"Aunt Airi was telling me you skipped cleaning duty on the temple," Dag teased, leaning back and enjoying watching his best friend fidget and become impudent. It suited him.

Tadaaki rolled his eyes and crossed his arms. "I did, too, do the cleaning."

"I thought temple priests were supposed to be role models?"

The corner of his mouth turned up in a sly smile. Airi chuckled and nodded.

Did Tadaaki just squint at his aunt?

"Don't look at your aunt like that!"

Tadaaki gaped at Dag. "Like what?"

"Like you want to skewer her alive! She's your aunt, be nice! You can't treat her that way."

"She's not my—" Tadaaki stopped and shook his head, grumbling. "Yeah, I suppose."

Airi laughed louder. See? It was stuff like that that confused Dag to no end.

"She's old!"

"Hey!" Airi stopped laughing, and was now sullen, but Tadaaki began chuckling, sending his aunt a sly grin.

"You are," Dag replied, smiling himself.

"You two get out of here before I make you scrub the temple floors," Airi threatened with a wink, her voice playful. "You know I will."

Oh gods, no. He'd done that one too many times and had no desire to kill his knees today. Dag hopped up. "Leaving."

"Me, too." Tadaaki spun around and ran straight into Kou.

"Papa!" The little boy wrapped his arms around Tadaaki's legs.

He swooped down and picked up his son, a huge smile on his face. Tadaaki peppered Kou's face and swung him around, tickling his sides. The little boy giggled and squirmed, but didn't try to escape.

"No, stop, Papa!"

Tadaaki stopped.

"No, tickles!" The boy squealed as Tadaaki started tickling again.

When both were out of breath, Tadaaki put his son down. Happy as can be by the contented glow that radiated from them, Dag forced a smile as he watched the pair, sad, a tug in his chest reminding him that he and Tadaaki were in fact different in one small way.

Tadaaki stood back up, looking over his shoulder at Dag. "Want to step out for a bit?"

"Can you?" Dag glanced at Kou, who was now seated at the kotatsu. He wouldn't pull Tadaaki away from Kou. The two were inseparable, almost like he and Tadaaki used to be beforehand. He wasn't jealous per se. Not really. He understood Tadaaki had to look after his kid. Dag just missed his friend sometimes.

"I'll, uh, look after Kou," Aunt Airi offered. "You all know how much I love spending time with my great-nephew."

"Are you sure?" Tadaaki asked, still holding onto Kou.

Kou leaned over and narrowed his eyes at Dag. The two were so alike it was kind of creepy. "You can go."

"Gee, thanks." Dag bowed with a flourish, then stood back up.

Kou bared his teeth at Dag. Dag scooted back, afraid of getting bitten... again. He was the only one Kou ever bit and it sucked.

"Would you two stop," Tadaaki said with a sigh. "You're always at each other's throats. It'd be nice if my best friend and kid got along for once."

"He started it," Kou and Dag said together, pointing at each other.

"You both started," Airi declared. She swatted Dag and gave Tadaaki a push. "Now you two run off. I'll get Kou his dinner."

The kid brightened at the mention of food. "What's for dinner?"

Dag pulled Tadaaki out the door and laughed when his head whipped around at the mention of his favorite tofu dish. "Want to go back?"

"Nah, it's okay," Tadaaki said, following Dag outside. "I haven't seen you since your last break."

"Yeah, it's been awhile."

"I've missed you."

Dag snorted, the pain rearing back up. "You've been too busy to miss me." He then added with a mumble, "Have been forever."

"Hey." Tadaaki grabbed Dag's arm. "You okay?"

"Sorry." Dag closed his eyes, willing himself to be excited that Tadaaki actually made time for him instead of being mad he hadn't had any yet. "I know it's not your fault. I'm just being pissy."

"Really, Dag, what's up?"

Black eyes like the night sky, worried, staring straight at Dag, were there to meet Dag's when he opened them. He forced a smile. He was really being selfish wanting Tadaaki for himself, but they never got time together. They'd be getting even less when Dag started medical school in the fall.

"It's nothing. I'm just tired from all the traveling." Dag shifted, clearing his throat. He rubbed the back of his neck. "Can we just hang? Not drive into town?"

Tadaaki frowned, his brows pulling together. "Really, Dag, is everything all right?"

"Yeah," Dag answered with a rough tone. Damn. It always made his voice sound deeper than it normally was. "I just… I just need it to be the two of us. I do have news."

Worry immediately occupied Tadaaki's eyes.

"It's nothing bad," Dag assured him quickly. "Really, it's not."

Tadaaki's shoulders slumped. "Fuck, Dag, you had me worried for a minute."

"Well, it's not like my naked toddler showed up at school in the middle of AP Chem our junior year looking for me," Dag replied, biting his tongue when he was finished. Damn. He was just all sorts of foot in mouth today. He really needed to get his head in the game.

"Where'd that come from?" Tadaaki asked, rounding on Dag. Fury had his nostrils flaring and eyes narrowing.

Dag closed his eyes again. He hated seeing Tadaaki upset with him. It'd happened so much over the past five years. They continued to grow further and further apart, going their separate ways, becoming different people. It made Dag want to hold tighter and never let go… but Tadaaki was never *his*.

Firm, callused fingertips pulled on Dag's chin.

"Dag, please." Tadaaki's voice had softened. "Something's obviously wrong."

"You don't want to hear it." Dag didn't want to say it. Being jealous of a kid was stupid and just made him an ass. Tadaaki pulled Dag into his arms, holding him awkwardly since Dag was now bigger than he was.

"Dag, I'm your best friend."

Those words said it all and none of it.

"Dag. You're scaring me."

"Let's go for a walk," Dag said as he stepped back. Dag blinked rapidly as he opened his eyes. He had to swallow several times before making his throat open up and work probably. The whole getting the words out and such. "Come on, this way."

Not waiting for Tadaaki, Dag circled around the house to a badly overgrown path. No one used it, which was a shame. It led to one of the most beautiful spots in their busy town.

"Dag, I don't think—" Hesitance filled Tadaaki's voice.

"Just come."

"I—okay, Dag."

Footsteps followed him through the trees and brush. Dag sighed in relief. He wasn't sure Tadaaki would come along. He avoided this path as much as he could and only came when Dag asked him to.

"Thanks, Tadaaki."

"Sure."

They walked in silence up the forgotten path and quickly reached the bluff overlooking the town. The bright lights clashed with the darkening night sky, but you could see for miles and Dag loved the view. He came when he could, which wasn't often enough.

They sat down on a log Dag had found and rolled to the bluff when they were in junior high. Tadaaki's expression was blank and focused out in front of them. Dag, as usual, got distracted by Tadaaki's closeness. He wanted to reach out and hold Tadaaki's hand like when they were kids.

It couldn't hurt. Not one more time.

He reached out and took the hand he'd been longing for, wrapping his own around it. Tadaaki jumped at the contact but didn't pull away. He grinned at Dag.

"Scared of the dark?"

"It's not totally dark yet," Dag answered.

"So you are?"

"Do I get to hold your hand if I am?" Dag queried.

Tadaaki shook his head but his eyes were filled with mirth. "If you want me to give you a bath and read you a bedtime story."

"Sure, why not, everyone could use a little love sometimes."

Tadaaki jolted, gave Dag a questioning look, but didn't say anything and went back to watching the town. He also didn't let go of Dag's hand. The warm tingling sensation that he always felt when Tadaaki touched him flowed from his hand to his heart, making it thud a little quicker and a little harder. The sun's descent continued until the black sky hung over them and stars peeked through the veil.

With a deep breath in, Tadaaki turned to Dag. "You want to tell me what's up?"

Ah. The quiet had been so nice and being able to hold Tadaaki's hand without getting teased—or a flustered best friend—had been good while it'd lasted. Dag shot Tadaaki an apologetic look.

"I got accepted."

Bewilderment struck Tadaaki's beautiful face until comprehension dawned. "You made it in? To Berkeley's medical school?"

He nodded, contented because of the amount of pride rolling off Tadaaki as he jumped up and yelled.

"That's awesome! So fucking cool, Dag! I can't believe it! Well, I can, you're determined and focused like that, but oh gods, we have to celebrate." Tadaaki paced around the log, waving his hands. "We have to call the gang, and maybe we can—"

"No."

"We—wait, what?" Tadaaki stopped and stared at him. "Why don't you want to celebrate? You've worked so hard for this. You've wanted this since I broke my leg that summer you were seven."

"Yeah, I hated not being able to help you," Dag agreed as he stood up. "You've always been what's most important to me."

"That's what best friends are for," Tadaaki said, sidestepping Dag's comment. He bounced in excitement. "And for throwing parties to celebrate each other's awesomeness."

Dag frowned. No, that's not what he meant. Tadaaki knew that.

"We should throw the party at the temple. Oh, we should call the gang and get planning. We've got lots—"

"No."

Tadaaki sighed and threw Dag a nasty face. "Why?"

"Because I'm celebrating right now with the one person I want to be with."

"Don't be silly, everybody wants a party."

"Not me." Dag grabbed Tadaaki, whose stunned expression should have warned him. "I want this, here, with you."

Wait, no, that wasn't how it was supposed to come out. Wording wasn't happening right.

"I told you, I am celebrating, right now. Here. With you."

"Like that's a celebration."

Dag pulled Tadaaki into his arms. "For me it is."

"What're you doing?" Tadaaki pushed against him, but Dag held on tighter, burying his nose in the crook of Tadaaki's neck.

Gods, he was going to miss this man so much. Despite their differences and fights over the years, they kept coming back to each other. Dag just yearned for more. The sparks got bigger and better every time they touched. It was like a jolt that went to his heart every time. It sucked he was the only one feeling it.

"Dag." Tadaaki chuckled, fidgeting in Dag's death grip. "You're being really weird tonight."

"I know." He did. Dag was just all out of sorts knowing he'd really be leaving Tadaaki behind this time. Coming home was only going to get harder. If they'd had more of a connection, he'd feel better about going away. "Sorry."

"Just tell me what's wrong."

211

Dag squeezed harder.

"Dag!" Tadaaki coughed.

He let go, but only enough to put Tadaaki at arm's length. Dag swept his thumb across Tadaaki's jaw, smiling at the disbelief Tadaaki wore. It was all he could do. Had done for years. Ever since Kou showed up. Gods he was a jumbled mess right now.

"I'm sorry Kou and I fight so much."

"Uh, wait, we—" Tadaaki stepped back. "That's not what we were talking about."

"I know."

"You're all over the place tonight."

"Yeah." Dag laughed, but it wasn't a happy one. "I am. I'm really leaving this time."

Shocked silence met his statement. Tadaaki watched him, unmoving, eyes wide.

"With medical school, how often do you think I'll get to come home? See you?" Dag inhaled sharply. "Fuck, the next time I come home you'll probably be married to some girl. Then we'll just be strangers waving hi at Target as we pass."

"Excuse me?"

"You heard me," Dag answered, frustrated as all get out. "Kou's getting older; just because his mom's out of the picture doesn't mean you'll be single forever."

"But… I—no—wait," Tadaaki stammered. "You're not making sense."

"I know. I do think it's great how good of a dad you are." Dag put a hand through his hair and pulled on the long locks. "It just sucked we went in different directions so soon. I think that's part of the problem. Knowing we're not the same. I… I always thought we were? When I see Kou, I'll apologize."

Tadaaki bent his head, openly staring at Dag like he was nuts. Maybe he was. He felt so much, for one person, and he couldn't show it. Tadaaki never gave him the chance and now he was going away, not just months, but years.

"Dag, you're so not making sense."

212

"It's all jumbled. I can't word it right now."

Tadaaki snorted. "Obviously, but there's something more going on."

"Gee, can you tell?" Dag snapped, regretting it immediately when Tadaaki flinched. He blew out a deep breath, working hard on reining in his jumbled emotions. It was hard. It was like all of them wanted to spill out tonight whether he wanted them to or not. Maybe somewhere deep inside his subconscious he finally wanted an out-and-out rejection so he could move on. Not that he believed he really ever could.

"Why are you mad?"

"Because I want you and I can't have you!" Shit. Foot to mouth.

Tadaaki's rigid stance and wide eyes made him look like a scared animal about to be shot down.

"I'm sorry, I shouldn't have said that."

"Why did you say that?" Tadaaki asked as he moved away from Dag.

Gods, every step was a knife in the heart. They really were getting older, going their separate ways. Dag always believed they'd be together forever when they were young. Every part of him screamed out to grab Tadaaki and never let him go. Not this time.

Too many times he watched Tadaaki walk out a door, a room, a friend's house and wished he had the courage or the ability to make him stay.

"You know I'm gay. Have been since forever," Dag said. "I've been out and proud since junior high."

Tadaaki chuckled nervously. "You never pussyfoot like this, Dag."

"And I've… you…" Dag yelled in frustration. "And you have Kou. You're straight."

"I—oh."

Tadaaki was close to the path back to the shrine now. Dag jumped over the log and grabbed hold of Tadaaki's hand. He brought it to his forehead. "Do you know how much of a shock it was to find out you knocked up some girl and kept it from me?"

213

There it went, Tadaaki's nervous laugh again. Dag lifted his head, the ache from loving Tadaaki splitting him in two.

"Look at me, Tadaaki! Really look." Dag bit the inside of his cheek. Gods, he wanted to cry. All he wanted to do was celebrate getting into med school with his best friend, and he had to fuck it all up. But there was no going back now. "I am who I am, and I wouldn't want to be any other way. I live in a time and place where I can be me, but I can't have you. It hurts."

Apprehensive eyes filled with wonder stared back at Dag. If only he could say what he wanted to, but his throat grated so bad he couldn't speak. He laid his hand against Tadaaki's heart.

"Always."

"What did you say?" Tadaaki's pitch twisted and his voice shook.

Why couldn't he get the words out? Three stupid little words, and he couldn't say them. Dag pressed harder. "Always."

"Always?"

Dag nodded, closed his eyes against the pain.

"Dag, look at me."

He shook his head. He couldn't.

"Please."

So he did. Dag found excitement facing him. Cautious, wary optimism. It confused the fuck out of him. This whole night did.

"Just, let me…" Tadaaki trailed off. "It's… Kou. Things aren't what they seem."

What did that mean? Did… was Tadaaki? Hope rose.

"Don't ask."

The hope faltered. "Ask what?"

Tadaaki pressed his palm against Dag's chest, closed his eyes, and pressed his lips together in concentration. Dag glanced down when a heat sunk into his shirt. A weird glow came from Tadaaki's hand. When did he grab a glow stick? A sharp intake of air had Dag looking back at his best friend. The anxiety from before was gone. In fact, a new, totally different emotion had replaced it.

"I know this light," Tadaaki murmured as his voice caught. His gaze, filled with so much awe, zeroed in on Dag.

Why was he crying?

"I know this light." He hiccupped. "I've seen it before."

"Um…" Dag's confusion grew. Had Tadaaki hit his head on a low branch?

"I know this light." Tadaaki wrapped his arms around Dag. "It's the same. Still so good. So warm. Why didn't I see it before?" He shook his head, talking more to himself than to Dag. "Because I was afraid. A fool. So much time's been wasted."

"Tadaaki?"

Not that he was going to complain about his best friend holding him. It was Dag's dream come true. His heart was jumping for joy and wanted to sing out to the world that Tadaaki was finally looking at him. Like he loved Dag. Maybe Tadaaki wasn't as straight as Dag had assumed. That kind of thing… not everybody figures it out as quickly as Dag did. Some people struggled with it. Had Tadaaki struggled?

"Tadaaki, you okay?" He wanted to make the tears stop. Dag wanted more than anything to make Tadaaki smile.

"Yes," Tadaaki mumbled before sliding his head so he could look up at Dag. "I've missed you so much."

His heart soared. Dag shouldn't be happy, but he was. Those really were tears.

"You have no idea how much I've missed you."

Was that? No, Dag must be seeing things. People did not have tails.

Tadaaki laughed. "Guess third time's the charm? Although in this case, it's really a second chance."

"What are you talking about?"

Tadaaki shook his head. "I'll explain later."

"Are we getting together? 'Cause I'm getting mixed signals here, and I want to be clear about what's happening." He needed the words, the reassurance.

"We'll figure it out, Dag."

"What about school? The temple?"

Tadaaki chuckled again and squeezed. "I said we'll figure it out." He cupped Tadaaki's cheek, his heart clearly thinking he was trying to run a four-minute mile. So many different emotions radiated off Tadaaki. What was going on? The change in Tadaaki confused him.

"You came back."

"Of course I did." Dag brushed a hair away from Tadaaki's face, seeing love there and wanting for the world to taste it. Could this really be happening? Finally. After all this time? "I'll always come home to you."

Tadaaki pressed his lips together and nodded. His chin thumped against Dag. Tears fell steadily from his eyes.

"Tadaaki, you're freaking me out."

"I'm sorry—" He gulped. "I really am. It's been so long. I nearly gave up waiting."

"For what?"

"This." Tadaaki kissed Dag. A soft, gentle kiss on the mouth. One Dag felt crackle down to his toes, to the ends of his hair and straight into his heart. Fuck, he could barely breathe. Tadaaki pulled back. "Welcome home, Dag."

He nodded, dazed, and reached for Tadaaki. He'd never felt anything like that before, and Dag wanted to feel it again. But Tadaaki shook his head.

"Close your eyes."

"Why?"

"Please."

"Anything," Dag answered, closing them as requested. This was really happening. "For you, anything."

"I know," Tadaaki said softly. "I really do know."

Why was there so much pain in those words? Dag wanted to fix it.

Dag heard the rustling of clothes. Confusion battled it out with the exhilaration riding him as his heart and mind tried to figure out what was happening. He never thought... he... hell, Dag was so muddled he couldn't think straight.

"Open them."

"You sure?"

Tadaaki laughed nervously. "Yes."

He did. Complete and utter disbelief made him a little woozy. He sat down. Tadaaki leaned over him, wearing worry once again.

"Dag?"

"You have tails."

"I do."

"You have tails," he said again, fixated on the soft fluffy white behind Tadaaki.

"Yes."

Wow. Tails. Nine of them. "You're a kitsune?"

"I am."

"The stories... they're true?" Dag looked up, his mouth dry. "You have tails."

Tadaaki grinned. "Back to that?"

"Can I pull them?"

Tadaaki choked on his laughter.

"I'm serious."

Tadaaki pulled Dag against him. "I'm sure you are."

Dag slipped a hand down Tadaaki's back to his ass. They really were tails. His best friend was a kitsune. Did it matter? Dag closed his eyes. No, he'd wanted Tadaaki since forever. Loved Tadaaki since forever. He and the kid would figure it out for Tadaaki's sake. They both loved the same person, after all. Dag would eventually process that Tadaaki had tails.

His hand slipped down one.

They *were* furry and soft. The coarse fur felt good against… shit. He pressed his head against Tadaaki's and squeezed his best friend tighter. He wanted to do something, tell Tadaaki everything. But none of it would come. So he said what he could.

"Love."

He just hoped Tadaaki understood. *Please let him understand.* A kiss was pressed against his chest. Dag opened his eyes, staring at the one person who he'd been in love with since before he was born.

"Always love."

Tadaaki smiled so big the sky could've opened up and rained down stars and not even compared. "Always love."

Chapter Sixteen

The euphoria was bound to wear off sooner or later. It had to. Tadaaki had gotten dressed and they cuddled against the log, but sitting out on the bluff on the rock got cold, and there were all those lingering questions from earlier: like the whole 'I know this light' thing and why suddenly Tadaaki was more than happy to snuggle up and kiss when he never, ever let their relationship go that direction before. The inconsistencies niggled at the back of Dag's mind and wouldn't let go.

"Hey." He nudged Tadaaki. "We should get back before we're missed."

"Hmm?" Tadaaki pushed back into Dag. "I'm comfy."

"Well, I think we need to talk."

Tadaaki immediately stiffened in his arms. "About what?"

"I dunno. Things." Dag didn't want to fuck things up but two plus two wasn't equaling four. Something felt *off*. "How can you suddenly be okay with us? With this? What was the whole 'I know this light' thing about? I want to be happy that our relationship is going in the direction I want… but it doesn't make sense."

A longsuffering sigh came from Tadaaki before he stood. "All right."

"All right what?"

"We'll talk."

"I think we need to Tada."

"I know. I know." Tadaaki curled his arms around his waist. "You always have been too inquisitive for your own good."

"I think that's an attribute." Dag stood, staring at Tadaaki. He had a feeling, and it wasn't a warm, fuzzy one. "Don't you?"

"Most of the time."

"But not this time?"

"I know you, and well… " Tadaaki trailed off.

"Well, what?"

"I had just hoped for more time before we did this," Tadaaki answered.

"You do want a relationship, right?" Please say yes.

"I do. More than anything," Tadaaki said quietly. "For so long."

"Now, see, that's what doesn't make sense." Dag frowned. "You have never indicated you liked me."

"I thought I had to look out for you."

"Why would you need to do that?"

"To repay Berg for everything he did for me." The ache in Tadaaki's voice was so real, so torturous.

"You are so not making sense." And the way Tadaaki was talking… something about it scared Dag.

"I know. I just don't know where to start."

Dag understood the feeling but if they were going to figure out how to make this work… they needed honesty. "Start with the light."

"I dunno. I think… oh, all right." Tadaaki sat down on the log, curling up on himself. "You know how all life has energy?"

"Yes."

"People carry specific energy signatures."

"Okay." What was the queasy feeling in his gut for?

"I know yours."

"Okay." Dag scooted over next to Tadaaki. He wanted to reach for his best friend but felt he shouldn't.

"You were Berg."

For a moment, Dag froze. He thought nothing, he felt nothing, and he wasn't sure he even saw anything. Something about that statement was bad.

"My energy came from Grandpa?"

Tadaaki shook his head.

"My energy is my grandfather's?"

Tadaaki nodded. "You're his reincarnation."

That should be cool, but instead a different emotion planted itself inside Dag. He just didn't understand why he was angry.

"How would you know that? Because you're a kitsune?"

"Kinda, yeah."

"I hear a 'but' coming."

"I know you're his reincarnation because I knew Berg."

Several things clicked for Dag at the same time. The inside jokes, the comments, the slip of the tongues—all of them made sense. So did the implication of what Tadaaki said about knowing Berg, and the statements about Tadaaki waiting for so long. All of the puzzle pieces came slamming together and threatened to tear Dag apart.

"You knew my grandfather?" His voice shook.

"Yes."

"Those pictures… the two on your dresser. The ones with Berg and Tadashi?"

"Are of me and your grandpa," Tadaaki finished—Tadashi finished—whatever. Dag's head spun.

It hurt to breathe. Other pieces of the past hour clicked into place. It wasn't him Tadaaki—Tadashi—fuck it, Tadaaki had been so excited over. He had been ecstatic to see Berg, not Dag. Tadaaki kissed him because he was Berg's light.

Dag pushed from the ground and turned to the path. Tadaaki called after him but the words bounced off Dag. He couldn't process them. His heart had been ripped from his chest. Tadaaki didn't want him. His best friend wanted his dead grandpa.

Branches, twigs and all sorts of stuff whipped into Dag's face but he kept going, determined to get away from Tadaaki.

So much pain. So much misery. Was it really worth it? Dag didn't think he could stand being a dead man's replacement. That pushed him too far. The whole kitsune thing, yeah, he could've gotten used to it. The glow trick with the hands? Dag would've found a way to make it fun. The replacing a dead guy?

No.

Just no way. Not ever.

Dag stumbled out of the trees onto the temple grounds. Tears stung his eyes and cheeks. He blamed it on the lighting. He had to get out of here—

"No!"

Dag stopped, closed his eyes, and prayed he would not be thrown into jail for murder. "I don't need your crap right now, Kou."

"You cannot hurt him again!"

"Excuse me?" Dag opened his eyes and stared down at the little pest. "What are you talking about?"

Kou's lips quivered, but his black eyes held determination. His arms were flung wide and his legs were spread apart. The brat had the gall to jut his chin out, too.

"Move, Kou. I am not in the mood." Dag stepped to the side and hoped he wasn't about to get bitten.

"No!" Kou jumped Dag, bowling him over. The little pest had more strength than Dag had given him credit for.

Winded and feeling worse for wear, Dag lay on the ground as Kou squatted on top of him. Dag's back and chest hurt something fierce. Could the little kid have actually done some damage? Talk about an ego blow. Wait. Was Kou a kitsune too?

A little finger went in Dag's face. "Your death almost killed him."

"*My* death?"

"Yes. Yours. Berg's. It's one in the same." Kou's voice shook. "I almost lost my Papa because you had to play hero. For days he wouldn't eat or drink. Grandpa Mizuno finally had to force water down his throat. He wasted away to almost nothingness. I cried for days and days, worried he wouldn't come back to me."

"Fuck."

Kou punched Dag in the chest. "You are not allowed to hurt him again!"

"And I refuse to be some replacement!" Dag shouted back, anger coiling inside him. "I am me, not some dead—"

"Dag?" Tadaaki's panicked call interrupted them. Luckily it sounded farther away. Dag still had time to get away.

Pain exploded inside Dag and he went silent. So many emotions mashed together inside him. Anger at Tadaaki. Humiliation. Desire. Love and regret. Loneliness. Why couldn't Tadaaki want him?

"He loves you. Does it really matter why?" Kou asked, looking down at Dag, tears in the little boy's eyes.

They seemed to hold much more than a kid his age… he had said 'cried for days and days'. "How old are you?"

"Older than you."

"Then why do you always bite me?" yelled Dag. "Do you know how much that sucks?"

Kou actually smiled and shrugged. The damn kid looked smug. "It's a squirrel thing."

"A what?" Dag began, but was stunned silent as Kou transformed on top of him. "No way."

"Why is it so hard for you to believe?"

"There is no way I was taken down by a talking squirrel."

"I can bite you," Kou threatened. "In some really sensitive spots, too."

Dag scrambled up, knocking the squirrel off him.

"Hey!"

He stomped at it. "I must be dreaming. I have to be. I am back at my apartment at school having a meltdown."

The squirrel jumped on him, hanging onto Dag's shoe and chirping at him. "Why do you freak out every time?"

"Every time what?" His voice went up a notch as Kou scrambled up his leg.

"Every time we meet you freak out!"

"You're a talking squirrel!"

"That's not an excuse!"

"Yes it is!" Dag brushed at Kou, trying to get the little demon off him. He got a bite in return. "I'm gonna get rabies! I just know it. Fuck, I'm gonna die of rabies."

"Stop being a jerk!" the squirrel squeaked. "You're going to make my Papa cry again. I'm tired of you making him cry."

"I never wanted him to cry! I've always loved him!" *But Tadaaki didn't love me back.* The thought was like a punch in the gut and gave the damn squirrel an opening.

Kou scrambled inside Dag's shirt. Teeth sunk into his side. Dag yelped in pain and fell to his knees.

Dag yanked his shirt off, and luckily, the damn squirrel flew off with it. He stood on two shaky legs and pointed at Kou. "You have never liked me from the start. Why are you trying to stop me?"

Kou's little head poked out of the shirt. He pointed at Dag. Fuck, that was weird. "No, I didn't like you, because I knew your light before my Papa had time to recognize it. He was always so worried about protecting your family that he couldn't see past his duty, and besides, he cried enough over you the first time.

"If he had fallen in love with you again and you rejected him—" Kou looked like he was about to cry. How could a squirrel look so pitiful? "It would've broken him. I couldn't let that happen. He was finally willing to live again. Do you know how many decades it took my Papa to stop mourning Berg?"

"I am not Berg!" Dag hated the comparison.

"Yes, you aren't!" Kou squeaked.

"I—wait, what?" Dag hadn't expected the demon squirrel to agree.

"You aren't Berg. Just his light. You could've fallen in love with someone else," Kou answered, kicking off the shirt and standing. "I saw him falling in love with you, and if he knew you were Berg's light, it would've killed him if you didn't love him back."

"But I do love him!" So damn much. That's why he couldn't stand the thought of Tadaaki thinking he was Berg.

"I know!" Kou huffed, then skittered back to Dag. "I know…"

Gods he was confused. What the hell did the squirrel want from him? "What do you want, Kou?"

"Do you really love my Papa?"

"Yes. That's why—"

Kou held up a paw. Gods, he was being shushed by a squirrel.

"Hear me. He was falling in love with you, not Berg. You being Berg's light has just given him another reason to love you more than he already does." Kou really knew how to throw punches. "Does it really matter?"

Dag thought so. That was the problem. He was Dag, not Berg. Kou edged closer to Dag and put a paw on his shoe.

"Think hard, Dag. Does it really matter that my Papa has been given another reason to love you even more?"

"Then why didn't he tell me before?" The question popped out of Dag's mouth before he had the chance to think.

"Because he was scared. Because he thought he was being disloyal." Kou sighed. "Dag, do you really think you can let him go again?"

"I don't want to," he confessed.

"Then don't."

Dag wasn't so sure it was that easy.

"Dag!" Tadaaki's shout was close that time.

He turned and saw his best friend tumble out of the woods. Worry and fear were etched across Tadaaki's face, panic in his eyes. It made Dag's chest tighten uncomfortably. He hated making Tadaaki worry. The moment their eyes met, Tadaaki rushed toward him.

"Oh, thank the Gods, Dag. You're—" Tadaaki reached for him then stopped. It was like a knife tore through him.

Dag went to his knees.

"Shit. Dag!" Tadaaki reached for him again.

"Stop!" Kou yelled. Tadaaki listened, watching Kou carefully.

The squirrel turned to Dag, his beady black eyes serious. "Do you love him?"

"Kou, what are you—" Tadaaki started before Kou gave him the paw, too.

He was really good at shutting people up that way.

"Dag, do you love my Papa?"

"Yes," Dag choked out. "Always."

"Then the rest is just details."

"I don't—" Dag said before biting his tongue. "Ouch."

Tadaaki knelt down next to him. A tentative hand cupped his face. It was cold and clammy and shook a little. "Dag."

Black eyes like the night sky pleaded with him. Love was there. It had probably always been there. Hidden just from sight.

Could he live with Tadaaki loving two hims?

"Dag." Tadaaki pressed their foreheads together. "Can we start over? Do this again?"

"I don't understand." Do what again?

"Hi," Tadaaki said. "I'm Tadaaki. I'm a really old kitsune from Japan. This is my son, Kou, a demon squirrel. We're temple priests for the god Inari."

"Will you explain how a fox ended up with a squirrel for a son?" Dag asked, peering over at the little menace.

Tadaaki smiled. Gods, Dag loved that smile. Was all the rest details? He didn't know. He wanted to believe things would work out. If a demon from folktales could be true, couldn't happy endings be true too?

"And I love you."

Dag's head shot up. He regarded Tadaaki for a moment, then reached for his hand. This was his best friend. The boy he'd fallen in love with during Obon. The man he'd loved since who knows when? Could he let him go?

Relief swept Tadaaki's face and he squeezed back.

"I love you," Dag said. "I want to figure this out. I do. But I want you to see *me*."

Tadaaki gulped and nodded. A little fear crept back into his eyes. Dag wanted to dispel those worries. There had to be something he could do.

"Will you tell the story of how we fell in love? The first time?"

THE END

Dear Reader

Thank you for downloading Freddy's **Internment**. We hope you enjoyed it. (You should ask Freddy about how Kou really ended up in the story. All Angel & Toni's faults.) Please consider leaving a review where you purchased this ebook or on Goodreads. Reviews and word-of-mouth recommendations are *vital* to independent publishers.

If you're a fan of gay fantasy, you may also enjoy Freddy's *Snow on Spirit Bridge*, or you may want to dig your teeth into Angel Martinez's SFF humor series, *Brimstone*. And if you've ever felt you've had a devil on one shoulder arguing with an angel on the other, Mathilde Watson's *Shrug It Off* will leave you satisfied.

We love hearing from our readers. You can email us at mischiefcornerbooks@gmail.com. To read excerpts from all our titles, visit our website: http://www.mischiefcornerbooks.com.

Sincerely,
Mischief Corner Books

Freddy MacKay

Eternity
in the Tides

www.mischiefcornerbooks.com

www.mischiefcornerbooks.com

MBC

Potato
Surprise

A Brimstone
Prequel

Angel Martinez

www.mischiefcornerbooks.com

About Freddy MacKay

Freddy grew up in the Midwest, playing sports and running around outside. And honestly, that much has not changed since Freddy was small and throwing worms at other kids, expect worm throwing has been replaced with a healthy geocaching addiction. Freddy enjoys traveling and holds the view a person should continually to learn about new things and people whenever possible.

Freddy's contemporary LGBTQ book, *Incubation: Finding Peace 2*, won 3rd Place - Best Gay Erotic Fiction in the 2012 Rainbow Awards. In 2013, Freddy's story, *Internment*, tied for 3rd Place - Best Gay Fantasy in the Rainbow Awards. Freddy's steampunk/ SF story, *Feel Me*, was a finalist and honorable mention in the 2014 Rainbow Awards for SF. The 2015 Rainbow Awards saw Freddy's *Snow on Spirit Bridge* become an Honorable Mention and Finalist in the Best Gay Fantasy category. You can email Freddy at: freddy.m.mackay@gmail.com

Website:
http://freddysstereograph.weebly.com

Twitter:
https://twitter.com/#!/FreddyMacKay

Also by Freddy MacKay

Awakening
Dirty Little Secret
Feel Me (The Marduk Expanse)

DEEPER THAN BLUE UNIVERSE
Eternity in the Tides
Internment: Spirit Threads 1
Enhearten: Spirit Threads 2 (Coming Spring 2017)
Snow on Spirit Bridge

FINDING PEACE
Beginning Again
Incubation
Days Gone By (Coming Soon)

FINDING HOME
Moving Mountains
Snowed In

TALL TALES OF HOOPER'S TOWN
Sock Poacher & the Shower Thief

IMP UNIVERSE*
The Nut Job (Coming 2017)

*shared universe with Angel Martinez

STRIKING THE RIGHT CHORD
Notes of Oblivion

About Mischief Corner Books

Mischief Corner Books is an organization of superheroes… no, it's a platinum-album techno-fusion group… no, hold on a sec here…

Ah yes. Mischief Corner Books is a diverse group of authors who met on a mountain in Tennessee and decided since they were probably too easily distracted to rule the world that they'd settle for causing a bit of mayhem instead.

In addition to making mayhem, we publish books with a diverse range of genres and topics... we live to break molds.

MCB. Giving voice to LGBTQ fiction.

Website:
http://www.mischiefcornerbooks.com